'What a beautiful, heartbreaking book ... a gentle uncovering of what it really means to be human.'
Lip Magazine

'A novel in three voices about the inner turmoil — and beauty — that people keep walled behind flawless surfaces.' **Tiffany Tsao, author of The Majesties**

'Dazzling.' **Foyles**

'Like Japanese brush painting, the author's simple, clear prose captures Miwako's vulnerability and complexity. Also vividly drawn are Fumi and Chie, each having built their own unusual protective personas that are gradually revealed. An eerie and elegant puzzle.' **Kirkus Reviews**

'A novel that lingers in the mind thanks to its poetic delivery, layering of ideas and an engrossing tale, all led by vivid characters.' **Bad Form Magazine**

'A subtly fantastical story, driven by themes of love, loss, and grief ... There are mysteries that tease at you and lies you'll be told, all in service of a complex, intense story that ebbs and flows so beautifully. It's a wild ride, and a delightfully satisfying one.' **Books & Bao**

'Written in clear, simple prose, Goenawan's novel presents the intriguing mystery of Miwako Sumida through the eyes of three characters who try to piece together her puzzle while struggling with their own questions of meaning and identity. This story about youth, friendship, grief, and trauma invites us through secret doors, ready to discover more.' **Intan Paramaditha, author of Apple and Knife**

'Murakami without the male gaze – a feminist Murakami, perhaps ... An engrossing tale clearly influenced by Japanese women writers such as Risa Wataya and Banana Yoshimoto, *The Perfect World of Miwako Sumida* is about the crushing weight of secrets and how the long arm of history returns to haunt a person. In this novel, young women straitjacketed by the standards of mainstream society demand: give us a closer look.' ***The Saturday Paper***

'The way these characters' lives intersect makes for a complex and satisfying tale, one that's sad at the same time as it's lively and warm.' ***Book Riot***

'Goenawan, like any skilled novelist, manages to elegantly reveal both the pain and beauty of unraveling a life after loss. This is only her second novel to date, and she's already been compared to the wizard of world-building, Haruki Murakami.' ***Lambda Literary***

'A quietly powerful meditation on the destructive power of secrets, as well as the power of truth to heal even beyond death.' ***The Nerd Daily***

'Goenawan does an expert job of getting to the core of this university student with a mysterious past, and on how people grapple with the death by suicide of a loved one.' ***Alma***

'A vibrant and at times surreal exploration of lost love, death, trauma, and friendship in Japan in the 1980s/90s ... This novel is beautifully created and provides a mature look into suicide and its impacts on those left behind.' ***Good Reading*** ****

THE PERFECT WORLD OF
MIWAKO SUMIDA

Clarissa Goenawan is an Indonesian-born Singaporean writer. Her debut novel *Rainbirds* won the 2015 Bath Novel Award and was shortlisted for three further prizes. Her short stories have won several awards and been published in various literary magazines and anthologies. *The Perfect World of Miwako Sumida* is her second novel.

CLARISSA GOENAWAN

THE PERFECT WORLD OF MIWAKO SUMIDA

SCRIBE
Melbourne • London

Scribe Publications
2 John Street, Clerkenwell, London, WC1N 2ES, United Kingdom
18–20 Edward St, Brunswick, Victoria 3056, Australia

Published by arrangement with Soho Press, New York, with the assistance of
Rights People, London

Published by Scribe 2020
This edition published 2021

Interior design by Janine Agro
Printed and bound in the UK by CPI Group (UK) Ltd, Croydon CR0 4YY

Scribe Publications is committed to the sustainable use of natural resources and
the use of paper products made responsibly from those resources.

9781913348847 (UK edition)
9781922310286 (Australian edition)
9781925938463 (ebook)

Catalogue records for this book are available from the National Library
of Australia and the British Library.

scribepublications.co.uk
scribepublications.com.au

PROLOGUE

Ryusei and Chie returned to the pathway. Tall grass had given way to dense trees, so close together they almost blocked out the sun. Some of their leaves had fallen, covering the dark mossy ground. Tiny white mushrooms were scattered around their roots. The sound of trickling water had faded away, but every once in a while, a bird chirped in the distance. Amidst this endless wave of trees, it seemed as if they were the only two people left in the world.

"Do you think this is where Miwako hanged herself?" Ryusei asked.

Chie stopped walking. The question sparked a series of troubling thoughts. *Had* Miwako died here? Now that the thought was planted in her mind, the mountain felt anything but peaceful.

She could almost hear the forest spirit calling her, beckoning her to join souls with it, just as Miwako had, to remain here forever.

Stay here, so you can be free. You no longer need to carry this burden.

PART ONE
RYUSEI YANAGI

Before I knew it had happened, I'd fallen in love with Miwako Sumida.

Whenever I was on campus, my eyes unconsciously sought her out. I constantly watched where she went, what she did, what she wore. How she tied her long hair back and adjusted her glasses. When Miwako read, she would tilt her head, resting it on her slim fingers as if it were too heavy. She always looked like she was daydreaming.

One afternoon, she took the seat next to me in the library. I kept my eyes on my book, but she was so close I caught a whiff of her shampoo. The sweet scent of summer strawberries, ripe and bursting with flavor.

Eight months later, Miwako Sumida hanged herself.

But I wouldn't let her death slip past me. She'd wanted to tell me something, and I had to find out what it was.

1

Like
a
Long-Lost
Friend

March 15th, 1989

I met Miwako Sumida at a goukon organized by Toshi, a friend of mine.

I had never been interested in group dates. They were desperate measures for desperate people, but Toshi *was* desperate. He'd been trying to gain the attention of a pretty, short-haired girl in his swimming club. I didn't want to ruin his excitement, but the girl had probably agreed to come because Jin—our other friend, popular and a total charmer—would be there. Toshi and I had been hanging out since our first year at Waseda, so I felt obliged to participate.

The goukon was scheduled for noon at a family restaurant near our campus. At a quarter past twelve, the girls were still nowhere to be seen. We ordered milkshakes and continued to wait, listening to Oricon singles from the restaurant's only speaker.

"Are you sure those girls haven't ditched us?" Jin teased Toshi.

"Don't say that; they're just late." Toshi tapped his fingers on the table. "They'll be here any second."

"No matter what, you're picking up the tab like you promised. We'll give them another five minutes before we order food."

"Shut up."

Yawning, I gazed out the window. Wet leaves sparkled in the bright sunlight. It had poured yesterday afternoon and all night, but the rain had stopped right when I'd left the house that morning. The scent of fresh soil lingered, mixed with the fragrance of plum blossoms.

Suddenly, Toshi stood and waved. I turned toward the door and saw three girls walking toward our table.

The one in front was the beautiful freshman Toshi was after, and the two girls behind her were a study in opposites. One had long, silky black hair and a serious expression behind a pair of old-fashioned thick-rimmed glasses. The other was glamorous, with bleached, permed hair and a body-hugging dress that emphasized her curves. The blonde was one-hundred percent Jin's type, so I knew I'd be expected to make conversation with the glasses girl.

Before anyone else could say a word, Jin spoke.

"I can't believe you're here, Sumida," he said.

The girl with the glasses gave him a thin smile. "Me neither. I'd never have guessed I'd see you again. I'm surprised you remember my name."

Jin chuckled. "Come on, my memory isn't that bad."

"You know each other?" Toshi asked.

"We were high school classmates," Jin said quickly. "Apologies. I've done things in the wrong order, haven't I? Please, ladies, take a seat, and then we can do the introductions."

The three of them made themselves comfortable on the long sofa. The pretty girl was named Sachiko Hayami, the stylish one was Chie Ohno, and the one with the glasses was Miwako Sumida.

"Sachiko, Chie, and Miwako," Toshi repeated. "Do you mind if we use first names?"

"Of course not," Chie said in a cheerful tone. She was so

friendly, probably one of those girls everyone had an easy time getting along with.

Toshi ordered some light snacks, and we made the usual collegiate conversation. What are you studying? Oh, interesting. Are you in any clubs? I've been thinking of checking that one out. What about you, Ryusei? Any fun hobbies? Oh, me too. I listen to the radio all the time. Music, mostly. I have pretty eclectic taste. Wow, people have said that about me too! Have you seen any good movies recently? What did you think of it? Wait, don't tell me the ending. I haven't watched it yet.

As the exchange went on, I became fascinated by how different these girls were. Sachiko and Chie were chatty, while Miwako gave cursory answers to everything anyone asked her, like she didn't want to be there. Then again, I too was only there to pad the numbers.

After a while, it became obvious that Miwako *really* didn't want to be there. She wouldn't stop looking at her watch, which seemed too big for her thin wrist. As expected, Sachiko was more interested in Jin than Toshi. But what piqued my interest was the tension between Jin and Miwako. He seemed overly conscious of her, glancing at her every now and then before averting his eyes. She, on the other hand, openly stared at him whenever he looked at her.

When the girls excused themselves to go to the washroom, Toshi wasted no time in grilling Jin.

"You've gone on a date with Miwako, haven't you?" he asked.

Not bad for Toshi. He was surprisingly sharp that day.

Jin slurped his chocolate milkshake. "No way. She's not my type."

"I don't believe you. She kept looking at you."

"Glaring, you mean?" said Jin, laughing. "If you must know, we do have an unpleasant history. I'm not going to be the one to spill it, so don't bother asking." He lowered his voice. "But the other girl, Chie. She's hot."

"Yeah, and nice, too." Toshi seemed to have forgotten his question. "So you're going for her? Ryusei, I think you'd do well with the—"

"The mature type," Jin said. "You prefer older girls, don't you?"

"I've never said that," I said, stirring my drink with a straw.

"Look," Jin said. "Just go along with it unless you've got a violent objection."

I didn't respond. Even without them suggesting it, I would have chosen Miwako over the other two. She seemed sensible. A girl like her wouldn't expect too much from a setting like this. Regardless of whom I ended up talking to, we would probably go to karaoke together as a group, exchange numbers out of courtesy, and part ways, never to see each other again. She would forget me, and I would forget her. That was all.

But when it came to Miwako Sumida, nothing was as I expected.

AS PREDICTED, AFTER WE finished lunch, Toshi announced we would be heading to a nearby karaoke joint.

Miwako sighed. "How long will this take?"

Chie twisted her hair around her finger. "Two to three hours at most?"

"I'm going take my leave. I don't like singing in front of people, and I need to go to the bookstore."

"But we'll be short one girl!" Sachiko protested.

I stood. "Don't worry, I'll go with her. I have to pick up a book too."

Jin snickered. "How convenient."

"Any violent objections?" I asked, parroting him.

He flashed me a smug smile. "No objections. All good. We'll see you tomorrow."

"Miwako, are you okay with that?" Chie asked.

"Why not?" she said, grabbing her bag.

The two of us left the restaurant together, Miwako walking in front while I followed a few steps behind. After we were a couple blocks from the restaurant, she stopped and turned to me.

"Ryusei Yanagi, isn't it? You can stop trailing me now."

I was impressed she'd remembered my full name after only hearing it once.

"We've walked far enough. Your friends won't notice if we go our separate ways now." She added, "Unless you want to exchange numbers, in which case I'm not interested."

I decided to humor her. "Me neither. I actually just want to go to the bookstore."

She furrowed her brow. "Fine, but don't be a bother."

"If you feel that uncomfortable being seen with me in public, we can pretend not to know each other."

"I didn't say that, but the place I'm heading to is a little run-down. You might not like it."

I didn't respond, even though I knew exactly where she planned to go based on where we were walking.

An old man named Ikeda owned a small secondhand bookshop around the corner. Screw holes marked the place where the shop signboard should have hung. The placard had fallen down a long time ago, and he had never bothered to fix it. Regulars simply called the place Ikeda Bookshop, and I'd frequented it since high school.

At the front of the shop, the old man stacked his newer stock, forming book towers that threatened to topple at any moment. Inside, wooden shelves and crates crammed with yellowing paperbacks and hardcovers stood close to each other. Two adults wouldn't be able to walk side-by-side between the shelves at the same time, and the whole shop had the comforting smell of old paper.

Ikeda stored even more books at his house. If I wanted a particular title, I only needed to tell him. The next time I showed up, the book would be waiting at the counter like a long-lost friend.

Somehow, Ikeda Bookshop stocked only books in English. According to rumors, Ikeda used to be a rag-and-bone man and had stumbled upon a vacation home in Azabu owned by a British lord. The nobleman had passed away, leaving an enormous collection of English books and no heir to claim them. Old man Ikeda had struck a good deal with the caretaker, buying up the entire library.

The story sounded like something a regular had made up on the spot for a friend they'd brought to the place, but it was also somewhat plausible. How else could old man Ikeda have gotten his hands on such an extensive collection?

Miwako peered into the shop. "Excuse me."

"Yes?" Old man Ikeda appeared from between the shelves and adjusted his thick circular glasses. "Ah, it's you," he murmured. "Give me a minute."

Dragging his feet, he pushed a stool and climbed it to retrieve a book from a wooden crate atop a shelf. After that, he went behind the counter and returned with another book. I always enjoyed watching him pull out books. Despite the chaos, he knew exactly where every title was located.

"The one you asked for," he said, handing a book to Miwako and another to me.

Miwako had a novel with an upper-class European lady and a well-dressed aristocratic gentleman on the cover, while I had requested Oscar Wilde's *The Picture of Dorian Gray*.

"I owe you an apology," Miwako said after we left the shop. "I thought you were making it up. You know, about wanting to visit the store."

I laughed. "Why is that? Do I seem like I don't read?"

"Yes," she said without skipping a beat. "You seem pretty frivolous to me."

"Frivolous?" I turned to her, taken aback by her frankness. "Really?"

"Do you go there often?" she asked, ignoring my remark.

"Once or twice a week, at least," I said. "It's a nice place. You never know what you'll come across. They have quite a few gems."

I recalled the favorites I'd collected there over the years—an illustrated copy of *Alice's Adventures in Wonderland*, an autographed copy of *Fahrenheit 451*, and the original 1966 edition of *Flowers for Algernon*, all prominently displayed on my bookshelf. Each time I pulled one down, it brought me back to the day I'd stumbled upon it inside a wooden crate.

Outside of the classics, I sometimes picked one or two titles I'd never heard of that seemed interesting. More often than not, I found myself well rewarded.

"You know that satisfaction you get when you come across something really good? It's almost like treasure hunting. I could spend hours doing that there," I continued.

"Did you want to stay longer?" Miwako asked. "Sorry, I didn't know."

"No, it's all right. I go there all the time."

She glanced at the book in my hand. "What did you buy?"

I showed her the cover.

"What's it about?" she asked.

"A handsome young man preserves his beauty by selling his soul to the darkness. Instead of him aging, his portrait does. And every time he does something terrible, the painting becomes more hideous and twisted."

"That sounds awful." She turned to me. "Why would you pick a book like that?"

"Well, why not?" I said, unsure what to say. "What about you? Did you buy that romance book because you have dreams of being a runaway princess?"

For the first time, she struggled to come up with an answer. We both went quiet, and I started counting the number of steps we took.

When we reached twenty-seven, a ping shattered the silence. Two steps later, a bicycle shot by, splashing dirty water from a puddle onto my pants. Luckily, they were a fairly dark wash. I looked around for the offending cyclist, but he had already disappeared into the crowd. Somehow, we had already arrived at the metro station.

"Are you taking the train too?" Miwako asked.

"No, just walking you here," I said. Though I had no idea why.

She stared straight at me. "But you're not going to ask for my number."

I nodded and smiled. "That's right."

"Then give me yours," she said, taking out a notebook and a pen. "Let's go to Ikeda Bookshop again. Next time, we'll take our time browsing." She paused for a moment. "Unless you prefer going there by yourself?"

While I did always go to Ikeda Bookshop alone, a change might be nice. "No, of course not. I'd love to go with you."

As I watched Miwako enter the station, I wondered if she would ever call.

Just a few days after that initial walk, Miwako and I returned to the Ikeda Bookshop. This time we stayed for several hours, until closing. Almost every week after that, one of us would ask the other to go together. Ikeda Bookshop became our weekly Thursday affair, and eventually, I caught myself looking forward to it soon after the last Thursday had passed.

Since freshman year, I'd spent a lot of time at the university library. Apparently, so had Miwako, though prior to the goukon, I'd never noticed her there. After getting to know her, I began to look for her at the library. Whenever I saw her, I chose a seat at the same table.

We didn't talk much, but I enjoyed quietly stealing glances at her, watching her read. She always tilted her head slightly, resting it on her left hand and caressing the corner of the page with her right thumb and forefinger. She had long, slim fingers, and the way she handled books was so gentle. From time to time, she would adjust her glasses and push her silky black hair behind her ear. Sometimes, she would tie her hair up into a ponytail with a black rubber band. She had an elegant, pale neck. When I looked at her, I always thought, *She looks so peaceful.*

A month later, Toshi and Chie became a couple, and not long after that, Jin started dating Sachiko. Because the six of us were always together, people assumed I was going out with Miwako, though I wasn't. From time to time, I did wonder about the possibility. Life was brighter with Miwako, even when we weren't doing anything in particular. And whenever she was around, my heart beat faster.

Dear Ryusei,

By the time you read this, I will no longer be in Tokyo. Please don't look for me. I had to get away.

    This must be confusing, but I'll explain it properly soon.

    Thank you for everything. The times we've had together are some of the most precious of my life.

    Take care, Ryusei. And please send my apologies to Fumi-nee.

Miwako

2

A Woman Who Wants a Man in Her Life

The first time Miwako saw my sister was when Fumi-nee came looking for me at the university library. I had accidentally left my house keys in the studio.

"Stupid." My sister dropped the keys on top of my book. "How can you be so careless?"

I looked up and frowned. "How did you know I was here?"

"You were carrying a stack of library books." She rolled her eyes. "Doesn't that seem like a dead giveaway?"

"Well done, Sherlock Holmes."

She leaned in and whispered, "The next time you forget your keys, Ryusei Yanagi, you're sleeping in the hallway."

I inched away from her. My sister glanced at Miwako, who was looking at us from across the table, but didn't speak to her.

"I'll see you for dinner," she said before leaving.

Once she was gone, Miwako asked, "Was that your girlfriend?"

I wanted to laugh but decided to tease her instead. "Why, are you jealous?"

"Yes."

I felt a lump in my throat. I had hoped Miwako would get flustered and deny it so I could make fun of her, but her tone was so serious that I felt like she was mocking me.

"Your girlfriend is so pretty," she continued. "Not to be rude, but isn't she a bit older than you?"

"She is. She just turned twenty-nine."

Miwako raised an eyebrow.

"I like older women. They're more experienced."

"Uh-huh," she said, seemingly undisturbed as she returned to her newspaper. It was the first time I'd seen her read anything other than school textbooks and romance novels.

"What are you looking at?" I leaned over and saw the advertisements section for part-time jobs. "Ah, so you're broke."

She glared at me. "No, I'm not. And even if I were, that's none of your business."

"Come on, I'm just kidding," I said. "What kind of job are you looking for?"

"I don't know. Something not too difficult? Preferably not a night shift. Maybe waitressing or looking after a shop. I just want a part-time job for the school break."

I involuntarily pictured Miwako in a waitress uniform. She was so hardworking—her colleagues would definitely like her, and romances were always starting at those jobs. The thought made me depressed.

"You're so strange," I said. "Most people would prefer to sleep in and relax at home during their holiday."

"Not everyone is as lazy as you."

"So, Miss Hard-Working, have you found the job you want?"

She shook her head. "I've seen a couple of openings near my apartment, but their hourly rate is too low. I'm hoping to find one with better pay. I really need to save up."

"Do you want me to introduce you to the boss at my part-time job? There's enough work for both of us."

"I didn't know you worked part-time," she said. "What kind of job is it?"

"Nothing too difficult. Just helping out. I'm sure you could do it too."

"And how much do you get paid to 'just help out'?"

Leaning in, I whispered the amount.

"That much?" she asked, a little too loud. People looked up at us, and the librarian shot us a warning glance.

"I'm sorry." She lowered her voice, then turned to me. "So this job, where is it?"

"Pretty close by. I'm heading there later. If you don't have classes this afternoon, you can come with me, but there's no guarantee my boss will hire you."

"Don't worry. I'll do my best to convince him."

IT WAS CHILLY OUTSIDE when we left the library. The maple trees lining the pavement were yellowing, signaling the beginning of autumn.

That day, Miwako was wearing a loose beige sweater and a long pastel-colored chiffon skirt. The wind shifted her hem as she stepped onto the fallen leaves. When she walked, she almost tiptoed, like she was dancing. The airy motion reminded me of cotton candy. She probably did it without even realizing it.

I kicked at some gravel, wondering what people thought when they saw two university students alongside each other. Surely it looked like we were on a date. The thought made me flush.

"What are you smiling at?" Miwako asked.

I turned to her. "Nothing."

"It's creepy."

Still grinning, I quickened my pace and turned onto a side street. Old warehouses flanked the quiet alley, each enclosed by a tall wooden fence. I looked for unit twenty-three. The gold plate had been taken out, replaced by a number spray-painted in black covering the entire gigantic blue door. I climbed over the fence and unlocked the gate from inside.

"What are you doing?" Miwako hissed. "People will think we're trying to break in."

"This is the only way to get in. The door can only be opened from here," I said. "I assumed you wanted me to open it for you, or would you prefer to jump over in that pretty skirt?"

She frowned at me.

"Come on," I said, leading her around to the back of the building.

The warehouse was almost empty. One of the walls had been partially knocked down for ventilation. Two bicycles rested against the wall. Nearby, buckets of paint and cans of spray paint lay atop stacks of old newspapers. But even with a huge ceiling fan providing some much-needed circulation, the air was thick with a sharp chemical smell.

The other side of the warehouse contained a small partitioned office. The door opened and my sister came out, wearing her work apron. It was stained by so many different paints that it was impossible to determine its original color.

"Ah, we've got a guest," she said, coming over to us. "You're the girl from the library, aren't you?"

Miwako didn't answer.

"Yes, she is," I said. I gestured for Miwako to introduce herself, but when she remained silent, I ended up doing the talking. "This is Miwako Sumida. She's studying at Waseda too."

My sister furrowed her brow.

"She's looking for a job," I continued, nudging Miwako with my elbow.

She bowed nervously. "Good afternoon."

My sister forced a smile. "One moment," she said to Miwako before dragging me off. "Didn't I tell you to bring in someone who could help with my work?" she whispered.

"I did."

"What are you talking about? That's just your girlfriend," she said, a little too loud. "She's tiny. How do you expect her to help paint a giant mural? It's hard labor, you know that."

I flashed her a smile. "You're a girl too, aren't you?"

She was quiet for a moment before continuing. "Look at her clothes. Is she planning to work in those?"

"Isn't it you who always says not to judge a person by their appearance?"

My sister rolled her eyes. "Fine. I'll let her give it a try, but don't blame me if she ends up crying and running home."

I laughed. "She's tougher than she looks."

My sister walked over to Miwako, who had a smile that looked entirely forced.

"You can call me Fumi-nee," my sister said. "I'm Ryu's older sister and the owner of Studio Salt. Welcome to my place."

Miwako's eyes widened. "Excuse me?"

"Studio Salt," she said. "Does the name strike you as odd?"

"No, not that. It's just . . . Ryusei told me you were his girlfriend."

My sister burst into laughter. "Me, his girlfriend? You're joking. I'm not interested in boys who've just entered puberty."

"Hey, stop it," I said. "I didn't say you were my girlfriend. She jumped to that conclusion. I'm not into cougars."

My sister ignored me. "You're so cute, Miwako. Ah, may I call you Miwako?"

"Yes."

"And I happen to be single, so if you have a kind and handsome older brother, you can introduce me to him." She flashed Miwako one of her signature smiles. "Now, you're probably a pretty good painter. Are you planning to start today?"

Miwako looked at me. "Actually, I still have no idea what the job is, and . . ." Her gaze shifted to my sister, who was now staring at me. "I'm not good at painting."

"You didn't tell her anything about this, Ryusei?"

"I told her the job was to help you, which is true."

"Useless." My sister sighed. "Well, I'm a painter, and I'm on commission for an outdoor mural at an orphanage. It's quite a big wall, so I'll need some help laying the foundation by painting the whole wall a base color, then tracing over the lines I draw and filling in the colors. It's exhausting work, very labor-intensive. Are you up for it?"

Miwako nodded.

"Then let's start today. We can walk there—it's about fifteen minutes away on foot." My sister tilted her head. "But are you going to be all right painting in that outfit? Your clothes might get dirty."

"It's all right. I can start now."

"Great. Let's pack up." As she walked off, my sister called over her shoulder, "If you haven't quit by the end of the day, I'll hire you until the project is finished."

THE SUN WAS HIGH when my sister left us to go buy lunch. We had begun painting the wall with a white base.

Despite the cooling wind, Miwako was drenched in sweat and had taken her sweater off. Underneath, she had on a lavender tank top, which was now smeared with paint. She'd tied her hair up, but stray wet hairs kept sticking to her face. She was so focused on painting the wall that she didn't bother to brush them off.

"It's tiring, isn't it?" I dipped my brush into the paint bucket. "You can rest for a bit. I won't tell my sister."

"No way. I'm being paid to do this," Miwako said.

That was just like her. I used to think it was sheer stubbornness, but I'd grown to admire her resilience.

I glanced at Miwako and was surprised to find her gaze already on me.

"What are you staring at?" I asked, looking away.

"Now that I've gotten a proper look, there really is a resemblance between you and Fumi-nee," she said. "You have the same features, especially the nose. Both of you have a sharp nose, which gives you a nice side profile."

I became flustered. "It almost sounds like you're saying I'm good-looking."

"I never said you weren't. Your face is well proportioned, and you have nice eyes."

I laughed half-heartedly at her clinical compliment. "You should also say you like my personality."

She laughed too. "Of course I do. I'm not the kind of person who'd spend this much time with someone I don't like." She looked into my eyes. "I don't think I've ever said it out loud, but I do enjoy our time together at the bookshop."

Before I could stop myself, I said, "Miwako, will you go out with me?"

She stared at me, then she shook her head. "No. I can't."

I swallowed. "Why not?"

"Because it's you."

I thought I heard her wrong. "Excuse me?"

"You're too important as a friend. If we were to go out, sooner or later things would turn sour, and we wouldn't be able to spend time together anymore. It would make things awkward for the rest of the group too."

"What makes you so sure things would turn out that way?"

"Some things are bound to fail," she said, then looked up at me. "I'm sorry." She made the confession as if presenting a straight-forward set of facts.

I stood there in stunned silence, wishing I could sweep away my feelings for Miwako like she wanted. But denying that I was in love for the first time didn't make it true.

"Your sister is really cool," Miwako said, changing the topic. "It's so bold of her, choosing an unconventional career as an artist."

I forced myself back into the conversation. "Don't be so quick to assume. She wanted to be a doctor."

"Why didn't she pursue it?"

"Not everyone has the money to attend college, and medical school is particularly expensive." I continued to paint broad white lines along the wall. "My sister happens to be talented at drawing. She taught sketch classes for children at an art school and eventu-ally set up her own studio, but she never planned on becoming a painter. It just happened."

"I see."

"She doesn't hate her job, but it's not her dream," I said, trying not to think about what my sister had sacrificed for us—for me.

"What does she envision for this mural?" Miwako asked, dipping her brush into the paint bucket.

"I'm not sure. It will probably be of the kids and the pastor who live here," I said. "The children will be back soon, so you'll be able to play with them."

She looked down. "I don't like children."

"Really? That's surprising, since you look like one," I teased. "Just wait until you've got your own."

"I'm never having kids. I would hate them." Her tone had gone so sharp, it was almost frightening.

"What are you two talking about?" my sister asked, coming over with two big plastic bags.

I ignored the question, though I was glad she had returned. The three of us went into the orphanage, and my sister led us to the dining area.

"You seem familiar with this place," Miwako said to Fumi-nee as we sat at the table.

My sister opened the first plastic bag and took out three lunch boxes. "Ryu and I have spent a lot of time here."

Miwako passed out the disposable chopsticks. "Ah, you volunteer? That's nice."

I looked up. My sister gave a thin smile to reassure me that it was okay, but I didn't want to hide this from Miwako.

"We used to live here," I said.

My sister's eyes widened.

"It's fine, Fumi-nee," I said. "You can tell her."

"We were here for a couple years," my sister explained, snapping her chopsticks apart. "Our parents died in a car accident."

"I'm sorry, I didn't mean to bring it up," Miwako said.

"Don't worry, it was a long time ago. And it is what it is." Fumi-nee opened her bento—chicken katsu with vegetables, my favorite. "That aside, I've taken a look at your paintwork, Miwako. You seem so organized, but you're actually a bit clumsy."

Miwako bit her lip.

Fumi laughed. "Don't worry, Ryu will show you the ropes. But I can't help thinking, being with you, my little brother would have a challenging life."

"Wait, there's been a misunderstanding. There's nothing going on between us."

Miwako looked at me to corroborate her statement, but I only shrugged and opened my bento box. We all had identical sets.

"I want a boyfriend too," my sister lamented, ignoring Miwako's protests.

"You're so beautiful," Miwako said. "I'm sure you'd have more suitors if you weren't so intimidating."

I gaped at her bluntness.

"Miwako," I said, cutting her off. "Why don't you start on your food?" I turned to my sister. "She didn't mean it like that."

"I know." My sister sighed. "But maybe she's right. And I really do want to find someone. I've been feeling so lonely lately, and I'm not getting younger. Finding a boyfriend isn't as easy as it used to be."

I sighed too. "Didn't you just break up with your last one a week ago? It's a little too soon to be looking for a replacement."

"The best way to get over past love is by starting a new romance," said my sister indignantly. She turned to Miwako. "Don't you agree?"

Miwako raised an eyebrow but nodded.

"Oh, come on," I said, groaning. They both laughed.

My sister shook her head. "My poor, clueless brother doesn't understand a woman's heart."

"Shut up," I hissed.

"He might look like a player, but the truth is, he's never gone out with anyone since he started college."

Miwako's eyes widened. "Is that true?"

"It's not," I said, looking away. "I don't introduce my sister to every girl I date."

My sister covered her mouth, stifling a giggle.

"So it's true," Miwako said.

She always saw right through me. But I hoped this would help her understand that I really was serious about her.

"Sounds like you've had a lot of relationships, though, Fumi-nee," Miwako said.

"Of course," my sister said, unashamed. "I like having a man in my life. Being pampered."

"And that's why you end up with a smooth-talking jerk every single time." I took a bite of my cutlet. "Your criteria need to be questioned. You're terrible at choosing men. You trust people too easily."

"Who says?"

"Remember that so-called trader? You should've gone to the police."

Fumi-nee glared. "Stop it, Ryu."

Miwako turned to me. "What happened?"

"Don't tell her."

"I *will* tell her, so she knows how bad your judgment is." I put down my chopsticks. "Listen to this, Miwako. My sister once dated this guy who pretended to work for a trading company. Turns out he was a con artist. He ran off with her life's savings." I looked into Fumi-nee's eyes. "Tell me that didn't happen."

My sister stared blankly ahead. "That was in the past. I've learned my lesson."

"Then you should've gone to the police, especially after I tracked him down. But no, you would never do that. You shouldn't take pity on people like him. He didn't care about you. He never loved you. He only saw you as a source of income, just wanted your money. A man like him—"

I felt Miwako's hand on mine.

"That's enough," she said in a soft voice.

Next to her, my sister was silent.

I stood up. "I'm done. Thank you for lunch."

MIWAKO AND I FINISHED painting the base coat way past dinnertime. I treated her to supper at a nearby yakitori stall, where we ate way too many grilled chicken skewers. After that, we returned to the studio to tidy up.

My sister told me to walk Miwako home. Miwako didn't want me to at first, but Fumi-nee insisted.

"It's not for you. It's for me," she said to Miwako. "It's late, and I want to make sure the young girl I've employed gets home safely. If you say no, I can't in good conscience hire you. Do you still want to work here after today?"

"Of course I do."

My sister kept her word and officially took on Miwako as an assistant. The only casualties of the day were Miwako's tank top and skirt, which were covered in white paint.

"It's okay, I bought them on sale in Shinjuku," she told me when I walked her home. "And if you look at them from a certain angle, don't you think the paint spots look a little deliberate?"

I shook my head. No one would think that. "If you want, I can paint something to match the paint spots," I said. "But I'm not as good as my sister. No promises on how it'll end up looking."

"It will be fine. I trust you."

I trust you. Her words made me ache.

"What do you even need the money for?" I asked. "You're not in debt to a bunch of loan sharks or something, are you?"

Miwako tilted her head. "What do you think?"

"Knowing you, it's probably for more romance novels."

"Yes, of course," she said.

"One can never have enough books."

"True. The question is where to put them."

"Get a new shelf?"

"What if there's no space for it?"

"Get a bigger house."

She nodded. "Sounds like a plan. Let me figure out how many hours I need to work for that."

We both laughed. Finally, we reached her neighborhood.

The night was quiet, the street empty. All I could hear was the occasional rustle of leaves. I looked up as I stretched my arms. The moon was bright and perfectly round, lighting up the cool dark sky.

As a kid, I used to imagine what sort of people lived on the moon. My mother told me the tale of Princess Kaguya, who was discovered as a baby by an old childless bamboo cutter inside the stalk of a glowing bamboo plant. He named her Kaguya, and she grew into an extraordinary beauty who captured the hearts of many men. Kaguya was revealed to be a celestial princess from the moon and eventually returned to her home, leaving her adoptive parents in tears.

Kaguya was supposed to be a princess, but I'd always pictured her as a fairy, with a floating robe and steps so light it was as if she were dancing in the air, jumping from rooftop to rooftop as she made her way back to the moon. *One, two, three . . .*

"Your sister really is pretty," Miwako said, startling me.

"You've said so quite a few times already," I said.

"She's like a fashion model, and so tall." She turned to me. "Isn't she almost your height? How tall are you, Ryusei?"

"About six feet, I think."

"Your sister must be at least five-ten. That's so tall for a girl."

I chuckled, though I felt crazy doing so. She had no idea how close she was to the truth about Fumi-nee.

"What's so funny?" she asked.

"Nothing," I said. "You always say what's on your mind, don't you?"

She shrugged. "Is that bad?"

"No, it's one of the things I like best about you. You shouldn't change."

She went quiet, probably embarrassed.

"This is my building," Miwako said and stopped walking. "You can go back now."

I looked at the apartment in front of us. A modest four-story structure painted white with rows of doors close to each other, probably only one-bedroom units.

"You live by yourself?" I asked.

She nodded. "My family's house is too far from campus. I didn't want to spend that much time commuting."

"I see," I mumbled. "All right, I'll see you tomorrow. Good night, Miwako."

"Good night, Ryusei."

She smiled at me, then started up the stairs. I pretended to walk away, but after two steps, I looked back. Miwako was looking at me too. We both laughed.

"Go home already!" she shouted.

I waved at her and took eight steps before turning around one last time. She was entering a unit on the second floor, the third from the right. I wondered if Miwako's apartment was number twenty-three, the same as the studio.

On my way home, I stopped at a convenience store for a bottle of umeshu. I drank quietly, alone in my room. My sister must've seen the empty bottle when she cleaned the next morning, but she never said a word.

As I drank, I thought about what I'd learned about Miwako

that afternoon. That she was clumsy at painting and bought her clothes from the bargain basements in Shinjuku and disliked children.

These were tiny steps. But if I continued to take them, I thought that one day, I might finally reach Miwako Sumida.

Dear Ryusei,

How are you? I hope things are well.

At this time of year, the leaves in Tokyo must be starting to fall. It's probably windy and cold there, especially at night. I know you usually wear thin clothing. Please at least put on a scarf when you go out, so you don't get sick.

I'm in the village where my great-grandmother grew up. I was nervous about coming here, since it's quite remote—only accessible on foot—and I'd never visited before. But it's so beautiful and peaceful here. We're at the top of a mountain, so the air is crisp and refreshing. There aren't many people here, perhaps about thirty families, mostly farmers.

I'm staying with a distant relative of mine who's set up a health clinic here. In the afternoons, she also holds free lessons for local children. In return for food and lodging, I help out with the day-to-day operations for this special school of sorts. We have students from as young as six to teenagers who will either leave soon or end up here forever.

My aunt—I call her that, though she's really more of a cousin—is named Miss Sugi. She's a single woman in her forties and the only doctor here. I hear she used to work at a big university hospital in Tokyo. Sometimes volunteers, usually university students, come to help out. But right now, it's just the two of us, so we get pretty busy.

Every day, I wake up around 5 A.M. to do the cleaning. I'm in charge of the state of the clinic's building and the house next to it, where Miss Sugi and I live. According to Miss Sugi, the house doubles as extra hospital lodging when needed, though we don't currently have any live-in patients. I also cook and prepare lesson plans for the students. After that, I tend to the kitchen garden and feed the cattle. The clinic has two cows, four goats, and a dozen chickens. Would you believe I've learned to milk cows and goats? It was a bit messy at first, but I've finally gotten used to it.

The lessons start in the afternoon, after most of the students are back from helping their families in the fields. They come around noon and eat lunch together, then divide into groups and do the exercises we give them.

I've noticed that what they're learning is years behind what we studied at their age. But according to Miss Sugi, it's good enough. Most of them will remain in the village their whole lives and take over their families' farms. A few might go to work in the factories, where basic literacy skills will come in handy.

Once in a while, we have a student who dreams of moving to the big city, and those who leave never come back. Miss Sugi hopes it's because they're too busy with their new lives, but I wouldn't be surprised if many of them are struggling to find full-time employment and are too embarrassed to return.

I teach here as well. I'm in charge of the art classes. Remember how Fumi-nee always laughed at my drawings? I'm the first to admit I'm not as talented as you, but your sister has coached me well in the past few months. I'm so much better now. I've passed along several of Fumi-nee's pointers to my students. Some have a knack for painting. I told Miss Sugi we should go to an art market in the city to sell their work. She said it was a good idea, except for the logistics of how to bring their paintings down the mountain. We'll have to think of a way around it, but I'm excited about the possibility.

After classes end, this place becomes quiet. Normally, I clean up and Miss Sugi prepares dinner. At the very end of the day,

Miss Sugi knits. She tried teaching me once, but I'm terrible at it. I wonder if it's for the same reason I'm not a natural artist.

It's past midnight. I have to get up early tomorrow, so I'll end here. I'll write to you again soon, Ryusei.

Miwako

3

On a Lovely Afternoon in July

A year after the first time I met Miwako, I attended her wake. When I arrived at the funeral home, a substantial number of visitors had already gathered. The first familiar face I saw was Sachiko's. Clutching a white handkerchief, she was sobbing. Chie went over and hugged her, both their eyes red and swollen. Not far from them, Toshi and Jin stood side by side in their stiff black suits. When they saw me and my sister, they bowed awkwardly, and we returned the gesture. It felt strange to see them looking so solemn.

"Let's go in," I said to my sister.

The room was packed with mourners in black, facing a coffin decorated with carnations and chrysanthemums. A framed photograph of Miwako was displayed on the altar. In the photo, which looked like it had been pulled straight from her student ID, she was unsmiling.

As I stared at the photo, it finally dawned on me that even though I was at Miwako's wake, it didn't seem like she was gone, just away for a while, like she had been for the past few months. That framed picture looked nothing like the Miwako I knew. When I closed my eyes, I could still hear her sharp, stubborn voice and surprisingly unbridled laugh. I recalled the second time I'd asked her out last summer.

We had been reading in the park on campus when Miwako said, "Those girls thought we were dating. Why didn't you say anything?"

I looked up from my book. A group of girls was walking away, giggling and whistling at us. I recognized them as juniors from my high school.

That summer, the weather was good—breezy and cool. Miwako and I had decided to read books on a park bench instead of our usual spot in the library. She'd tied her long hair up with a plain black hairband, but the wind had made it messy.

"They're going to spread rumors," Miwako said.

"Oh," I mumbled and looked up at her. "But that's fine, isn't it? Doesn't seem like something you'd care about."

She clicked her tongue. "Is it so you'll have fewer girls to bother you?"

I continued to read, or rather, pretend to read, absorbing none of the words on the page.

Leaning in closer to speak to her, I caught a strawberry scent; she always used the same shampoo. "What do you think?" I whispered. "Shall we put those rumors to rest?"

Miwako moved away, shrugging. "How exactly would you do that? Talk to every single one of them?"

"That—that's not what I meant," I stammered.

She looked into my eyes, and my heart pounded again. I took a deep breath and thought about the line I'd practiced so many times on the nights I couldn't sleep. The words came tumbling out.

"I like you," I said.

She frowned.

"I'd like us to be a couple," I said hurriedly. "Will you go out with me?"

She was silent, though her face had turned red. Better than her non-reactions, at least.

Miwako finally said, "That's not funny."

I swallowed hard. "I didn't mean it to be."

She stood. "Enough, Ryusei. You've gone too far."

"Miwako, I'm serious. You already know that."

Her posture was tense. I knew I should stop, but I couldn't.

"Please, let's at least give it a try," I continued.

"No," she said sternly. "I told you, it wouldn't work out between us."

And then she stood up and walked away without looking back.

Dumbfounded, I tried to refocus on my book to calm down. But it was no use. On a beautiful afternoon in July, for the second time, I had confessed my feelings to the girl I loved, and she'd turned me down without a moment of hesitation.

THE BUS RIDE BACK to Ueno seemed to last forever. The passengers took too long to board, and the driver navigated too slowly. The creaking of the doors as they opened and closed at each stop made me sick, and the noise of the teenagers at the back of the bus was headache-inducing.

The air-conditioning blasted away, chilling the inside of the vehicle. But when I leaned against the window, it was warm, baked by the afternoon sun.

The bus stopped again, and a bald middle-aged man in a suit came onboard. Carrying a tattered leather briefcase, he glanced around the bus and chose the empty seat in front of me. Once the journey had resumed, he took a newspaper out of his briefcase. The date read April 21, 1990.

Miwako Sumida had been dead for three days, but the world kept on as normal. The late cherry blossoms bloomed, lining the streets with a cotton-candy hue. Children in uniform ate their vanilla ice cream by the roadside, and birds pecked around at the park ground.

A falling petal stuck to my window pane. I traced it with my index finger, but the bus moved and sent the split-tipped petal to the ground.

"Ryu, are you all right?" my sister asked.

"I'm fine," I said after a moment, still staring out the window. "Of course I'm fine."

My sister sighed. I snuck a glance at her. She was nervously fiddling with her fingers. The polish on one of her nails was chipped. I made a point not to look at it. My sister wouldn't like it if she knew I'd seen the chip. She put so much effort into maintaining a flawless appearance. "Looking good is the first step toward feeling good," she always said.

The bus stopped again, and a group of boys got on. Sporting soccer uniforms from a neighborhood high school, they stood near the door and talked rowdily. Two of them were stealing glances at my sister, but she didn't seem to notice.

"You've got some admirers," I whispered.

"Oh," she mumbled, not even bothering to look.

At times, I would catch my sister staring intently at nothing in particular, which I'd always reasoned as one of her quirks. But on this particular occasion, she had me worried.

I reached for her hand. "Fumi-nee, are you all right?"

"I don't know." She turned to face me. "It's so sudden, isn't it? It feels like if I were to go to the studio and wait for Miwako, she would turn up any minute."

I looked straight ahead. "Should we do that, then? Let's go to the studio."

My sister nodded. I squeezed her hand.

I paused. "Why?"

"You don't have to tell me if you don't want to." She picked up another photograph to frame. "It's just that I've got plenty of time to listen to your story, and he sounds intriguing."

Hearing that, I envied Kenji a little. I knew it was a silly, petty jealousy, and that I was reading too much into her curiosity. And Miwako was right. We had plenty of time. So I told her about Kenji Ishihara.

4

A
Strawberry
Field
on a Warm
Summer
Day

Kenji had lived at the same orphanage as me and my sister.

"My sister says an orphanage is like a pet shop," I said. "The youngest puppies have the highest chance of being bought. But the older they get, the lower the probability anyone will want them."

Miwako stared at me. "That's pretty harsh, isn't it?"

"Yes, but it's true. The younger children are usually adopted quickly."

When our parents were killed in that car accident, my sister was fifteen and I was seven. She was almost too old to be in the orphanage. Nobody would adopt her. Some couples expressed interest in me, but only me. *He's a sweet, well-behaved boy*, the pastor in the orphanage told prospective parents. *We've always wanted a son just like him*, they replied. *Come live with us, Ryusei. We'll be your new family.*

But I didn't want to leave without my sister, so I turned all of them down. I wouldn't exchange the only real family I had for a group of strangers. It wouldn't be fair to her if I were the only one who found a new home.

"I didn't realize you were so thoughtful," Miwako said.

I stared off into the distance. "You're wrong. I wasn't being thoughtful. I was being a burden. If I had considered things properly, I would have realized my sister was better off without me."

"What makes you say that?"

"Because I wanted us to be together, she took me with her once she was a legal adult and had to leave the orphanage. If she hadn't had me dragging her down, she could've had a better life. Instead, she had to work day and night to support me."

Miwako was silent for a moment. "But that was the decision she made. I'm sure she wanted to be with you too."

I said nothing. I didn't tell Miwako I used to wake up in the middle of the night and see my sister sobbing silently, hand over her mouth to stifle any cries. Or how she would stare intently into an empty space sometimes, seemingly lost in her own world. *What weighed on you so much? Do you regret taking me with you? Do you wish you had abandoned me?* These questions constantly floated through my mind, but I could never bring myself to ask them. I was too afraid to hear her answers.

"What about Kenji?" Miwako asked.

"He's originally from Okinawa. He told us he used to live near the beach. I never asked when or how his parents passed away, but he came to Tokyo to live with his uncle, the owner of this studio. They stayed together for a couple of years, but eventually his uncle passed away from illness. None of his remaining relatives were willing to take him in, so he ended up living with us in the orphanage. Kenji said his uncle used to be a bicycle repairman."

Miwako gestured at the two rusty bicycles in the corner. "Did those belong to his uncle?"

"One of them. The other is Kenji's, but he never used it after his uncle's death." I glanced at the bicycles, which had stood against the wall for ages. "He said it would be too sad to ride it alone."

"So this studio was his inheritance when he got a little older."

"Yeah." I stretched my neck. Sitting down for so long to insert the photographs into the frames had made my whole body stiff. "Kenji is around the same age as Fumi-nee. The two of them were the oldest children in the orphanage. Maybe that's why they got along so well.

"After my sister and I left the orphanage, we were low on cash. We couldn't afford to rent a place in Tokyo, but my sister was adamant about not moving out of town. She didn't want us to live too far away from my elementary school. Thankfully, Kenji let us stay in the studio."

"You used to live here?"

"Yeah, sleeping bags and all that. It was really cold at night," I said, laughing. "Later on, my sister received more commissioned work, so we moved out to our current place. But she still comes back here to do her work. She says she's more productive outside the house."

"And she probably needs the space. Her paintings are huge."

I nodded. "That too."

"Where's Kenji now?"

"He vanished," I said. "He used to joke that once he saved up enough money, he was going to visit all the best surf spots in the world. Maybe he's doing that right now? Riding the waves in Bali, Hawaii, the Gold Coast. Who knows?" I shrugged. "He's a little crazy. I could never tell whether he was joking or not. But he's quite resourceful, and tough, so I'm sure he's fine wherever he is."

"Uh-huh." Miwako wiped the sweat off her forehead. "Do you think he's in love with Fumi-nee? And that's why he let her use the studio?"

I chuckled. "No, that's not possible."

"Why not?"

"It's just not."

Miwako shot me an intense look. "You know, normally, you're pretty open-minded, but you're so overprotective when it comes to your sister. Why are you convinced no man apart from you can sincerely care about her or make her happy?"

"What do you mean?"

"You're so intent on keeping her from getting a boyfriend. Fumi-nee is smart, talented, and beautiful. It's only natural for someone like her to date," Miwako said. "You can't stop her from exploring her options. She should be allowed to make her own decisions."

"She *is* making her own decisions," I said. "Her own stupid decisions."

Miwako crossed her arms. "You're just being mean."

"I have my reasons."

"Oh, really? Why don't you explain those to me?"

I said nothing.

She sighed. "Come on. How long are you going to hang on to your sister?"

"Forever, if I have to." I stopped, realizing how controlling I sounded. I took a deep breath and continued. "I'm not trying to hang on to her for too long."

"You just said forever. That seems pretty long to me."

"What I mean is, I'll be here to support her until the right person shows up. But only if they're the right one."

Miwako shook her head. "She might have made some bad decisions in the past and still do so once in a while, but she's not a kid. There's no need to protect her from everything and everyone. If you want to be a good brother, just be there for her when she needs you."

"I can't." I looked up. "Maybe I'm doing it for myself. But as annoying as it is, I don't want her to get hurt."

Miwako averted her eyes. She resumed her work quietly, as if what I'd said disturbed her. Had she somehow misunderstood? True, what I had said could have come off wrong, but I couldn't explain any further without revealing the truth about my sister.

I took another photograph and fixed it to a base. We had only gotten a third of the way through the stack.

"I'm so jealous of you," Miwako said. "Not only is your sister beautiful, she's intelligent and kind, and she loves you. I have an older brother, but I always fantasized about having an older sister. Someone to go shopping with and to share clothes with. I'd sneak out from my room at night and go to hers so we could talk about girl stuff. She would even let me try on her makeup."

"You have an overactive imagination," I said.

She shrugged. "I guess. But you simply can't do things like that with a brother."

I paused. "Have you tried?"

"Of course not."

"Then maybe you should."

"Don't be silly," she said. After a moment, she asked, "What about you, Ryusei? Do you ever wish you had a brother?"

Miwako's words cut me deeply. She hadn't meant anything by them—how could she possibly know?—but that didn't make them less painful. I hadn't planned to say anything, at least not for a while. I'd never told anyone, especially after what had happened to my sister. But this was Miwako. Maybe she would understand.

I swallowed hard. "Can I tell you something?"

She tilted her head. "Hmmm?"

"It's about my sister," I said, avoiding her eyes. "She was born as a boy."

Miwako scowled. "That's not funny."

"I didn't mean it to be."

"You mean . . ." Her words trailed off as the realization hit her. "I see."

"That's why I don't necessarily want her to date," I said. "There might be someone out there who will truly love her for who she is, but that possibility is slim. I don't want my sister getting hurt over and over. She's the only family I have."

I waited for Miwako's reply, but she didn't say anything. There was a long, awkward silence.

"Do you still think I'm lucky, Miwako?"

"Yes," she said. "You've had both a brother *and* a sister."

I smiled. Only Miwako would think like that.

"Actually," I said, leaning my back against the wall, "I always saw Fumi-nee as a sister, not a brother. I felt it even then. When she turned eighteen and we were about to leave the orphanage, she told me she was going to live as her true self. I couldn't have been happier."

I recalled the day we had that conversation. We were in our room, packing. I was getting ready to move out. It must have been very hard for her to bring it up then, but she was unflinching.

"That afternoon, she looked into my eyes and said, 'Ryu, I want to be the best version of myself. Not for anyone else, but for me.' Seeing her make that decision, I couldn't help but think, this person is so strong and beautiful. I'm really proud of her."

Miwako put her hand on mine. "She must have been proud of you too."

I nodded. "I appreciate you not being judgmental about this. It hasn't been easy. Fumi-nee has been through a lot." Pausing, I hesitated for a moment. "Besides everyday discrimination, I think she might have been bullied in school. But that was a long time ago and I was young, so I could have been mistaken."

"It must have been hard for her."

"Yes, but not as hard as hiding who she is."

"True."

"I couldn't have asked for a better sister. Sometimes, I feel I don't deserve her. She works so hard to put me through school."

Miwako reached for my hand and squeezed it. "She's a good person, isn't she?"

"Fumi-nee always said she only had two goals in life. One of them was to see me graduate from university and get a job at a good company," I said. "This has become my goal too, to get a high-paying job in sales or consulting so my sister can stop worrying about money. She wouldn't need to juggle so many projects anymore."

"That's really nice. What's Fumi-nee's other goal?"

I averted my eyes. "You should be able to guess."

"I'm not a mind-reader."

"I know, but . . ." I paused, unsure how to word it. "Well, she used to say that one day, when she had saved enough, she would go in for—"

"Gender reassignment surgery?"

I was surprised she had put it so plainly.

"Yes, something like that that," I muttered. "That's why she's taken on a second part-time job at night."

"What does she do?"

This was another piece of information I hadn't intended to volunteer, but the words had already slipped from my mouth.

"Fumi-nee is a hostess," I said.

"I see," she mumbled. "Well, she's certainly beautiful and charming. She must have a lot of clients."

I looked straight at Miwako. Her eyes were clear and bright. "You're beautiful too, you know."

She laughed. "You don't need to say that just to make me feel better."

"That wasn't why I said it."

Her face turned bright red. She continued with the task at hand but nearly dropped a glass case.

"Be careful," I said, secretly pleased.

"It's fine." She brushed me off. "So is Fumi-nee close to reaching her second goal?"

"I don't really know. After all these years, she should have quite a bit saved up, even after what her ex-boyfriend stole. Sometimes I wonder what's stopping her. But money is a sensitive topic in our household, as is her situation, so I can't really bring myself to ask."

Miwako lined up the photograph with the frame's edges. "Maybe Fumi-nee wants to keep things the way they are. Maybe she's realized she's perfect exactly the way she is."

She rendered me speechless again with that one musing. How could someone who had met my sister no more than a few weeks ago understand so much about her? On the surface, Miwako seemed blunt, never mincing her words. I would never have guessed she had so much compassion beneath. I wondered what had made her that way, and whether I would be the one to find out.

KENJI'S RUSTY BICYCLES WERE still sitting around in the studio. They looked much worse than they had when Miwako had first come.

Seeing that they were unlocked, and it was so easy to jump over the barrier, I wondered how long it would be before those bicycles met their end. Would someone eventually steal them, or would they simply break down, left to themselves? They must have been very nice once, but left to the elements, they'd become unsightly. Yet those bicycles gave me a kind of solace. They seemed to reflect the passage of time—how in the end, nothing was permanent.

"Ryu," called my sister from the office. "Don't just sit there. Help me move these canvases."

Getting up, I loosened my tie. "What are you looking for?"

"Those paintings Miwako did."

I felt a lump in my throat. "What do you need those for?"

"Hmm, I don't know," she said. "I just want to see them. Will you give me a hand?"

I hung my suit jacket on the back of the chair and entered the office. It was a small area, partitioned off by flimsy plastic walls. A fan stood in the corner of the room. On one side was a table with two folding chairs facing one another. On the other was a large stack of canvases. I went over and helped my sister shift the paintings around. Most were hers, but there were also a few of mine.

"When did you paint this?" my sister asked, singling out a canvas. "I never saw it."

I peeked over her shoulder. It was a painting of a strawberry field on a warm summer day. There was nothing else, just a seemingly endless field of red, ripe strawberries. Looking at it brought pain to my chest.

"It's beautiful, Ryu. Where did you get the idea?"

"I copied it from a calendar." I lied, not wanting to tell her it was a painting of Miwako, or rather, her fragrance. That shampoo she used, I still didn't know what kind it was. A couple of months ago, I'd gone to the supermarket and sniffed every brand of shampoo on the shelf to catch its scent, perhaps desperate to find a piece of her. But I couldn't find anything close.

At that moment, I could still remember the fragrance so clearly. But as the years went by, would it become less and less distinct until I forgot it completely? Would my memory of her warp and rust like those bicycles?

My sister put the canvas down and we continued to search in silence.

"Ryu, look. This one is Miwako's," she suddenly said.

The painting Fumi-nee had found showed two headshots next to each other. They were drawn far too symmetrically, and the colors lacked depth.

"This is the first painting she did." My sister stared at the canvas with a longing smile. "They're supposed to be us."

"Us?" My chest felt heavy.

"She was getting better. See here."

My sister took another canvas depicting the two bicycles in the warehouse, without the rust. I couldn't say the painting was impressive, but it was definitely a step up from the previous one. I had never seen Miwako paint, so she probably had done these with my sister when I hadn't been around.

I scanned the rest of the canvases. Despite never possessing the slightest desire to be an artist, my sister definitely had the talent for it. Fumi-nee did mostly abstract painting, but there was a peculiar quality that pulled people into her artwork. Her bold strokes gave off a sense of alienation and desperation, but her choice of muted colors conveyed a hidden loneliness. My sister had mastered the application of intricate details to her pieces. At the same time, she took extra care to make sure nothing was overwhelming. I recognized a delicate balance, a sense of equilibrium in all of her pieces. What my sister couldn't tell anyone, she whispered into her work.

"Ryu, have you seen this before?" my sister asked.

She was pointing to a painting of a cat sitting on a countertop next to a sink with running water. Behind the cat stood a vase filled with yellow daffodils. Judging from the rough strokes, it was another of Miwako's paintings.

I shook my head. "This is the first time I've seen it, but that cat must be Tama."

"Yes, it must be," she said. "I wonder what will happen to Tama. I didn't see her during the wake."

"Don't be silly. You can't bring a cat to a wake."

5

My
Own
Life Is
Anything
But
Romantic

Miwako had picked up Tama on a rainy day. I would never forget that morning, because it was the first and only time Miwako and I had slept together.

It happened a week before the new term started. I hadn't seen her for a while, as she had gone home to stay with her family for the winter break.

On the day she told me she would be back in her rented apartment, I decided to drop by to give her some apples. The orphanage received a large donation of apples every year from a patron in Aomori. There were far too many for them to eat, so the staff usually sold the rest to fundraise. My sister and I always bought a crate and shared the apples with our neighbors.

I hadn't yet reached Miwako's apartment when I spotted her leaving a convenience store. Instinctively, I called after her.

She looked up at me, surprised. "Ryusei, what are you doing here?"

I walked over to her. "We've got a lot of apples at home, so Fumi-nee asked me to bring you some." A white lie—of course, the idea had been mine.

"Let me help you," I said, taking the plastic bag from her hand and nearly dropping it. "Wow, what did you buy? It's so heavy."

"Some beer."

"Having a party?"

A grin slid across her face. "Yes, a party for one. With the new term starting, I thought I should celebrate."

"I'll join you," I said. "Two is always better than one when it comes to drinking."

Miwako laughed, which I took as a sign of agreement. We walked side by side to her apartment. I wasn't sure if it was my imagination or just that we hadn't seen each other in a while, but Miwako looked pale and thin, her collarbones more pronounced than I remembered.

"Really?" she exclaimed when I mentioned it. "No, I don't think I've lost any weight, but thanks."

"I didn't mean it as a compliment. I don't find stick-thin girls attractive."

"So you prefer curvy ones like Chie, with big breasts and all."

"I prefer everything in moderation."

We turned into her apartment building and took the stairs to the second floor. Next to the door was a decorative mailbox with a wooden bird perched on top, one of its wings chipped. Underneath was the number twenty-three, scribbled in black marker. So I'd guessed correctly.

"I must apologize, the place is a mess," Miwako said. "I haven't had a chance to tidy up."

I took off my shoes. "You can't possibly be messier than Toshi."

Coming in, I realized she was only being modest. Miwako's apartment, as I had guessed, was extremely neat. Small but cozy, it was a typical one-bedroom with a separate living, dining, and kitchen area. There was a wooden coffee table in the middle of the living room with a few circular cushions around it. A tall white bookshelf stood against one wall, and the other side of the room had a small television and a stereo set.

Miwako opened the windows. "Sit anywhere you want."

"Where's the fridge?" I asked.

"Let me take care of that. You're the guest." She took the plastic bag from my hand. "Just wait here. Make yourself comfortable."

Miwako disappeared into the kitchen, and I took the opportunity to peek at her bookshelf. The top row was full of textbooks, but the rest had only romance novels. Most in English, a couple in Japanese. Miwako and I had gone to Ikeda Bookshop together so many times, and on every occasion, she had left with a romance novel. I'd known she was into the genre, but for some reason, I'd expected to see other books here too.

She returned with an ice bucket full of Asahi Super Dry. "Sorry for the wait."

I frowned. "We're starting now?"

"Yes." Miwako put the bucket on the table and sat next to me, her legs folded in front of her chest. "Have you changed your mind?"

"No, it's not that," I said. "It's just that . . . it's only ten in the morning."

She shrugged. "Who cares?"

Miwako cracked open two of the cans and passed one to me. We toasted and drank together. The beer was crisp and clean, its coldness refreshing.

"You really like romance novels, don't you?" I asked.

Miwako laughed. "You're spying on me."

"It's hardly spying when your books are out on display for everyone."

"Hey, I don't invite everyone here," she said, laughing again.

"But you're not wrong. I do love romance novels, even if my own life is anything but romantic."

"When's the last time you had a boyfriend?"

She paused. "I've never dated anyone."

"Why not?"

She smiled. "Let's just say that there are two types of people. Those who are meant to date and those who aren't. I'm the latter."

"How can you know if you haven't tried seeing someone?" I took a sip of my beer.

"Like who? Are you volunteering?"

"I already did—twice—and you turned me down both times," I said. "If you've changed your mind, I'm still here. But I have to warn you, the vacancy won't last forever. I'm pretty popular, remember?"

We burst into laughter. When that died down, I looked into her eyes.

"Miwako, I'm serious. Just give me a chance."

She seemed like she was about to protest, so I added, "You don't need to give me an answer now. But please consider it. Okay?"

She looked away without responding. Not even a nod.

The sky was darkening. In the distance, thunder rumbled.

"Should we close the windows?" I asked.

Miwako shook her head. "Let's let it be. You don't mind, do you?"

I shrugged. "Why would I? It's your apartment."

"Uh-huh."

I turned to her. "Do you like rain?"

"Yes, I do," she whispered. "I always leave the windows open. I like watching the rain wash things away."

There was a long pause before she went on. "You know, lately I've been noticing all those little sounds. The creaking of doors opening and closing, water trickling from the tap, low coughs, approaching footsteps, soft knocks on the door, heavy breaths."

"Is that so?" I wondered if the alcohol and dark clouds were making her sentimental.

The white curtains on the windows flapped violently as the wind grew stronger.

"What are you thinking about?" she asked me.

"Nothing." I sipped my beer. "I'm not thinking about anything."

Miwako straightened her legs out in front of her to stretch, pointing her toes. She wiggled them before folding her legs up again. Resting her chin on her knees, she tilted her head slightly as she reached for her beer.

The rain started, and drops of water came in. Darkened splotches appeared on the curtains. I glanced over at Miwako, but she didn't seem to care. Drink in hand, she continued to stare blankly ahead. The wind caressed her long black hair.

Then she put down her beer and took off her glasses. My heart skipped a beat. Her round eyes looked brighter, almost like they were sparkling, and her sharp nose was more apparent.

"You should get new glasses," I said. "Those frames don't suit you."

She looked at them. "I don't wear these because I need them. They're a memento from my father."

"Your father?"

"Yes. I mean, my birth father. He passed away when I was young," she said, pausing. "He had cancer. By the time the doctor diagnosed it, his illness had already reached a terminal stage. These glasses are one of the last things he left me."

I felt a lump in my throat. "I'm sorry to hear that."

"Don't be. I still have my mother, just like how you still have Fumi-nee." She glanced at me and smiled. "It's not that bad."

I cleared my throat. "What are you talking about? I would give anything to have my parents back. I'm sure you feel the same way."

Miwako lowered her head. Her smile was gone.

"I'm sorry," I said. "I didn't mean to imply that I understand what you've been through. I know our situations are different."

She looked up. "My mother remarried a few years ago."

"Do you resent your stepfather?"

"No, it's the opposite," Miwako said, shaking her head. "He's a very nice man, but I . . ."

She stopped talking. Still sipping my beer, I waited until she was ready.

Outside, the rain grew heavier. The roaring thunder moved closer and closer. I thought of my sister, who was supposed to be in the studio. I hoped she'd thought to bring an umbrella. But knowing her, she most likely hadn't. She would just stay there and work until the rain stopped.

"When you told me you had refused to be adopted so you could stay with your sister, I felt ashamed," Miwako continued.

I turned to her. "Why would you say that?"

"I always thought it was going to be just my mother and me. But after a while, she told me about a colleague she'd been seeing. To be honest, I was too shocked to reply."

I looked at Miwako, but she was still staring into the distance.

"Later that week, she introduced me to Mr. Sumida. He seemed kind and sincere, which he *is*. He's also one of the few people who makes me feel comfortable. I've never admitted it to anyone, but from the first time I saw him, I wanted him to stay with us. I hadn't seen my mother look so happy since before my father's passing."

"What's the problem, then?"

She turned to me. "Sometimes I wonder if I'm betraying my father by replacing him with someone else."

"Miwako, don't be silly." I put my hands on her shoulders and drew her close. "Your father would have been happy to know you and your mother are doing well."

She leaned in toward me. I moved my hands to her back and embraced her. Closing my eyes, I breathed in that familiar summer scent in her hair. She was usually so strong and opinionated, but then there were moments like this, when it felt like she was much younger, confused and lost.

"You really don't think my father would hate us?" she asked.

"Of course not," I said. "Imagine if you were in his position. What would you think? Wouldn't you be happy the family you left behind was doing all right? Living your life well is also a way to cherish his memory."

She nodded, smiling slightly.

I smoothed her hair. "You said that once, you thought it would only be your mother. Does that mean that your brother . . ."

"Yes, he's my stepbrother. My new father's son. Mr. Sumida's first wife ran away with another man, leaving him with Eiji, who's a few years older than me."

"Is he good to you?"

She stared off into the distance again for a moment. "Yes, he's a great brother. Very caring and understanding. Everything is perfect. I couldn't ask for more."

"That's good. I'm sure your father would be relieved too. He would be at peace knowing you've got yourself a good family."

Miwako buried her face in my chest. I touched her hair, running my fingers slowly through it. I moved one hand down to her waist. She pulled back and our eyes met. Inching forward, I kissed her. Our first kiss tasted like beer.

Then our lips met again. One hand still at the back of her head, I pulled her closer to me. She closed her eyes. Tentatively, I slid my right hand up toward her chest. She didn't resist. Her breast fit perfectly in my hand. I felt blood rush to my ears.

Then I stopped myself. Was this really what she wanted?

"Do you want to keep going?" I asked. "We don't have to. It's all right. We can stop."

Her eyes still shut, she said, "No, don't stop. This is what I want."

"MIWAKO."

I whispered her name again, but she remained quiet. She lay on the bed with her back to me. I looked at the curve of her spine, mentally tracing her backbone. Soft sunlight filtered into the apartment, shining on her pale skin. Her bare back was so lovely, but she still somehow seemed so small and lonely.

The curtains had stopped flapping. The rain had turned to drizzle, and the air brought in the smell of fresh soil. I could almost imagine the wet leaves outside, torn and broken and scattered in the drain.

I got dressed and went to the living room, picking up the empty beer cans on the floor. I wiped up the rainwater near the window using an old rag I found in the kitchen. When I returned to the bedroom, Miwako was still lying in the same position, but she was too still to actually be sleeping.

Sitting on the bed, I whispered, "I know you're up."

She didn't respond.

"Come on, let's go for lunch. You must be hungry," I said. When she didn't respond, I asked, "Are you okay?"

Finally, Miwako turned to face me. "I'm fine."

"Uh-huh," I mumbled, averting my eyes from her naked chest.

She got up and went to shower, leaving the bathroom door open. I could see her outline behind the frosted glass. She felt so distant, even after what had just happened. Had I taken advantage of her in a moment of weakness?

I cleared my throat. "Miwako, can I ask you something?"

"Yes?" she replied, her voice clear.

"Why did we, you know—"

"Why did we have sex?"

"Um, yeah." I cracked my knuckles.

She took a while to answer. "You wanted it, didn't you?"

"Well, yeah," I mumbled.

The sound of running water floated through the bathroom doorway. As I continued to gaze at her blurred outline, an unbearable dread hit me. Did Miwako not think of what had just happened as significant in any way?

Miwako stepped out of the shower, clad in a bath towel. Her skin was damp. Droplets of water fell from her hair, creating a trail on the floor. She walked over to her wardrobe and asked, "What are we having for lunch?"

I forced a smile, trying not to look shaken. "You can choose."

"Anywhere is fine. You decide."

"What about the little yakitori stall we went to last time? It's close by," I said. "You said you like their chicken."

"Yeah, that place is good."

She took the towel off, and I immediately turned away, my face flushing. I was making a fool out of myself, acting as if it was the first time I'd slept with anyone.

Then I remembered something.

"Miwako," I said softly. "This wasn't your first time, was it?"

"No, it wasn't," she said. "Is that a problem?"

I felt a lump in my throat. "Not at all. You just mentioned earlier that you'd never had a boyfriend before. Was that a lie?"

"No, it's true."

Miwako sat next to me, now fully dressed in a loose white cotton T-shirt and denim shorts. She had lovely collarbones. As she looked into my eyes, I tried to analyze her expression, but came away with nothing.

It was none of my business, but I asked, "Who did you sleep with?"

"Someone in high school," she said. "He wasn't my boyfriend. Just a classmate."

I had slept with a girl in high school too—my second girlfriend. Hardly unexpected. A number of us had. I wondered why I had asked the question. I swallowed and said, "So you liked him."

Miwako shook her head. "No. I told you, we were only classmates. I didn't have any romantic feelings for him."

"I don't understand. Then why did you sleep with him?"

"You're really asking that?" she said, chuckling. "Are you sure you want to know the answer? You're not going to like it."

"Just tell me," I said.

"Fine, if you insist." Miwako crossed her arms. "I slept with him out of spite. He was a nice enough guy, a quiet student. Some of the girls in school thought he was good-looking. He had a girlfriend at that time, and he was friends with the popular kids, but . . ." Her words trailed off.

"But what?"

"He had this older sister," she said. "She loved to cook. She made all his lunches from scratch, and they looked amazing. He would bring the most elaborate homemade bento boxes to class."

I frowned, confused. What did that have to do with sex?

"I guess I was jealous," she continued. "My mother worked long hours; she never had the time to make me a fancy lunch box. I told you, I've always wanted a sister."

I waited for her to continue, but she said nothing more.

"That's it?" I asked.

She nodded. "Yeah, that's it."

I tried to laugh, but I couldn't. I didn't get it. "You're telling me you slept with your classmate because he had a sister who made him bento boxes? What kind of reasoning is that?"

She shrugged. "Pretty silly, I suppose. I told you you weren't going to like it. You wouldn't understand."

"You're right, I don't. Is that why you slept with me?" It was hard to ask, but it wasn't out of the question. "To spite me? Because of Fumi-nee."

Miwako shrugged again and lay back on the bed. "I don't know," she said softly.

I should have been angry, but all I wanted to do was lie next to her, to take her into my arms again. I had no right to be upset. After all, it had been my idea. I'd kissed her first, initiated everything. I'd finally slept with the girl I had pursued for months, but I wished I could take it all back.

No. There was no way to have known what would happen after this.

"Hey Ryusei, don't you think Fumi-nee would make a bad sister-in-law for me if we ended up together?" Miwako asked. "She doesn't like me."

This time, I managed to laugh, trying not to read too much into the mention of us together.

"Even *you* can see she hates me," she continued. "So you should know she's not the reason I slept with you."

I could tell Miwako was lying. Despite their frequent bickering, Fumi-nee liked her. My sister had mentioned more than once how much she loved Miwako's bluntness. Miwako was just trying to make me feel better, and while I appreciated it, it didn't make it easier to process that what had happened meant nothing to her.

Nothing personal. Just sex.

Miwako got up and grabbed my hand. "Let's go. I'm hungry."

I looked out the window. "It's still drizzling."

"I don't mind, do you?"

"Yes, I do." I didn't want her to get sick.

She shrugged. "There's an umbrella by the door."

MIWAKO STOPPED WALKING. SHE glanced at me and said, "Did you hear that?"

"Hear what?" I asked, tilting my head to listen.

Without answering, she turned back and ran into the alley we'd just passed.

"Wait," I shouted, chasing after her. "Where are you going?"

The alley was sandwiched between two apartment buildings, and some residents had illegally dumped their rubbish there. An old television set, broken plastic chairs, and a tattered giant teddy bear with missing limbs were piled among cardboard boxes.

Stopping in front of one cardboard box, Miwako crouched down and opened it. There was a kitten inside. Its fur, white with patches of black and orange, was soaked. The tiny animal looked cold and frightened.

"Don't touch it," I said. "You'll only make things worse for it, since you can't bring it back."

Ignoring my advice, Miwako picked up the kitten. It purred and curled up in her arms.

"Don't worry. I'm going to take care of it," she said.

She had to be joking. "Are you even allowed to keep cats in your apartment?"

"No one needs to know."

"Don't be irresponsible. What will happen if your neighbors report you to the landlord?"

Miwako stroked its belly. "You're being paranoid. No one will find out. Even if someone did report it, I could always ask my mother for help."

"If you say so," I said, sighing. No matter what anyone said, once Miwako made up her mind, that was it.

She glanced at me. "Do you think we can keep it in the studio?"

"I don't think that's a good idea. The cat will climb all over the canvases and mess up the paints. Fumi-nee would never allow it."

"That's true," she said. "Anyway, I'll explore the options. I guess before we find it a permanent home, I'll just have to look after it."

Cradling the kitten, Miwako seemed so at ease. Her expression softened, and she was so calm and peaceful—it was the same look she had when she was reading. Perhaps keeping the cat wasn't such a bad idea.

"Is it a boy or girl?" I asked.

Miwako checked. "A girl, I think."

"What's her name?"

She prodded the box, searching for clues. "Nothing here. I guess we can name her whatever we like. Any suggestions?"

I took the kitten from her. "What about 'Tama' for 'jewel'?"

"I like that," Miwako said.

"She's like a treasure, isn't she? Because you dug her out from all that other stuff. Maybe I should get in an old box and see if you'd pick me up too."

Miwako glared at me. "Don't be stupid."

I laughed. "Doesn't she look like one of those lucky cat figurines?"

She nodded. "Hey Ryusei, do you know what a cat does with its nine lives?" She recited the old English proverb. "For three it plays, for three it strays, and for the last three it stays."

I chuckled. "Well, cats have good balance and reflexes, so they tend to escape from what would normally be deadly situations."

"No," she said, her expression serious. "Cats really do have lives to spare, and they can go between the worlds of the living and the dead."

I murmured in vague agreement, wondering why she was so adamant about this, though I found it endearing. "Shall we head back?"

She nodded.

For a brief moment, I managed to brush off what had happened between us. Miwako hummed as she carried the kitten back to her apartment, and I sheltered them with a translucent plastic umbrella, the sounds of our steps overlapping.

"WHERE DO YOU THINK Tama is now?" my sister asked, still looking at the painting of the cat.

"Probably at Miwako's mother's house," I said. "She told me that if her landlord found out about Tama and threatened to evict her, the family would put her up there."

"Tama must miss Miwako."

"We all do, don't we?" I said, and my sister started to cry.

I offered my hand to help her up. "Should we go home? It's getting dark. Or do you want to stay here a while?"

She wiped her tears away. "No, let's go back."

We left the studio, walking side by side and holding hands on the quiet street. My sister said she didn't want to take the bus.

"Let's take our time," she said, and I mumbled in agreement. I wasn't in the mood to argue, even though the night was cold and windy. I offered my jacket to her, but she declined.

"Our bodies aren't so different," she said. "You don't need to be a gentleman."

It pained me to hear her say things like that, but I couldn't think of the right response.

"Did you keep those letters Miwako sent you?" my sister asked.

"No. I threw them away a long time ago." I lied, not wanting her to worry. "None of them said anything important. They were just the usual hellos, asking how I was doing. They could have been to anyone."

"Oh," she said. I caught a hint of skepticism in her voice.

"You know I'm not the type of person to keep letters, don't you?"

She gave a thin smile. "Of course not. You're not that sentimental."

Dear Ryusei,

This is my last letter. I'll say what I should have the first time I wrote to you.

It's about what happened the day we found Tama.

I know I hurt you. You probably thought I did it just because I could, without any thought about what it meant for you.

But that's not true.

Ryusei, I only did what I did that day because it was you. Yes, there was something that drove me to it, something I've been hiding from you. I can't go into detail, but I promise that when we meet again, I'll tell you the truth.

Miwako

6

She
Isn't
Cut Out
to Be
a
Model

When I opened my eyes, everything was bright. The white ceiling was blinding. The fan moved slower than usual. I counted its turns. One, two, three, four. I had to stop because my head hurt so badly.

The door opened. My sister entered in her pink pajamas, face covered with a homemade mask.

"I called for you so many times," she said. "Why didn't you come out?"

"I was sleeping." I tried to sit up, but my whole body ached. "What do you want?"

My sister leaned in closer and took a sniff. "Have you been drinking?"

"Just a little."

"You're still drunk."

"Stop raising your voice. My head hurts."

She crossed her arms. "Miwako's mother is on the phone."

I tensed, feeling instantly more alert.

"But since you're not in the right state of mind, I'll tell her you're still sleeping."

"No," I said, forcing myself up. "I'll take the call."

My sister shrugged and I walked past her out of the room.

"Ryu!" she shouted. "Go take a shower after the call. You smell awful."

"Shut up," I said, already aware I reeked of alcohol and sweat.

I tried to steady myself as I walked to the living room. Clearing my throat, I went to pick up the phone.

"Good morning, this is Ryusei Yanagi."

"Good morning, Yanagi," a woman with a muffled voice greeted me. "This is Akemi Kojima, Miwako's mother. We met during the wake."

Kojima. Had that been Miwako's previous family name?

"Yanagi?"

"Yes, I'm sorry," I quickly said. "What can I do for you, Mrs. Kojima?"

"It's about Miwako."

I waited.

"She left instructions for what to do with her personal belongings. Your name is on the list. I'm thinking of distributing her things this afternoon. I know this is rather last-minute, so if you have another engagement . . ."

"I'll be there," I said. "What time should I come?"

"Is five o'clock all right?"

"Yes, that's fine." I grabbed the pen and notepad Fumi-nee always left next to the phone. "Can I trouble you for your address?"

I wrote as Miwako's mother dictated. The house was in Katsushika. It would take me at least an hour to get there, probably more.

After setting the phone down, I sat at the kitchen table.

"Ryu."

I looked up. My sister held out a glass of water.

"Lemon water," she said. "It's excellent for a hangover. Make sure to finish it."

I sat up and took the glass from her hand.

"If you're not feeling better in an hour, I have some aspirin."

"This is fine," I said, gulping down the sour liquid. "I'm just a little dizzy. Nothing to worry about."

"When it comes to curing hangovers, you should trust me a little more." She winked. "Your older sister hasn't worked at a bar for the last seven years for nothing."

I laughed, but somehow it sounded like I was choking. Before my sister could say anything else, I returned to my room, not wishing to worry her.

THE FIRST THING I noticed upon arriving at Miwako's family's home was the nameplate out front. It bore the name Kojima, not Sumida. Other than that, the house was pretty much what I'd expected—a simple, single-story modern structure in an idyllic neighborhood in northeast Tokyo.

Just as I was about to go through the gate, I spotted Jin smoking by the roadside half a block away. I walked over to him.

"Hey," I called awkwardly.

He straightened his posture. "Oh, hey. What brings you here?"

"Miwako's mother invited me. What about you?"

"I'm here with my girl. She got a call too." He gestured to the house. "Sachiko and Chie are already inside." Jin held out his box of Hope Menthol. "Want a smoke?"

"Thanks," I muttered. I slid a stick out and leaned toward Jin, who lit it for me. I took a deep puff and exhaled the white vapor. I began to cough. It had been a while since I'd last smoked.

"Are you all right?" Jin asked.

I nodded. "I'm fine. A little out of practice."

"I didn't know you quit smoking."

"I didn't really. I just don't go out of my way to buy cigarettes anymore. My sister doesn't like it when I smoke around her." Even though nearly all her clients at the bar smoked.

"Ah, that sister of yours. She's gorgeous." Jin paused. "You know, I've wanted to tell you this for the longest time. There's something different about her. I can't put my finger on it, but it's definitely there. And I don't mean it in a bad way."

I said nothing.

"Let's just say she's special," Jin said.

"She is," I said.

Jin nodded but said nothing else. If the circumstances had been less somber, he probably would have teased me about how close my sister and I were. Instead, we continued to smoke in silence. Suddenly, I recalled the conversation with Miwako on the day we'd slept together.

"Hey Jin, remember how you told me you knew Miwako in high school?" I asked. "How the two of you didn't get along?"

"I can't believe you remember that." He chuckled. "But yeah, we certainly didn't."

"Why not?"

He shook his head. "You don't want to know."

"I do."

Jin stared at the cigarette in his hand. "Are you still in love with her?"

"Stop dodging the question."

"It's important." He took a puff and turned to face me. "If you're still not over her, you're not going to want to know."

A pain tugged at my chest. I forced myself to look nonchalant, though I doubted it was fooling anyone. "Did you sleep with her?"

He laughed. "No way. Don't be crazy. No offense, but she's not my type."

"Oh, right," I mumbled. "You're an only child."

"What does that have to do with anything?"

"Nothing. Forget it." I flicked the ashes off my cigarette. "Tell me this thing I wouldn't want to know."

"You just can't give it up, can you?" Jin blew the cigarette smoke slowly. "When we were classmates in high school, Miwako caught me and a good friend of mine smoking behind the school. She ratted us out to the teacher and we got in trouble. I thought she hated us, but in this strange turn of events, she ended up sleeping with my friend."

"Uh-huh."

"I don't get what was going through their heads, really," he continued. "My friend was dating a girl who—again, no offense—looked way better than Miwako. I thought they made a cute couple. The week after my friend slept with Miwako, everyone found out about it."

I was silent.

"If you ask me, I don't even think they liked each other. After that one encounter, they never spoke more than was necessary. As if nothing had ever happened."

"Miwako must've been furious that everyone knew."

"That's the thing. My friend isn't the type to brag about things like that," Jin said before taking a puff. "You might not believe this, but I'm pretty sure Miwako was the one who spread the news. What her goal was, I have no idea. But thanks to her, my friend got dumped pretty publicly by his girlfriend."

"Your friend didn't tell you anything?"

Jin shook his head. "Like I said, he wasn't the type to talk about private matters. When I cornered him, he only said he'd been curious. That's it. Curious. I couldn't believe that guy. He'd always been quiet. Not a loner, mind you, just didn't talk much." He stopped and stared at his cigarette.

"So that was why you didn't like Miwako? Because she slept with your friend for no reason?"

"I just found her appalling. You know, the way she did things. First off, did she really have to report us to the teacher? It was completely uncalled for. I have no issue with her choosing to sleep with my friend, but why tell everyone about it? I just don't get it."

Taking a puff, I told Jin, "Miwako had her own way of thinking."

"You're blinded by love, my friend."

"This has nothing to do with that."

Jin raised an eyebrow. "Oh, really?"

After taking a final inhale, I crushed the cigarette against the concrete wall. "I'd better go in now."

"Yeah," he said. "Take care. Let's catch up soon."

I nodded and walked toward the house. The iron gates were closed, but not locked. Beyond the entryway, several pairs of shoes were laid neatly in front of the door.

"Excuse me," I called out.

"One moment, please," said a soft voice from inside of the house.

A lady in a black kimono came out in a hurry. A surgical mask covered her nose and mouth, which explained why her voice had been so muffled on the phone. Even though half her face was covered, I recognized her as Miwako's mother. They had the same bright eyes.

"Good afternoon," I said, bowing.

She opened the gate. "Please come in. My apologies for asking you here on such short notice."

"Don't worry about that. I had no plans this afternoon." I took my shoes off. "Are you unwell, Mrs. Kojima?"

She shook her head. "It's the cat. I'm allergic."

"Ah, is Tama here?"

"That's the cat's name?"

"Yes."

"My daughter never told me she had a pet," she said, sighing. "So, you're familiar with the cat, Yanagi? I found it wandering in front of Miwako's apartment."

Before I could answer, Tama walked out of the house. The bell on her collar jingled. Mrs. Kojima kept her distance as Tama came straight to me. The cat purred and circled my legs. I crouched down to stroke her head.

"Hello there. How are you?" I greeted her. "It's been a while."

Tama purred again and curled her tail around her legs.

"You're good with animals, aren't you?" Mrs. Kojima said. She led me in while Tama followed behind us.

In the living room, Chie and Sachiko sat next to each other on a white sofa. Sachiko's eyes were swollen. I nodded at them and they responded in kind.

"Please, take a seat," Mrs. Kojima told me before excusing herself to retrieve the letter from her room.

I settled myself on the sofa across from the girls, a low square table separating us. I looked around, wondering where Mr. Sumida and Miwako's stepbrother were.

On my right, an old photograph stood atop a wooden cabinet. The photos showed a younger Miwako with her mother and a man, wearing the glasses I knew so well. I swallowed, barely able to breathe.

Tama came and curled up near my feet. Her warm belly calmed my nerves. I stroked her again on the head and then on her neck, comforted by her presence.

Mrs. Kojima returned with a white envelope.

"Miwako left me this letter," Mrs. Kojima said, opening it. "I'll read it to you all."

Dear Mother,

By the time you read this, I will be in a better place.

Forgive me for leaving so early. This has nothing to do with you. It was a decision I made myself. This is what I want. There is no one to blame.

If a reason is needed, then this is what I can say: I'm tired. So, so tired.

I hope you'll understand, and that you'll let me go.

Please live well and be happy—for yourself, and also for me.

Miwako

P.S. I know I have no right to ask any favors of you, but I hope you'll carry out these final wishes:

1. I'd like to donate all my personal belongings to charity, except for my romance novel collection. I want to give that to my friends, Chie Ohno and Sachiko Hayami.

2. I've been keeping a female calico cat. She ran away recently, but she might come back soon. I've attached a photograph so you'll recognize her. She has a red collar with a silver bell. I know you're allergic to cats, but if she returns, would you give her some food and keep her for a while? I want my friend, Ryusei Yanagi, to choose a home for her. I've enclosed a letter for him.

By the time Mrs. Kojima finished reading the letter, her eyes were red. Chie and Sachiko were crying too, and I felt like I was suffocating.

Wiping away her tears, Mrs. Kojima asked Chie and Sachiko, "Will you accept her books?"

Chie nodded. "Of course. I promise I'll treasure them."

Sachiko tried to answer, but no sound came out. She just kept nodding.

Mrs. Kojima turned to me and passed me a letter. "This is for you, Yanagi."

When I took the letter from her, a photo of Tama slipped out. I was the one who had taken that photograph.

SOMETIME LAST YEAR, MY sister had needed to document some of her paintings. I was resting in my room when she came in and told me what to do.

"Just take a snapshot of all the paintings you can find in the studio." She handed me a Nikon FM2. "It doesn't need to be fancy, but make sure you capture every single piece of artwork. Ask Miwako to help."

"What do you need these for?"

"An exhibition," she said. "The organizer requested photographs for the catalog."

I sat down and checked the camera. The film chamber was empty. "You don't usually do exhibitions."

"Yes, but this one's a little different. A lot of business owners go to that gallery to buy art pieces for their offices."

"Ah, there's potential money. No wonder Miss Yanagi is interested."

"Yes, so you'd better do this properly. I need the photographs by the weekend."

The next day, I bought three rolls of film and asked Miwako to help me. We spent half the day photographing my sister's paintings. By the time we were done, we had only used half of the last roll. I discreetly pointed the camera at Miwako, hoping to sneak a photo, but she noticed.

"Stop that," she said, glaring at me. "I don't like being photographed."

"Come on, don't let the rest of the film go to waste," I pleaded. "We still have a bunch of shots left, but I need to get the negatives developed today."

Her eyes lit up. "In that case, why don't you take some pictures of Tama? She's growing so fast. Soon, she'll be a fully grown cat, and I won't have anything to remember her adorable kitten days."

"You make it sound like Tama is your child."

"She *is* my child," Miwako said. "And if she ever goes missing, we can use the photograph for a missing cat poster."

"Don't be ridiculous. How would she go missing? She's in your apartment all the time." I got up and packed the camera into its bag. "But sure, let's do that. We can go to your place and take Tama's portrait."

What I'd said offhand turned out to be a difficult task. Tama wouldn't sit still. She hated the camera. Miwako and I tried everything from treats and toys to making childish noises. Somehow, the cat always managed to dodge the camera.

After a few hours of trying in vain, both of us collapsed on the bed. The whole apartment was in chaos, pillows and blankets strewn all over the floor.

"I don't think I could be a pet photographer," I said, catching my breath.

"Me neither," Miwako said. "Or maybe Tama isn't cut out to be a model."

I laughed. "That's another possibility."

Miwako rolled over and turned to Tama, who sat on her dressing table. "What do you think, Tama? We don't think you have what it takes to be a supermodel."

Tama purred. For once, she sat still and looked in my direction. I crawled out of the bed and reached for the camera on the floor.

"What are you doing?" Miwako asked.

"Shh," I hissed. "Don't make any noise."

Holding my breath, I aimed at Tama and clicked the shutter. It was only a split second, but I knew I'd managed to capture the shot. Tama immediately jumped off the table and ran to the living room.

"Did you get it?" Miwako asked.

"Yes," I said. "I'm pretty sure."

"Let me develop the film." She took the camera. "Tell Fumi-nee I'll give her the printed photographs this coming Sunday afternoon."

"That's not too much trouble for you?"

She shook her head. "Not at all."

In the end, Miwako told me the photograph never materialized. She said Tama's full body wasn't in any of the frames.

"I'm pretty sure I got her in my last shot," I said. "Are you sure you checked the negatives properly?"

She nodded. "I guess you've got a little too much confidence in yourself."

But now, picking up the fallen photograph, I knew it was the one I had taken of Tama that day. Why had Miwako lied about such a thing?

I stared at the folded letter in my hand, wondering if she had left me any answers.

7

The
Summer
Had
Forever
Left Her

"Ryusei Yanagi," my sister said, voice raised. "What on earth is that?"

"It's a cat," I said, putting the crate down and opening its door. "Tama, go greet Miss Yanagi."

Tama leaped out and went to my sister.

"I'm not blind. But why is she here?" Despite her harsh words, Fumi-nee kneeled and stroked Tama lovingly.

"She has nowhere else to go. Can't she live with us for a while?"

"I thought you said Miwako's family was taking care of her."

"That's no good. Her mother's allergic to cats." I crouched down. "Besides, I'm sure she prefers it here."

Tama curled up on my sister's lap.

"See? Look how comfortable she is," I said.

My sister shook her head. "You know pets aren't allowed in this building. The landlady lives on our floor. She'll definitely find out."

"What about the studio?" I took out Tama's bowl and a can of cat food from my bag. "It shouldn't be a problem for us to keep her there."

"The studio has a lot of openings. What if she escapes?"

"Don't worry. If Tama wants to leave, she'll get out no matter where you put her," I said. "Anyway, she's a smart cat. Even when she's been gone for a while, she always finds her way home."

I peeled open the lid on the can and emptied it into the bowl. Tama finally left Fumi-nee's lap and came to me.

"She looks hungry," my sister said.

"Miwako's mother didn't know what brand Tama normally ate, so she bought random cat food. Tama wouldn't touch it."

"Picky girl. Just like me." Fumi-nee stared at Tama, deep in thought.

I tilted my head. "So?"

After a long silence, my sister asked, "You promise to be responsible for her? Buy all her food and clean up after her?"

"Yes, I promise. We can put your paintings inside the office and lock the door, just to make sure Tama doesn't ruin any of them."

"That's a good idea," she said. "All right, I'll let Tama stay in the studio temporarily. But if she misbehaves, or you don't keep your word, she has to leave."

"Deal."

"But how long are you planning to keep Tama there?"

Pausing, I remembered Miwako's letter. "Until I decide who should keep her."

My sister raised her brow. "What do you mean?"

I took a letter from my bag and handed it to her. "Miwako left me this."

She looked at me. "Do you want me to read it?"

"Yes, go ahead."

Dear Ryusei,

I'm sorry to ask you for help, but you're the only one I can trust to do this.

It's about Tama. She's still missing. When she returns, please help her find a new home with someone who will cherish her even more than I do.

Goodbye, and take care.

Miwako

My sister looked up. "Tama went missing?"

"She did," I said, trying to remember when. It had been a few weeks before Miwako left Tokyo.

THAT NIGHT, MIWAKO HAD turned up at the studio. My sister had gone to meet one of her clients, so I was the only one there. I hadn't expected anyone, but what surprised me more than Miwako's unannounced visit was her appearance. Her hair was in disarray, and she was wearing a pair of house slippers.

"Tama's missing," she said, her voice small. "She was still around when I left my apartment. But when I came back, she was gone. I don't know what to do."

I paused, taking in the news. "Why don't you come in?"

Guiding her inside, I pulled a plastic chair out for her. Miwako sat, trembling. I went into the office to get her a cup of warm water. She took it but just held it in her hands.

"Are you all right?" I asked, crouching down in front of her.

Miwako looked at me. After a long moment, she mumbled, "Yes."

I pulled up a chair and sat next to her. "Do you want to tell me exactly what happened?"

She bit her lip. "I left after feeding Tama in the morning. She was asleep on my bed. But when I came home, I couldn't find her anywhere."

"Did you lock the door?"

"I did."

"Was it unlocked when you got back? Do you think someone could've broken in?"

She shook her head. "No, it was still locked."

"Are you sure Tama didn't slip out when you were leaving the house?"

Miwako frowned. "I would have realized something like that, don't you think?"

"Well, it's one possible explanation," I said. "Could she have escaped through the window?"

"I keep all the windows closed whenever I leave the house."

I nodded slowly. "Have you been searching for her?"

"Yes, I went around the neighborhood. I even brought out her food bowl."

I sighed. "Do you want to go look for her together?"

She quickly nodded.

Getting up, I offered her my hand. "Don't worry, we'll find her. Any idea where she might've gone?"

"She's never left my apartment. Not since I first brought her in."

I looked at her house slippers. They were stained with mud.

"Do you want to go back to your apartment and change into proper shoes first?"

She looked down, but the question didn't seem to affect her. "I'm okay. Let's look for Tama first. What if she got hit by a car or attacked by a dog?"

I forced a smile. "You worry too much. Tama probably just followed some handsome male cat home."

Miwako was silent. Taking her hand, I led her toward her apartment. I discreetly scanned our surroundings for Tama, but the cat was nowhere. In the distance, I heard thunder rumble.

"We should stop by your apartment first for an umbrella," I said.

"Is it going to rain?" She looked completely disoriented now. "What if Tama gets caught in the storm? And it's so late. She must be starving."

"Miwako, listen," I told her sternly. "You want to find Tama, don't you? Panicking won't help. You need to get ahold of yourself."

She looked like she was about to cry. "I'm sorry. I'm just worried."

"So am I. But we need to stay calm so we can think properly."

Cold droplets fell onto my arms.

"Let's go," I said. "We need to find shelter."

Still pulling her along by the hand, I headed toward a nearby park, remembering a shelter not far from the entrance. But by the time we reached it, our clothes were already wet. The drizzle had become a downpour in only seconds. We sat down on a stone bench.

I turned to Miwako. "Are you okay? You look cold."

She didn't respond.

"Let's wait here until the rain stops."

She stared out at the rain, dazed.

"Miwako," I said sternly. "Are you all right?"

This time, she stood. "I'm going to go look for Tama in the alley where we first found her."

I looked at her, disheveled and soaking wet. "Do you really need to do that right now? It's pouring. If we just wait for—"

"I know, but . . ."

I sighed. "You wait here. I'll go check."

"But Ryu—"

I ran straight out into the terrible weather. Sprinting toward Miwako's apartment, I shouted Tama's name.

"Tama! Tama! Where are you?"

But all I heard was the sound of rain. There was no way we would find Tama in this weather. And from the start, I'd been unable to shake the feeling that our search was futile. But I kept going, if only to satisfy Miwako.

Finally, I reached the alleyway of abandoned junk. Rummaging through its piles, I shouted her name again.

"Tama! Are you here?"

She wasn't. I groaned in frustration but tried to take my own advice to Miwako. *Think clearly, Ryusei. If you were Tama, where would you go?*

I ran to Miwako's building and searched the perimeter. I shout Tama's name over and over, losing track of time. I wouldn't have realized the rain had stopped if Miwako hadn't found me.

She stared at me for a moment before speaking. "Ryusei, did you . . . ?"

Her words trailed off when I shook my head.

"You're drenched," she said. "You need to change into dry clothes, or you'll get sick."

I followed Miwako to her apartment. She ran a hot bath for me. When I came out, she handed me a pair of drawstring pants and a black T-shirt that were clearly hers.

"Your clothes are still drying," she said. "I know these are too small for you, but please bear with them for now."

I put on the pants without a word. As for the T-shirt, there was no way I could fit into it.

In the end, I spent the night at Miwako's apartment. I had wanted to leave, but she wouldn't let me. She didn't say a word, but she wouldn't let go of my hand. I gave up and told her I would leave the next morning. She nodded and muttered a soft thank-you.

"I'm sorry for making you stay. I just don't want to be alone tonight," she said.

I patted her head and said, "It's fine. Don't apologize. Just let me call my sister."

I told Fumi-nee I would be staying at Jin's place. She gave me an earful, saying she had already cooked both of us dinner. But when I told her it was to finish an important school assignment, her anger subsided. My studies had always been her soft spot.

After the call, I went to the couch to sleep, but Miwako asked me to come to the bedroom. She made a space for me in her single bed. Her mattress was too small for the two of us and we had to huddle close together, but that hardly mattered. The whole night, she hugged me tightly from behind and cried silently onto my back.

I'd known Miwako loved Tama, but I was surprised at how much the cat's disappearance had affected her. I asked every once in a while if she was all right. She mumbled that she was, but continued to cry. I wanted to turn and face her, but our cramped quarters made it difficult to maneuver, and the heavy air made me feel as if even a tiny shift would disturb her, so I remained still until we fell asleep.

The next day, I woke up with a terrible headache. I made an excuse to go home, not wanting Miwako to know I'd fallen sick. I didn't want her to feel guilty.

"Thank you for staying with me," she said. "I'll let you know if Tama returns."

I gently ran my fingers through her hair. "Don't think too much about this. You should get some rest. I'm sure Tama will come back soon."

After that, I was down with a bad case of flu. I couldn't leave the house for over a week. Miwako never called to ask after me. I felt a strange mixture of relief and disappointment. According to Fumi-nee, she hadn't turned up at the studio, either. She must have been busy looking for Tama.

A few weeks later, Miwako went missing herself.

THE SUMMER OF HER second year, Miwako Sumida took a break from university. The reason on record was poor health, but what that meant, I had no idea. She didn't say anything to me before leaving. Not a word of goodbye, let alone an explanation.

I found out on the third day of the semester. Chie ran up to me on campus.

"Do you know where Miwako is?" she asked. "Did she say she was planning to go somewhere?"

I frowned. "No. Isn't she in the same classes as you?"

Chie nodded. "Yes, but I haven't seen her since the new semester started. I thought she was sick, so I went to her apartment yesterday, but nobody answered. Earlier today I checked with the school administration, and they told me she submitted a temporary withdrawal form."

"You're trying to say she's gone?"

"I don't know." She shrugged. "I thought she might've told you something, so I—"

I didn't wait for Chie to finish. Grabbing my bag, I ran as fast as I could to Miwako's apartment. On my way there, terrible thoughts raced through my mind. Had she gotten into some sort of trouble? Was she in danger? But I tried not to speculate too much. Standing in front of apartment twenty-three, I knocked on the front door.

"Miwako," I shouted. "Are you there?"

I waited, but there was only dead silence. My anxiety grew and I kicked in the wooden door, which opened with a loud bang. I rushed into a completely bare apartment.

The wooden coffee table, the bookshelf, the mini television, and stereo set—all of them were gone. The only trace of Miwako was the pair of white curtains with yellow water patches, hanging motionless before the closed windows.

Groaning, I dropped to my knees.

That morning, I discovered that Miwako Sumida was no longer in Tokyo. But I could never have imagined that when I saw her again, it would only be her lifeless body, pale and cold to the touch.

The summer had left Miwako Sumida forever.

"WHAT ARE YOU GOING to do now?" Fumi-nee asked me.

I stroked Tama's fur. "I'm taking Tama to the studio."

"I didn't mean about Tama. I meant about Miwako. What are you going to do about her?"

That familiar ache returned, deep in my chest. "What are you talking about? She's gone."

"It doesn't seem like you've come to terms with her death."

"Then what do I seem like?"

My sister crossed her arms. "Like you're about to do something crazy."

"You're just making weird assumptions," I said, eager to get away from her. "I'm going to go take a shower now. Can you look after Tama?"

"Hey, I'm not done talking."

Ignoring her protests, I headed to my bedroom. My sister was right. I should resign myself to what had happened. Nothing would bring Miwako back to life. But I had to find out what had happened in her final months. She'd said she wanted to tell me something. Maybe I could find out what, if I traced her path somehow.

But I had no idea where Miwako had been. When I received her letters, there had never been a return address on the envelope.

Something had happened while she'd been away, enough to

convince her that life was no longer worth living. I wondered if anyone else ever found out what the reason was. Miwako could be so closed off about her worries—I doubted she had confided in her family.

But maybe her closest friends, Chie and Sachiko. Between the two, Miwako had known Chie longer. They had become friends in high school, and Chie had been the first to notice Miwako's disappearance.

Perhaps she knew something.

PART TWO
CHIE OHNO

Most people don't remember their first day in kindergarten, but Chie recalled hers all too well. A girl in pigtails had come up to her and asked if they could be friends.

"Yes," Chie said, trying to hide her nervousness with an easy smile.

Shortly afterward, the teacher asked the class to split up into groups of three. Chie went up to her new friend, but to her surprise, the pigtailed girl had already joined a group.

"I'm sorry," she said, "we already have enough people."

The class had thirty-one students, so one child was bound to be left out. Chie ended up partnering with the teacher. She tried not to seem upset, but really, she was devastated to be the only one without a group on the first day of school.

From that day onward, Chie didn't believe in friends. People would only seek you out whenever it was convenient for them. When it came to the crucial moments, they would drop you immediately to save themselves. Chie promised herself never to trust anyone and thereby never to get hurt again. But years later, she broke that vow for Miwako Sumida.

Though Miwako was cold and at times strange, Chie was unquestionably drawn to her. They spent most of their free time together, and people started calling them best friends.

Chie would never admit it, but she loved that phrase. *Best friends.* Had she actually longed for one all those years? Probably, if she were honest. And she did think she and Miwako would be friends forever. Or at least, for many years after they graduated from university, after they got married and started their own families. Maybe even after their hair turned white, they could still be together, exchanging tears and laughter.

But none of that happened.

Because when they were twenty, Miwako Sumida ended her life.

8

Transparent People

The train came to an abrupt stop, jolting the passengers inside.

"What's happening?" Chie asked Ryusei, who was sitting next to her.

He got up and left the train car. A few minutes later, he returned.

"There was a minor malfunction," he said. "Service will resume once the crew makes sure everything is all right."

"Uh-huh." She looked up. "How much longer until we get there?"

He checked his watch. "Another three or four hours. You should go back to sleep."

"I wasn't sleeping," she whispered, but Ryusei couldn't hear her. He had already left the car.

Pressing her face against the cold glass, Chie scanned their surroundings. She had no idea where the train had stopped. As far as the eye could see, there were only trees. On a typical day, she would have marveled at the feast of greenery. But not now, not in the middle of a journey in memory of her dead best friend.

Didn't we promise to solve all of our problems together?

Chie closed her eyes and tried to nap. She hadn't been sleeping well recently. Even when she tried to keep herself occupied, all she could think of was Miwako.

Miwako, I knew you better than anyone else in this world, didn't I? But I don't understand what was running through your mind in those final moments. Why did you slip that noose around your neck?

Chie heard chattering sounds in the distance. It had to be that group of elementary school children she'd seen in the station. They looked like they were on a class trip, carrying matching hats and water bottles. Where were they headed? It was odd to see so many young children from the city on this unpopular route.

A petite lady in her twenties walked by, waving a flag and singing a children's song. The students followed her, and there was another teacher not far behind. Only two teachers? No, there had to be at least one more for such a big group of children. Chie watched them pass and saw a pair of transparent students, a boy and a girl.

Each classroom was bound to have at least one transparent person. Chie knew this well because she used to be one of them.

Transparent people, by all accounts, were normal. So normal, in fact, that they simply tended to fade into the background. If you looked carefully, you could spot them toward the end of the line during school outings, but they would never be last. In class, they sat in the middle, usually near the wall. They didn't get the nice seats with a view by the windows. They weren't the best students in the class, but they were doing well enough to pass their exams.

To sum up, they were the average of the average. They got along well enough with a few classmates, but none were real, close friends. They lived a quiet life in high school, college, and later on, in the workplace. They tended to marry each other because others might pull them closer to the spotlight, and they never got used to being the center of attention. They were, after all, almost unseen.

"You're still not asleep?" Ryusei's low voice roused Chie from her thoughts. "Looks like the train's going to be stopped here for quite some time."

Chie stood up to stretch.

"I wouldn't go to the restrooms now," Ryusei said. "Those schoolchildren are down the hall using them. There are thirty-two of them. It's going to be a while."

She shook her head. "Ah, no, I just need to stretch my legs."

He looked out the window. "I see. Do you want to take a quick walk?"

"Maybe later. The hallway will be crowded while the train stops here. Let's wait."

Ryusei chuckled.

Sitting down, Chie furrowed her brow. "What's so funny?"

"It's just . . ." He tilted his head. "I never knew you were so level-headed."

She sighed. "I know, all of you think I'm scatterbrained."

"Hey, I never said that," he protested.

Now it was Chie's turn to laugh.

"I guess you're right. I owe you more credit than I've given you," he said. "I mean, we never really talked, did we?"

"Even when I talked, you hardly listened. Your full attention was always on Miwako."

Ryusei's smile turned stiff.

Chie looked down. "I'm sorry. I shouldn't have brought her up."

"It's fine. We can't avoid talking about her forever, especially not now that we've planned this whole journey for her," he said, still facing the window. "Thanks for accompanying me. I really appreciate it."

"Don't mention it. I was planning to make this trip even before you approached me." She let out a sigh. "But there's no point now, is there? I still regret not trying to find her earlier."

"You shouldn't. There's no guarantee that finding her would have made a difference."

Ryusei smiled as if trying to reassure Chie, but something about the way he did it made her sad. She leaned her head against the window too.

Miwako, you really are one stupid girl.

"How did you meet Miwako?" Ryusei asked Chie. "Were you two classmates in high school?"

She turned to him. "Not classmates, but schoolmates."

"So you knew Jin too."

Chie shook her head. "Miwako transferred to our school after her mother remarried. Jin must have known her from her first high school."

"What was she like back then?"

"What do you think?" She laughed. "Serious, unfriendly. The same as always. She gave off a don't-come-near-me vibe wherever she went." Chie paused, clasping her hands together. "But she was a good friend."

"You were so fond of her."

She tilted her head. "Compared to the way you felt about her, it was nothing. You really liked her, didn't you?"

Ryusei paused. "It doesn't matter. She never saw me as anything more than a friend."

Chie looked away. That was exactly the problem with guys, especially ones like Ryusei. They only saw what was right on the surface. But she couldn't blame him, since he knew nothing about Miwako's past.

Her secret was what had drawn Chie in, but she had no idea

what about herself could possibly have attracted someone like Miwako.

Noise flooded the hallway as the group of schoolchildren returned to their seats. Chie craned her neck to look for the two transparent students. She failed to find the boy, but she caught a glimpse of the girl, absentmindedly holding on to her backpack straps.

"Do you like children?" Ryusei asked.

"Of course. They're so sweet," Chie said, turning to face him. "What about you?"

"I do too. I volunteer every couple weeks at an orphanage." He was quiet for a moment before he continued. "Miwako told me she hated kids."

"That's not true. Miwako loved kids."

"She definitely told me she hated them."

"I'm not going to argue with you, but Miwako loved kids. She was just terrified of them. You . . . Never mind." *You don't understand*, she wanted to say, but she didn't want to hurt his feelings.

Ryusei looked like he was about to say something, but he didn't. He turned back to face the window. Chie closed her eyes and heard the soft rumble of the train engines starting. They began to move and she tried to sleep again, knowing it would be hopeless.

BEFORE CHIE OHNO MET Miwako Sumida, she had been living an unremarkable life as a transparent girl.

She got along well with everyone but was close to no one. She did well enough in everything, though nothing could be considered an achievement. Most of her teachers, except her homeroom teachers, didn't remember her name. Most students knew her as Ohno. No one called her by her first name. Chie was perfectly fine with that. It was a peaceful life, and in line with her goal to graduate painlessly. She didn't want to get involved in unnecessary high school complications.

But one day, her life completely changed.

Everything started when her older sister married her colleague and moved to her husband's hometown near Osaka. She had previously subscribed to a number of indie zines and tabloids, and for a short time, the mailman continued to deliver them to the Ohno family home.

Though Chie and her sister had a good relationship, they had never been particularly close. Her sister worked long hours in a supermarket, and when she was home, she would lock herself in her room. Chie often wondered what her sister did behind that closed door. Finally, she found her answer in these alternative music and art magazines, which she spent days poring over.

Chie found a particularly fascinating weekly indie zine called *The Secret Diaries*. Her sister already had a few volumes, so she was probably an existing subscriber. Chie never asked her about it. It seemed inappropriate somehow.

The zine was entirely composed of diary entries. In practice, it was the opposite of what one would normally call a diary, made completely public to its surprisingly large pool of subscribers. These entries were printed, bound, and distributed on a weekly basis, along with a postcard readers could tear out and use to vote for their three favorite entries. The most-liked diaries would be featured up front. The "diarists"—this was what the zine editor called its contributors—regularly posted entries in a bid to be placed in the front pages.

Anyone could submit their diary entry. All they had to do was to fill out a different form from the zine and send it to the office with a photograph or a drawing to accompany the entry. The form

damage her reputation at school. But Chiyo could do this, because she didn't exist.

Miyu was probably angry, just like Chie had been a few weeks ago. Shortly thereafter, she stopped posting. With her disappearance, Chiyo became the uncontested top diarist for months.

As for Chie, without realizing it, Chiyo's color had slowly bled into her transparent life. Part of it was probably the many fashion magazines she'd been reading in the name of research. Or perhaps it was simply a biological process. Her uniform began to feel a little tighter on her chest, thanks to her hormones. Once she dyed and permed her hair, put on some makeup, and altered her school uniform, girls began to talk to Chie, and boys started to steal glances.

A boy came up to Chie after school to ask her out. She was flattered, but she turned him down. He was too nervous, and it made her uncomfortable. She regretted it almost immediately. It was the first and only time anyone had ever asked her on a date. She should have said yes, but what was done was done. She thought she would once again become unnoticed.

But to the contrary, more boys professed their feelings for her, including an upperclassman with a pretty face. He was a little too dressy for her liking, but she said yes because she wanted to experience dating. She was under no impression that they were in love, but they definitely had good times together. They even had sex. Chie's boyfriend didn't know it was her first time, and she saw no reason to tell him. He was obviously much more experienced, which made the whole thing more than bearable.

Then the inevitable occurred. While Chie was inside one of the stalls in the girls' bathroom, she overheard several classmates talking about her.

"Do you see how Chie behaves?" one of them asked. From her voice, Chie recognized her as one of the girls she usually had lunch with. "Hanging on to her boyfriend's arm all the time and rubbing her boobs on him."

Another girl chimed in. "Do you think they're fake? They're not a normal size for a high school student."

One girl burst into laughter, and the rest followed.

"Hey, don't be so loud. What if someone hears?"

An impatient *tsk* followed. "If we hate her that much, why don't we kick her out of the group?"

Chie felt like she'd been stabbed in the chest. She clenched her fists.

"That's no good," the first girl said. "She gets a lot of attention, even if she attracts boys for all the wrong reasons. Anyway, she's already with someone, so she's not competition for us. And she's, you know . . ."

"Cheap?"

"Exactly. No one takes her seriously. Think of her as a lure."

They laughed again, and Chie remained still as she heard the door open and close. Back to silence. Chie came out of the stall and washed her hands. Facing the mirror, she stared into her reflection.

This is nothing to be upset about, Chie Ohno. You get along with everyone, even if you have no real friends. It's the same as before. You just get more attention nowadays, that's all.

A girl came out of the stall next to the one Chie had been in, startling her. The bathroom had been so quiet she hadn't realized anyone else was there. The girl had short black hair and nice bone structure, obscured by thick, old-fashioned glasses.

The girl washed her hands without even glancing at Chie. On her left wrist, she wore an oversized black men's Casio watch. Her boyfriend's? Probably not. She was too plainly dressed and serious-looking to be fooling around with a boy.

Or maybe not. Someone like her would go out with a

bespectacled college student—a mature, soft-spoken older boy who threw out old-fashioned lines like, "I would like us to date, with marriage in mind." But wasn't she too young for that? Chie chuckled, amused by her own wild imagination, honed by writing all those fake diary entries.

The girl turned to her. "Is something wrong?"

Flustered, Chie said, "No, nothing," and quickly left the restroom.

That was how Chie Ohno met Miwako Sumida, just a few days after Miwako had transferred to her school. Since Miwako was assigned to another class, Chie didn't know her name. She almost forgot about Miwako's existence. In all honesty, Miwako didn't seem like the type of girl who would hang out with a person like Chie.

Returning to her classroom, Chie was faced with two options:

1. She could confront the girls about what she had overheard in the bathroom, or

2. She could act as if nothing had happened. Everyone could continue to pretend to be friends.

It took her less than sixty seconds to decide that the second option was better in the long run. High school wasn't the time to make enemies. She had enough problems with homework and exams and didn't need additional trouble. Forcing a smile, Chie approached the girls.

One of them waved to her—the one who had called her cheap. "Chie, where have you been? We were looking for you."

"Sorry, I was with my boyfriend," Chie said, clasping her hands apologetically. "He asked if we could go on a date this weekend."

"That's so nice," the other girl commented. "I wish I had a boyfriend too."

An idea came into mind. "Why don't I ask my boyfriend to introduce you to his friend? Maybe we can double-date."

"Really? You would do that?"

Chie nodded. "I'll ask him later after school."

"Can I come too?" another girl asked.

"Of course you can. In fact, all of you should come."

"Oh, Chie, you're the best."

Hearing those words, Chie felt sick, but she had no right to feel that way. Her lies were even worse than theirs. She continued to suck up to these girls, playing the ignorant card. But this façade was in her best interest for now.

At home, Chie still wrote diary entries as Chiyo. Her diary was as popular as ever, but something in her had changed. She was no longer so thrilled about the popularity of "The Colorful Days of a High School Girl," perhaps because her own life no longer seemed to differ from Chiyo's.

Chie Ohno was no longer the transparent girl she had once been.

9

We're
in
a
Different
World

Chie felt a gentle tap on her shoulder and opened her eyes. Ryusei leaned in close to her. Way too close—she could see his long eyelashes.

"Wake up," he said. "This is our stop."

Rubbing her eyes, Chie stood up and stretched. Her neck was stiff. Surprisingly, she had managed to get some sleep.

"Are you okay?" he asked.

"I'm fine," she said. "I just fell asleep in a weird position, and now my whole body hurts."

He laughed. "Old woman."

Chie rolled her eyes and put on her sweater. Ryusei took both their rucksacks from the overhead compartment. She could have carried her own, but she knew he would insist on doing it, so she didn't bother. They left their carriage and stepped down onto the platform.

The train stop was quiet. A few other passengers got off too, none of them with much luggage. The station felt old, in serious need of refurbishment. The vibrating sounds of the train engines echoed all over the place.

"Where did that elementary school class go?" Chie asked.

"They got off earlier," Ryusei said. "Are you hungry? It's almost lunchtime."

She shook her head. "Not really."

"But we still need to eat." He scanned the station and gestured toward a ramen shop. "How about something warm?"

Chie shrugged and followed him.

The ramen shop was a small one just outside the gate, probably catering mostly to station workers. It had a long communal table with a few stools on each side. The only person in the stall was a plump man in a thin white T-shirt. His eyes were glued to a small television playing a game show between three idol groups.

"Excuse me," Ryusei called.

The man glanced over and stood. "What would you like to order?"

Ryusei and Chie looked at the menu, but there were only three variations of ramen.

"Number one, please," he said and asked Chie. "What about you?"

"I'll get the same."

The man nodded and gestured for them to take a seat.

"Where's the drink menu?" Ryusei asked.

The man replied with a grunt, "If you want bottled water, you can take one from the counter. If you need something fancier, go to the convenience store."

Ryusei turned to Chie. She shrugged. He took two bottles of drinking water and passed one to her. They settled at the table farthest from the platform.

"Not very friendly, is he?" she whispered. "No wonder it's empty here."

"Let's hope he's better at making ramen than greeting customers." Ryusei set the rucksacks down.

"Where are we going after this?"

"We need to leave the station and walk to the bus stop, but it's not too far."

Chie looked around at the nearly empty platform. "Really, that Miwako, what was she thinking, coming all the way here?"

She turned to Ryusei. He was staring off into the distance. His jawline seemed more prominent than before. Had he lost weight? She had never really thought about it before, but it was true—he was good-looking.

"Why did you like Miwako?"

Chie had asked the question aloud without realizing it. Ryusei turned to face her, seemingly caught off guard. Realizing she had just made a blunder, she quickly continued, "Sorry, if it's too personal—"

"No, it's not that," Ryusei quickly said. He chuckled. "You know, I could go on about that for hours and I'd still have more to say."

He looked at Chie, anticipating a response, but she waited for his answer.

"There were so many things about her," he said. "People usually misunderstood her, but she was a really sweet, caring girl. She always worked hard because she wanted to, not because anyone else was making her. She meant what she said. And she had her own way of seeing the world. She was so comfortable with being different."

Ryusei went quiet for a moment.

"When I was with her, I felt safe. I could be who I really was. I could make mistakes and count on her to tell me if I did something wrong. I trusted her completely."

"Uh-huh."

He took a deep breath. "You know, she just made everything

better. More intense. More colorful. When I looked at her, I used to think, 'Hey, maybe the world isn't such a bad place.'"

Chie felt a tug in her chest.

Ryusei shook his head. "Look at me, blabbering nonstop. Kind of silly, isn't it? Saying this after she's already gone."

"It's not silly," she said. "It's true."

"Thank you. I can see why you and Miwako were so close. You're really kind."

Their conversation was cut short by the arrival of their steaming noodles. The man handed over a tiny piece of paper with the total written carelessly in pencil.

Once the man left, they dug into the noodles. Chie couldn't tell whether the food was good or not. The train journey had left her feeling nauseous. She only ate half of hers, while Ryusei finished his entire portion. The noodles must have been decent, then, or he'd just been starving. After they were done eating, Ryu picked up both of their rucksacks again and led the way out of the station.

THREE DAYS BEFORE THAT, Ryusei had turned up in front of Chie's house.

His light-blue shirt was drenched with sweat. What was he doing here? Hadn't they just seen each other at Miwako's mother's house?

"Hi," he said awkwardly. "Can I come in?"

She opened the front gate. "You should've called first. What if I wasn't home?"

"Sorry, I wasn't thinking properly."

Putting down his backpack, he took his shoes off. The neighbor's seven-year-old son peeped over the wall that separated his house and Chie's.

"Chie is cheating on her boyfriend," he said. "I'm going to tell on you."

"Shut up," she shouted, but the boy ran off laughing. She turned to Ryusei. "Ignore him. That brat is always bothering me."

Ryusei nodded and managed a smile.

She invited him in. "What brings you here?"

Even before he answered, she knew the reason he was there. The only common bond between Ryusei Yanagi and Chie Ohno was Miwako Sumida. In Ryusei's eyes, there was only Miwako. It was as if no other girls existed. Now that Miwako was gone, Chie wondered what he would do with all the attention reserved for her.

"Please, take a seat," she said, gesturing at the sofa.

Suddenly she became aware of how bare her house was. A few weeks ago, her mother had read a book on Zen aesthetics and become inspired. She had gotten rid of most of the furniture and electronics, even the television. In the living room, all that was left were the unbleached cotton L-shape sofa, a round coffee table, and a pinewood shelf.

Chie turned to Ryusei. "What would you like to drink?"

"Don't bother, I won't be here for long." He looked around, placing his backpack next to his legs. "Is your mother home?"

"Not at the moment." Chie sat at the corner of the sofa. "She's gone for groceries, but she should be back any minute."

She waited for him to say something, but he just looked down and laced his fingers together.

Chie leaned toward him. "Ryusei?"

"About Miwako," he eventually said. "There's something I want to ask."

She nodded. "I figured."

He cleared his throat. "I'm trying to understand what happened. You must know something."

Chie struggled to remain composed. "I'm sorry. I don't."

"Something big must have happened for her to do what she did."

She swallowed. *Don't say anything, Chie. You have to protect Miwako.*

"You do know something, don't you?" he asked. "You look upset."

She crossed her arms and avoided his gaze. "You need to consider the possibility that she thought it was better for you not to know certain things, or else she would have told you." Chie turned to Ryusei. "I know you don't want to hear this, but Miwako is gone. Nothing you do will bring her back. There's no use chasing a shadow."

His expression hardened. "Is that all she is to you now? A shadow?"

The tug in her chest grew into a sharp pain.

"Please tell me what you know," Ryusei said.

She shook her head. "I can't help you." Had Ryusei always been this stubborn? Arms still crossed, she looked out the window, wondering when her mother would return. *I'm going to have serious trouble explaining why I let a boy in without her permission.*

"I need to figure out what happened when she left," he continued.

Chie sighed. "And how do you plan on doing that?"

"Do you know where she went?"

She swallowed again. "I have no idea."

"You're lying."

"It doesn't matter. You've got no business there."

"Let me decide that for myself."

Chie cursed silently. "She didn't want this, Ryusei."

"That's not true. Miwako told me she wanted to tell me something and I was waiting until she was ready." Ryusei opened his backpack and took out some envelopes. "While she was gone, she wrote me these letters."

"Ah." Chie should've known she wasn't the only one her best friend had kept in touch with.

He gave one to her. "I'm sure there's something important for me there."

The letter was short. So Miwako *had* hinted about telling Ryusei the truth. But in the end, she'd chosen not to. Wasn't that proof enough?

Ryusei looked into her eyes. "I know I can't force you to tell me anything, and I don't plan to. But if you ever change your mind, please give me a call."

She kept quiet. Why had Miwako left this decision to her?

"I'll take my leave now," he said, standing up and grabbing his backpack. "Sorry for coming here without warning."

She got up too. "Don't worry about it. You should go home and rest. You look tired."

"I'm going to Miwako's house first. Her mother might know where she was all that time."

No, not Miwako's mother—she can't handle it right now. "Why are you obsessing over this?" Chie asked, walking Ryusei out. "Even if you make it there, you won't find anything."

"I'm still going to try. This is the only lead I have," he said. "I'll see you around. Give my regards to Toshi."

Chie watched Ryusei put on his shoes. She empathized with him, of course, but she couldn't betray Miwako—she had to keep her promise.

But had Miwako really wanted this? She'd written that letter to Ryusei, after all. What if Chie had been wrong about Miwako's last wishes?

"Kitsuyama," she finally said. As she uttered it, the name felt heavy on her tongue.

Ryusei looked up. "Kitsuyama?"

"It's a tiny, very remote mountain village." Chie's jaw tightened. "Are you planning to go there?"

He was quiet for a moment. "Yes. I'll make my way there as soon as possible, probably stay in the village for a couple days. Miwako wrote about volunteering at a clinic there. I'll see if I can do that too."

They looked at each other.

"Chie." Ryusei broke the silence. "Would you like to come with me to Kitsuyama? Toshi can join us too."

His expression was earnest, almost pleading. Chie sighed.

"There's really nothing for you there," she said. "You shouldn't bother."

He put on his backpack. "I have to do whatever I can."

She paused, resigned. Perhaps going with him wasn't such a bad idea. She could at least keep tabs on what he was doing, make sure he didn't get too close to anything damaging.

"All right," she said eventually.

He smiled. "Thank you. I really appreciate it. Once I figure out lodging, I'll give you a call."

Their conversation was cut short by the neighbor's kid, who peeked over the fence again.

"Chie's planning to elope with her new lover," he shouted before running into his house.

Ryusei laughed. "We should tell Toshi before he hears that one."

Chie ran her hand through her hair. "About that, can you keep this to yourself? I don't want anyone knowing about this trip. I mean—" She struggled to find the right words. "Let's not complicate things." The fewer people who knew, the better.

He furrowed his brow. "I can't do that. Toshi is my friend. What if he thinks something's up between us?"

"That brat isn't telling anyone anything. Toshi won't find out about the trip unless you tell him. And you shouldn't, precisely because he's your friend." She looked Ryusei in the eye. "Consider this my only condition."

He went quiet for a moment, looking conflicted. Finally, he said, "Okay. But I'm not responsible for any misunderstandings, then."

"I doubt there will be any. But if there are, I'll be the one to explain." Chie closed the front gate. "I'll wait for your call."

THE BUS RIDE FROM the train station to the mountain was arduous. Ryusei and Chie were the only passengers. On the journey, the bus didn't make a single stop. The road wound through forests and fields and across bridges over rivers. Jizo statues stood by the roadside, some decorated with flowers.

Ryusei and Chie got off at the foot of the mountain. Once they stepped out, fresh air filled their lungs and took away their fatigue. Before them was an unpaved hiking path with a small, worn sign that read, THIS WAY TO KITSUYAMA.

"We should try to reach the village before the sky gets dark," Ryusei said, still carrying both their rucksacks.

Chie looked up at the towering mountain. "This will be good exercise."

Ryusei chuckled, and Chie took the lead. Not because she was familiar with where they were, but because there was only a single narrow path, just wide enough for one person at a time to walk comfortably. Hopefully there wouldn't be any groups coming down the mountain.

Their surroundings were just as Miwako had described in her letters to Chie: tall grass on both sides of the pathway, trees that looked like they had been there for a thousand years. Monotonous insects' hums echoed from all directions, a reminder that the area was still virtually untouched.

A gust of wind hit them, and Chie shivered. She asked Ryusei for her rucksack and took out a thick jacket, pulling the collar up over her neck.

"We need to move quickly," she said. "Miwako said the fog usually sets in once the sun goes down. It'll be harder to make the climb."

"Then you should walk faster. I'm just going by your pace."

He was right. Chie grunted and quickened her step. As they reached a higher altitude, her breathing became heavier. She had never been the athletic type.

"I was just teasing," Ryusei said, probably noticing her state. "You should go at whatever speed you want. If you faint, it's going to be difficult for me to carry you."

She turned to him. "Can we take a break?"

"Yes, but let's find a good place to stop first. The grass around here is too tall to sit on. There are more trees and less grass right up there. We should be able to find a spot."

Chie nodded, and they continued to hike. Her legs were getting weak, but she forced herself to walk faster. Not long after, she heard the sound of trickling water.

"There's a river ahead," Chie called out, turning around. To her surprise, Ryusei's face had lost its color. "Hey, are you all right? You look pale."

"I'm fine. Probably didn't get enough sleep."

She stared at him. "Really?"

"I've had trouble with that for the past couple of weeks. I took sleeping pills at first, but they've stopped working."

She walked on in silence, then recalled their earlier conversation at the ramen stall. "Hey Ryusei, can I ask you something?"

"Sure, go ahead."

"About what you said earlier, I don't doubt your sincerity. But at times, I wonder why someone like you fell for Miwako. Not to be cynical, but you're pretty good-looking. Don't you have other options out there?"

"What do you mean?"

"I don't know," she said, shrugging. "Prettier girls, I suppose? Or are you into plainer ones? That doesn't really make sense."

Ryusei laughed. "Chie, Miwako wasn't unattractive. But physical appearance isn't everything. Honestly, it might not even be a factor once you get to know someone. Their interests, life philosophy, sense of humor, even their taste in art and books and music. The other factors at play are endless." He paused. "What I'm trying to say is, you can't judge romantic interest based on superficial things."

"Are you saying you can be attracted to someone who isn't your type at all?"

"Of course," he said. "And what about you? Why do you like Toshi?"

She pondered for a moment. Toshi was certainly fun to be with. He never failed to make her laugh, and he was so understanding and caring. But was she really in love with him, or did she just like the idea of being in a relationship?

"I don't know," Chie said, glancing at Ryusei. "A little bit of everything." What a half-hearted answer.

The corners of his lips turned up. "Are you evading the question?"

"Maybe." She stopped walking and pointed to a rock by the river. "Let's sit. I'm tired."

The two of them sat on rocks a few meters apart on the riverbank. Chie took her shoes off and dipped her bare feet into the shallow river. The water was icy cold. Colorful rocks were scattered at the bottom. Ryusei called to Chie and threw her a packet of sweet bun, but she reacted too late. The bun fell into the light current. She bent down to scoop the packet out. When her fingers came out of the water, they felt frozen.

"Are you okay?" Ryusei asked. "Don't forget to drink some water."

Chie tore open the plastic packaging. She wasn't hungry, but her appetite had been a mess lately. Ryusei came over and sat next to her.

"Isn't it peaceful here?" she said, munching on the bun.

"Yeah, it's like we're in a totally different world," he said.

She held her breath. "What did you just say?"

"I said yes, it does feel peaceful here."

"No, after that. That this place feels like a different world. Miwako said something just like that in her letter. She . . ." Chie's voice trailed off. "I shouldn't keep talking about her. I'm sorry. It was inconsiderate of me."

"No, please continue," he said, staring off into the distance. "I want to hear."

Chie brushed her toes against the rocks in the water. "Miwako said the villagers believe the goddess of earth rules this mountain. She protects this place and cuts it off from the rest of the world. It becomes a completely different universe with a separate timeline."

"The goddess of earth . . ." Ryusei took a long, sweeping look at the scenery. "Not too hard to imagine."

Chie mumbled in agreement and dried her feet with her jacket. "Shall we continue?"

Ryusei and Chie returned to the pathway. The tall grass had given way to trees so densely packed, they almost blocked out the sun. Dried leaves covered the mossy ground, and tiny white mushrooms were scattered all over the tree roots. Chie slipped on a wet patch and nearly fell, but Ryusei was quick enough to catch her arm.

"Be careful." He helped her steady herself. "You don't want to twist your ankle in a place like this."

Chie mustered a thank-you and stepped more carefully. The sound of trickling water had vanished. Occasionally, birds chirped in the distance. Amidst the endless wave of trees, it felt like they were the only two people in the world.

"Do you think we're close?" Ryusei asked.

"We should be." She showed him her watch. "We've been walking for at least four hours, and we've barely rested. From what I understand, it's supposed to be a five-hour hike."

"Uh-huh," he mumbled, looking at their surroundings. "Do you think this is where Miwako hanged herself?"

Chie stopped.

"Sorry. That was inappropriate."

She didn't answer, but his question wouldn't leave her mind. *Had* Miwako committed suicide here? With the possibility taking root, the mountain felt anything but peaceful.

For a moment, Chie felt the forest spirit calling her, beckoning her to join souls with it and remain here forever, in this world where the goddess of earth ruled and everything was preserved for an eternity.

Stay here, so you can be free. You no longer need to carry this burden.

"Hey." Ryusei's voice roused Chie from her thoughts. "Is the fog setting in?"

"That can't be. It's only the afternoon." But when she looked ahead, she saw the faint blanket of white smoke. "You're right. We have a problem."

A Forest
Cat
and a
Typical
City
Girl

Chie quickened her pace and tried to push aside thoughts of Miwako. If she and Ryusei got lost here, there was no one to help them. At least not until tomorrow morning or even days from now. How often did people go hiking in a place like this? They hadn't come across a single person so far.

The trees had become denser. Only a faint tinge of light filtered through the foliage. Ryusei passed Chie a flashlight, which she shined onto the pathway. The ground looked different with thin patches of moss scattered around.

"Do you think we're lost?" she asked in a small voice.

Ryusei took the flashlight from her and checked their surroundings. "We're just on a different route. We should be fine if we continue to go up, since the village is at the top."

Chie tried to speak, but she couldn't. Her stomach felt like a wet cloth being wrung out.

Ryusei reached for her hand. "Don't worry, we'll get there soon."

He squeezed past her and led the way. The fog grew thicker, making it hard to see anything ahead. The greenery was disorienting. No matter how far they walked, all they could see were more trees. Chie's legs felt weak. She had a hard time keeping up with Ryusei.

"Hold on a moment," she called. "I think I need to stop. I'm so tired."

He turned to her. "Can you bear it for just a bit more? It's getting dark."

Chie knew Ryusei was just being logical, but she felt like she was on the verge of breaking down. She shook her head and pressed her lips together.

His brow furrowed. "All right, let's have some water. We'll keep going after that."

Leaning against a tree, Ryusei passed a bottle of water to Chie. She took a few sips as he ran the flashlight over their surroundings again. It was no use. No matter which direction they faced, everything looked the same.

"Maybe we should have brought a compass," Ryusei said with a nervous laugh. "I guess we'll have to spend the night here."

Chie lowered her head.

He grinned. "I'm only joking."

She sighed in frustration. "Is this really the time for that?"

Ryusei sighed. "Come on, don't you have a sense of humor? And it's true—chances are pretty high that we're going to have to spend the night in the forest. I have no idea which way we're supposed to go. You can decide, but we might end up wandering deeper into the woods, and then we'll be exhausted."

"Are you blaming me for this?"

"No, I didn't say that."

Ryusei took out another sweet bun packet from his bag. He opened it and handed it to Chie. She ate in silence and waited for him to open his own, but he didn't.

"Not hungry?" she asked.

He shook his head. "No."

Chie was about to finish her bun when she noticed Ryusei wasn't looking directly at her. He was fidgeting too much.

"This was the last of our food, wasn't it?" Chie asked.

"Smart girl," Ryusei said with a laugh. "Nothing escapes you, does it?"

"You should've told me. We could've shared."

"It's a small packet. Hardly makes a difference."

She couldn't believe his attempt at chivalry in this dire situation. "What do we do now?"

"We've got two choices, and you get to decide," he said. "One, we sleep here and resume our hike tomorrow after the fog clears. Two, we continue to climb and hope we reach the village somehow."

Chie buried her head in her hands. Neither option felt right. They shouldn't go on blindly, but the thought of spending the night in this dark forest frightened her, especially since she couldn't shake the thought of Miwako having hanged herself here.

She touched the ground. The soil was cold and damp.

Before she could decide, Ryusei stood and looked around.

"What is it?" she asked, getting up too.

"I thought I heard a cat," he said.

She narrowed her eyes. "A cat? Are you sure?"

"Shh," he hissed, staring into her eyes. "Can't you hear it?"

Chie listened intently, but the only sounds she heard were nocturnal insects and rustling leaves. Definitely not a cat. She shook her head, and Ryusei furrowed his brow. He gestured for her to follow him and stay quiet. She reluctantly obliged. *There's no cat here*. That much she was sure of. Chie tugged at Ryusei's sleeve, but he ignored her. He gazed intently ahead. She clicked her tongue, but then she spotted a trail.

"Is that a path?" she asked.

"Looks like it," he said, picking up his pace.

They followed the newfound trail, and a few minutes later, Chie stopped in awe.

Before them lay a deep valley, filled with colorful trees. Vibrant yellow and orange autumn leaves peeked out from the fog. It was like they were standing at the top of the world. Across the valley stood a majestic shrine.

"Hey Ryusei," Chie said, turning to face him. "If the goddess of earth had a palace, I imagine it would be that shrine."

He mumbled in agreement. "The village should be on the other side of the valley too."

"How do we get to it?"

"Good question." He squinted and pointed in the distance. "Is that a bridge?"

Chie strained her eyes. Finally, she caught a faint outline of a rope bridge. "I think so."

They trod carefully along a narrow pathway at the side of the valley. Chie was exhausted, but the view had rejuvenated her, and the prospect of not having to spend the night in the forest made her feel better. As they got closer, she noticed the bridge was made from chipped, mossy wooden planks and fraying ropes.

Chie took a deep breath. "Is this the only way to get there?"

"If we're willing to walk quite a bit farther, there might be another path down through the valley," Ryusei said. "But that could take half a day or more. This is all we have for now."

She swallowed. The bridge didn't look safe to cross. The fog made it impossible to see what was underneath, but it seemed like one wrong step meant a plunge into the abyss. Had Miwako mentioned the bridge at all? No, Chie was sure she never had.

Ryusei passed Chie her rucksack. "I'll go first. You hold on to your things. If something happens to me, don't panic. Stay here for the night. Tomorrow morning, after the fog is gone, go find help."

His words made her more nervous. "No, let's go together."

"The bridge looks old. If both of us fall, who's going to get help?"

"If you're not here, I won't survive the night."

Ryusei laughed. "Even so, I think it's better for one person to go at a time. Less of a burden on the bridge."

Again, she could see the logic in his proposal, but she didn't want to be left alone.

"Don't worry," he said. "I'll be fine."

Before Chie could protest again, Ryusei stepped onto the bridge. She wanted to tell him to be careful, but the words stuck in her throat. Left with no choice, she watched him carefully cross. After what felt like hours, he reached the other side of the valley.

"It's good," he shouted. "Walk slowly, one step at a time."

Chie took a deep breath and grabbed her bag. She gently lay her fingers on the well-worn ropes. They were cold to the touch, wet with condensation from the fog. Each wooden plank shifted with her next step, and the gaps between them were uneven. Chie tried to avoid the gaps, but she couldn't help looking down through each one, heart racing.

As she was about to reach the end of the bridge, Ryusei extended his hand and she took it with relief.

"You did it," he said.

"I did." Chie took a deep breath and started to laugh. "This is crazy. What are we doing here?"

He looked ahead. "It's all right, let's get moving. I hope we haven't crossed over to nowhere."

Feeling better, Chie walked next to Ryusei. They went up to the shrine, which appeared deserted. A musty odor hung in the air.

The pillars' paintwork had faded and chipped, and the building's wooden features had surrendered to the elements. There were cobwebs everywhere.

"Shall we go in?" Chie asked.

"Maybe not," Ryusei said. "Shrines are sacred, and some aren't open to outsiders. I'd rather not get into trouble." He looked around. "Also, I don't see a gate. I don't think this is the main entrance."

They made their way around to the other side. There was wild grass growing all over the yard. The stone pathway was slippery because of the damp moss and wet fallen leaves. Chie felt the fog fill her lungs.

Not long after, they found a giant torii at the opposite end of the shrine. Farther down, a steep flight of stone stairs led to a broad slope where the village sat. In the mist, Kitsuyama appeared to float atop a cloud.

THE CLUSTER OF TRADITIONAL houses looked like it was lifted straight from an ukiyo-e painting. At first glance, the clinic where Miwako Sumida had volunteered looked exactly like the other houses in the village, only bigger. The single clue as to its function was a small wooden sign in the front yard that read HAPPY CLINIC.

"Excuse me," Chie called. "Is anyone in?"

"Just a moment," someone replied.

A frail middle-aged woman in an indigo kimono appeared.

"Good evening," said Ryusei. "We're looking for Miss Sugi."

"That's me," the woman said.

He bowed to her, clearly not expecting a doctor to be wearing a traditional garment instead of the usual white coat. "I'm Ryusei Yanagi. We've corresponded before."

"Yes, you said you wished to volunteer for a few days." She looked at Chie. "And this young lady must be Miss Ohno."

Chie bowed to Miss Sugi. "Yes, good evening. I'm Chie Ohno."

"Our apologies for arriving on such short notice," Ryusei said.

"Don't worry about that. We have plenty of rooms here, and I always welcome the help. I should be the one thanking you for coming all the way from Tokyo." Miss Sugi gestured for them to come in. "You must be exhausted from the journey. Have you had dinner?"

"Not yet, but please don't trouble yourself," Chie said, trying to ignore her growling stomach.

"Oh, it's no trouble at all. There's leftover food in the kitchen. You only need to reheat it."

Stepping into the building, Chie took a good look at the interior. It had been a while since she'd last seen a house with tatami flooring and paper screens, though the place was definitely in need of restoration. The tatami mats were frayed, and there were water patches all over the yellowing ceiling.

"Do you want two separate rooms?" Miss Sugi asked.

"Yes," Ryusei said.

Chie blushed on hearing the question. *Do we look like a couple?* She knew for sure that he wasn't her type, and she was almost certainly not his either. He was far too serious for her liking, and if he'd fallen for Miwako, he probably considered Chie too flashy.

Miss Sugi slid open a screen door to reveal a small room. "One of you can stay here, and the other can use the room next door. There are folded mattresses inside the cupboard."

"Why don't you look at the other room first?" Ryusei said. "See which one you prefer."

"It doesn't matter," Chie said. "I'm sure they're the same. I can take this one."

"The bath is at the end of the hallway," Miss Sugi said. "I'll heat up your food."

They thanked Miss Sugi, and the older woman left. Chie felt so relieved knowing they would be sleeping with full stomachs and a roof over their heads. With a slight smile, she admired the building's stained wood structure.

"This place is charming, isn't it?" she said to Ryusei. "I've always wanted to stay in a traditional house."

He smiled. "You're such a city girl."

"Is that a thing?" she said, rolling her eyes. "Anyway, do you mind? I need to change."

Ryusei left the room and Chie closed the door behind him.

The wall separating their quarters was so thin, she felt awkward. She could hear Ryusei enter his room, drop his bag, and take out his clothes, as if they were sharing the same space.

Sighing, Chie wondered what awaited them in this quiet, distant place.

1 1

The
Little
Man

Barely a year had passed after the episode with Miyuta when "The Colorful Days of a High School Girl" was again threatened for its top ranking. This time, the shift happened gradually. The new contender was a diary called "Dirty Tales," written by someone under the pseudonym MK.

Chie had read thousands of entries by people from different walks of life, but "Dirty Tales" blew them all away. It was nothing like she had ever seen. The first diary entry was strange, but for some reason, it drew her in. She knew that before long, her own diary would be outranked.

> *Dirty Tales - Entry 01.*
>
> *Tonight, I had a visitor. A little man, so small he could creep through the gap under the door and enter my room. Illuminated by the moonlight, he climbed into my bed. He went under the blankets, in between my legs, and made his way inside me. He danced and danced there, despite my protests. But when morning came, he was gone. All that was left was a trail, tiny red footsteps all the way from my privates to the bedroom door.*

Chie quickly closed the zine and pushed it away from her. The words had made her shudder. What kind of person had written this? MK's entry was accompanied by a photo of a cup of steaming coffee. Compared to Chiyo's—a cute illustration of a bear Chie had painstakingly drawn—MK's was common. Of course, she knew MK could just as well be a perverted old man with a bulging stomach over his belt.

Whatever. I shouldn't concern myself with things like this.

Yet Chie found herself more and more drawn into MK's world, unable to resist her unsettling appeal. There was something in her writing, something Chie couldn't put into words. MK's diary wasn't just a collection of imaginative stories. It was the ultimate in strangeness.

Dirty Tales - Entry 07.

Today I spoke with the little man. I asked why he loves to dance inside me. There are so many others like me in the world—why me? He gave a little laugh. "Are you stupid or what, silly girl? Hehehe. I live just next door. You are the nearest, and just the right size for me. Hehehe." After saying that, he entered me, and this time, he did a wild prance. It hurt, but I kept quiet. I knew better than to say anything.

Chie couldn't imagine where MK had gotten the idea to write about a little man who danced inside her every night. It wasn't something just anyone would think up. MK kept writing about him, and, subconsciously, Chie started to wonder if the little man was real.

At night, she felt uneasy. What if the little man slipped through the gap under her bedroom door and crawled into her too?

Dirty Tales - Entry 13.

The little man was angry today. He was enraged. He tied me up to the bed frame using the phone cord. My wrists hurt, so I protested. "Shut up and spread your legs, silly girl," he shouted. "Wider, wider! Hehehe. Wider, wider, that's not wide enough! Hehehe." I told him he was too loud, that he would wake everyone up. He laughed again. "No one is here. No one is going to help you, silly girl. Hehehe. It will always be just the two of us, so you better get used to me. Hehehe." His laughter echoed in the room and continued to ring in my ears. Whenever I closed my eyes, I heard him laughing. Hehehe. Silly girl, wider, wider!

Chie felt her heartbeat race upon reading it. Every night, she thought about the little man and his sinister laughter. She had to stop reading these entries. They were affecting her in an unnatural way, but she still couldn't resist. She was addicted to MK's diary. She had trouble sleeping at night and started losing weight. Despite Chie putting on more makeup, her face looked pale.

"Are you sick?" her boyfriend asked when he came to see her during free period.

"No, I'm fine," she said. "Probably too much television and not enough sleep."

"You're looking thinner lately."

She mustered a smile. "Is that so? Then you'll have to feed me more. Let's go for ice cream after school?"

"Ah, okay. Actually, I was wondering if you wanted to come over later? My mother is working late today."

"Sure," she said without skipping a beat.

Chie knew what that meant. They always slept together when she went to his place. But what she didn't expect was for her boyfriend to take out the latest volume of *The Secret Diaries* after they had sex. She hadn't even read hers yet.

"What's that?" she asked, peering over his shoulder as he flipped through the pages.

"It's a zine," he explained, reading none other than MK's diary. "You know, one of those indie magazines they sell for cheap. This one is pretty cool. They publish a bunch of people's diaries."

"What kind of people?"

"Anyone, I suppose," he said, shrugging. "As long as you sub-scribe to the zine, you can fill in the form with your entry and send it to them. If they like what you've written, they'll include it in the next volume. A few of the entries are pretty terrible, but the good ones are really addictive."

Chie continued to feign ignorance. "But doesn't that defeat the purpose of having a diary? You're supposed to write your secrets in a diary, not publish them for the whole world."

He narrowed his eyes. "Come on, these are totally anonymous. No one would ever know it was you. That's the fun part."

"Do you ever send in anything?"

"I used to," he said and laughed. "I pretended to be an office lady, tried to come up with some steamy fantasy, but I lost interest after a while. It's hard to write about something you don't really know."

"But you still read other people's diaries?"

He whispered into her ear, "I guess it appeals to my voyeuristic side."

She nodded. "Voyeuristic."

"Some of them are pretty interesting, like this one. You should read this." He moved aside to give her a better view of the zine. "This girl, MK, writes about the most bizarre thing. A perverted little man who enters her body and dances inside her every night."

"Isn't that kind of creepy and gross?"

Her boyfriend laughed again. "You don't need to take it so seriously. But this girl, she's fascinating. Her entries are different."

"What makes you so sure it's a girl?" Chie scooped up her uniform from the floor.

"I'm pretty sure." He pointed to the photograph accompanying MK's entry. "This is a real photograph. Do you see that hand? It's too delicate to be a man's."

Chie looked at the image as she put on her clothes. A hand holding a cup of coffee. The cup was the same as the one in MK's first entry, but the watch on the wrist looked familiar. Chie tried to recall where she had seen it.

Where was it? Remember, Chie. Try to remember.

Ah, it was in the girls' bathroom at school. A short-haired girl had washed her hands, wearing the exact same watch as the one in the photograph. But that girl wasn't someone she knew, and she could no longer recall her face. Were they in the same year? Chie had no idea, but she knew she had to find her.

"What are you staring at?" her boyfriend asked.

"Nothing," she said, picking up her bag. "I have to go."

"Let me walk you home."

She shook her head. "No need to go through the trouble."

"Well, if you insist."

Her boyfriend turned to the next page. Of course, the second was Chie's diary.

"What about the rest of the entries?" Chie asked, curious. "Like this one. 'The Colorful Days of a High School Girl.'"

"Ah, that one." Her boyfriend frowned. "It used to be the most popular. I was a big fan. For some reason, I thought the girl was a student at our school." He glanced at Chie. "At one point, I even suspected she might be you."

Chie rolled her eyes.

"But it's so unlike you to read a cheap indie zine," he said.

She breathed a sigh of relief. "So you like this entry?"

"Not anymore." He scratched his head. "How can I put it? Compared to 'Dirty Tales,' it's kind of . . ."

"Colorless?"

"Yeah, something like that. It's plain."

Chie was hurt, but she tried not to let it show. Forcing a smile, she said, "I really have to go now, or my mother will get worried. I'll see you tomorrow."

She kissed him and left his house, but his words followed her.

Even my invented colorful diary pales in comparison. Next to "Dirty Tales," it becomes colorless.

All along, Chie had known this, but hearing it from someone else's mouth was different. It was like someone had thrust a knife into her heart and put their full body weight onto it, then twisted it around. What kind of person could MK be to render everyone else colorless?

Chie's search for MK began with curiosity, but soon spiraled into an obsession.

I want to find her. No, I need to find her.

In the weeks that followed, that was the only thing on Chie's mind. She spent her days looking for girls with short hair and glasses and checking their wrists, even ones she knew couldn't possibly be MK. Anyway, who *could* MK be? Anyone, supposedly, but Chie was sure there was something about her. Something special— something she didn't have, something that pulled everyone in.

WEEKS WENT BY, AND Chie still hadn't found MK. Staring at the sky from her school's rooftop, she wondered if she had been mistaken. Perhaps her memory was muddled. She'd never even gotten a good look at the watch. Or perhaps the girl had stopped wearing it? It really was too big for her, anyway.

Forget it, I'll never find her.

Why was she even looking for MK in the first place? What did she plan to do once she found her? It wasn't like she could march up to her and say, "Hey, guess what? I know about you and your secret diary."

What good would that do? Nothing would change.

The colorless will always be colorless.

Chie took a deep breath and looked up. The sky was so clear and blue that day, devoid of a single cloud. Closing her eyes, she enjoyed the breeze blowing onto her face and ruffling her long permed hair.

No one would be on the rooftop, even during recess. Rumor had it that the place was haunted. But Chie knew it wasn't true, because she was the one who had started that rumor. As the result, the place was almost always deserted, and it had become her private sanctuary. Up here, she could let her guard down. She didn't need to worry about her hair being messy or her makeup being smudged. She didn't need to look perfect. She could be herself.

Chatter came from the rooftop of a building across the way. The door opened and a petite girl ran out. A boy followed and overtook her. She squealed as he grabbed her hand. On his left wrist, the boy wore a purple and silver friendship bracelet. It would have been impossible for Chie to tell the item from that distance if she hadn't been wearing the exact same bracelet on her wrist.

She and the boy had bought the matching accessories two weeks ago when they had gone to Shinjuku for a movie. It was Chie's idea—she had read in a fashion magazine that friendship bracelets were about to be trendy again—but her boyfriend had chosen the color and the pattern. Sure enough, quite a few other couples followed their lead. Chie always prided herself on being among the select few who could start a new fashion wave at their school.

On the other rooftop, the petite girl shouted at Chie's boyfriend to stop, but she was laughing. He didn't retreat. Chie watched him kiss the girl's neck, and then her collarbone, as the girl tilted her head up a little. The girl's lips parted, and Chie felt anger surge inside her. Not toward her boyfriend, but toward herself. Did she make faces like that when they were fooling around? It looked so unbecoming.

"He's your boyfriend, isn't he?"

Beside Chie stood a bespectacled girl with short jet-black hair. The wind blew her hair into her face, and she used her left hand to tuck it behind her ear. On her slim wrist was a black Casio watch that was clearly too big for her.

Unable to control herself, Chie burst into laughter.

The short-haired girl narrowed her eyes. "What's so funny?"

"Nothing," Chie said. "I'm just happy."

"You're happy that your boyfriend is making out with another girl?"

"Not that. It's something else," she said, realizing that nothing she was saying would make any sense to the girl.

I'm happy to have finally found you, MK, and he hardly matters anymore.

MK gave Chie a strange look, probably thinking she'd lost it.

The bell rang, jolting Chie's boyfriend and that petite girl out of their embrace. They looked at each other. He grabbed her hands and they kissed again, and they laughed.

Chie remembered when she used to skip classes with her boyfriend. It had been quite often, in fact, but she couldn't recall the last time they did it. Guess he'd gotten bored with her.

"Class is starting," MK said. "I'm going to go downstairs."

"Wait," Chie called. "Don't go."

The girl turned around. "Are you worried I'm going to tell the teacher that you're here?"

"You can do that, I don't care. Just tell me your name."

"I'm Miwako Sumida. Is that all you want?"

Chie nodded. "I'm Chie Ohno from 2B. You can call me Chie."

"You'd better go now, Chie. I'm going to tell the teacher a student is up here."

After saying that, Miwako left the rooftop. Chie continued to stand there idly. *Miwako Sumida, Miwako Sumida.* She hadn't heard that name before. Was she a transfer student?

A friend had told Chie a new girl had transferred to 2A. Could that be Miwako Sumida? But her initials were MS, not MK. Then again, it was only a pseudonym. It could mean anything, like . . . what started with an M? Melon, milk, mushroom . . . Maybe MK stood for Mushroom King. Chie chuckled to herself at the thought.

"Ohno!"

Chie turned around and saw one of her teachers standing in front of the door. True to her word, Miwako Sumida had told on her. What a weird girl.

"What are you doing up here?" the teacher shouted.

"Ah, I . . ." Chie glanced at the building across.

Her boyfriend and the girl he had been fooling around with also noticed them. Chie's eyes met her boyfriend's, and Chie saw the two of them inch away.

"You two stay right there!" the teacher shouted. "Don't even think about running off. I know exactly who you are and which class you're in." She turned to Chie. "You too, Ohno. Follow me."

CHIE'S BOYFRIEND, THE PETITE girl, and Chie got an hour-long lecture from the disciplinary teacher. The three of them also had to clean the school swimming pool together.

As they did their chores, the atmosphere was tense. The smell of chlorine filled the space between them. Chie's boyfriend and the petite girl were silent. They didn't dare look at her. Chie thought it was sad, yet hilarious. Her boyfriend was usually chatty. And the petite girl, she knew her, although she had no idea what her name was. Her boyfriend and the girl were classmates. When Chie had come to their classroom to look for her boyfriend, she usually saw the petite girl giggling and talking loudly. Seeing her so quiet and docile now, she had to fight the urge to laugh.

Neither Chie nor her boyfriend said a word, but it was obvious their relationship was over. The strangest thing of all was that even after what had happened, they both continued to wear those matching friendship bracelets. Every time Chie was about to throw hers away, she found it sort of amusing to keep wearing it. And probably because she kept hers on, he couldn't get rid of his.

Being in the same school, the three of them were bound to run into each other from time to time. Whenever that happened, Chie's ex-boyfriend and his new girlfriend would avert their eyes and scurry away, clearly feeling guilty for committing a horrible act, which would have been the case if Chie had actually been serious about him. But she hadn't been in love, so no great harm was done. If the new couple had simply come up to her and apologized, she would've laughed it off and even made up a lie to make them feel better. Perhaps something like she'd also been seeing someone else, or was secretly pining for another guy. But they never said anything to her. Not a word of acknowledgment or apology. So Chie let that awkwardness remain until her ex-boyfriend and his new girlfriend graduated from high school.

1 2

A
Rabbit
and
an
Airplane

Since there was only one bathroom, Ryusei and Chie agreed that he would have his dinner first while she took a bath.

After she was done, Chie went to the kitchen to look for Ryusei. He was no longer there. She ate alone, did the dishes, and cleaned up a bit. She was tired, but for some reason, she didn't feel sleepy. Her body felt light and she was much calmer than when they'd arrived.

Chie walked slowly to her room, the wooden flooring cold against her bare feet. The screen screeched as she entered. She took out a futon from the cupboard, unfolded it on the tatami floor, and laid down sheets over it. The house was silent, save for the insect noises from outside. Wide awake, she stared at a small light bulb enclosed by a yellowing lampshade on the ceiling.

"Chie?" Ryusei's voice came from the other side of the wall. "Are you sleeping?"

She wanted to answer, but then changed her mind. The slight quiver in his voice made him sound sad. *He's going to try to talk about Miwako.* That kind of conversation would only sink him further into grief.

A moment of silence passed before he continued. "Somehow I keep thinking, I really didn't know much about Miwako."

Chie held her breath.

"The only thing I'm sure of is that she was different," he continued.

Yes, she was.

"What am I doing, talking to myself? You must already be asleep."

I'm sorry for not answering, but right now, I don't know a way to comfort you.

"You know, I really cared about her."

So did I. Even before you knew there was a girl named Miwako Sumida.

THE SUN HAD BEEN hiding behind the clouds when Miwako and Chie met for the third time in high school. Chie was on the rooftop again during her break, lying precariously on top of a water tank. Miwako climbed up and found her there.

"You're still here?" Miwako said. "Aren't you afraid the disciplinary teacher will find you again?"

Chie got up. "I doubt she'll check here. Criminals seldom return to the crime scene."

Miwako smiled. "You're funny."

"So are you. What kind of person reports her classmates to the teacher?"

"This kind of person." Miwako sat down next to Chie. "I like this place."

Chie stole a glance at Miwako's wrist. Miwako had replaced her huge watch with a smaller one. This time, it was a metallic gray Seiko watch, a ladies' cut that suited her more.

"It's eleven-thirty," Miwako said, assuming that Chie was checking the time.

"Oh," she mumbled. "You're Miwako Sumida, aren't you? I hardly ever see you."

"You wouldn't have noticed me. I'm not popular like you."

Chie laughed. She knew Miwako wasn't being sarcastic, but it sounded like she was mocking her. "Are you the new student?"

"I guess so."

"Why did you transfer here?"

"My mother remarried, so we moved into my stepfather's house."

Remarried. Could it be? "Did you change your family name?"

"Naturally, yes."

"Your previous family name started with K."

For the first time, Miwako looked properly at Chie. "How do you know that?"

"Ah . . ." Chie's voice trailed off. She couldn't think of a lie.

"Must be this, isn't it?" Miwako took out a dainty necklace hidden under her white shirt. The pendant bore the initial K. "I thought I'd hidden it."

Chie breathed a sigh of relief. "Yes. I caught a glimpse of it when we ran into each other in the bathroom some time back."

"Oh. I didn't notice."

"Is it weird?" Chie asked. "I mean, people suddenly calling you by a different name."

Miwako thought for a moment before answering. "I was pretty used to hearing my old classmates call me Kojima, so it was a little awkward in the beginning. But it's different here. Nobody knows I was ever a Kojima. To them, I've always been a Sumida."

Kojima. Miwako Kojima. I finally found you, MK.

Miwako tilted her head. "Do you come up here often?"

"Almost every day. At least during lunchtime, especially now that I don't have a boyfriend."

Chie thought Miwako would to say something like, "I'm sorry to hear that," but she didn't. That was only right, though. There was nothing to be sorry about. The breakup was a blessing.

Nowadays, Chie preferred to be alone. If she really wanted to be in a relationship, she would've accepted one of the guys who'd tried to court her since the breakup. But instead, she retreated to the rooftop to stare at the sky. Next to her, Miwako was enjoying the afternoon breeze.

"Don't you think that cloud looks like a rabbit?" Miwako suddenly said.

Chie squinted. "Which one?"

"The one over there." Miwako pointed. "See, that's the head, and those are the two ears."

"That looks nothing like a rabbit," Chie said. "It's more like an airplane."

"Are you kidding? It's definitely a rabbit."

"It's an airplane."

"How can an airplane have two ears?"

"I don't see any ears." Chie laughed. "But this is fun."

"I know," Miwako said. "When my father was still around, we used to do this all the time. You know, cloud gazing. That's what he called it."

"He must have had a lot of time on his hands."

"You could say that. There wasn't much else to do when he was lying in the hospital, waiting to pass on."

Chie felt a lump in her throat. She knew she was supposed to say, "I'm sorry to hear that," but she didn't. Miwako had probably heard those words a thousand times. The girl had to be sick of them.

Miwako turned to Chie. "Do you mind me joining you here during recess?"

"Of course not," she said, "just don't report us to the teacher this time. You gave me a lot of trouble. I had to clean the swimming pool with those two."

Miwako creased her brow. "Then you shouldn't have said you didn't care if I reported you."

"No one else would've taken that seriously."

"Well, I'm not them."

Miwako lay down and closed her eyes. Wrapping her arms around her knees, Chie sat next to Miwako and looked at her. The girl was surprisingly ordinary, which made her even more intriguing. Why would someone like her be writing such a strange diary?

Wind rustled through the leaves. A group of black birds flew out of the trees and disappeared into the distance. It was the perfect moment for Chie to say to Miwako, "Hey, I know about your diary entries as MK." Chie wanted to tell Miwako that it was all right. "I'll keep it to myself. Your secret is safe with me." But she couldn't bring herself to say any of it. She didn't want to upset Miwako and ruin the possibility of them becoming friends.

Friends.

She had never considered anyone a friend. But this girl, Miwako Sumida—somehow, Chie sensed they could be friends. She felt like she could open up to her. Or maybe not, seeing how she couldn't even tell Miwako about the diary.

Regardless, Chie pretended she didn't know anything about Miwako Sumida. But one day, she would tell her, when they were both older and things like keeping a secret diary didn't matter anymore.

From that day on, Miwako and Chie would slip up to the rooftop during their lunch break every day without fail. They would sit there idly, cloud gazing. Apart from frequent arguments about the shapes of the clouds, they didn't really talk, which suited Chie well.

As for her diary, Chie got bored with it. She sent in her entries less and less frequently. As expected, her placement continued to drop. Her diary was pushed further to the back. Eventually, her entry wasn't even published. But she didn't feel sad. In fact, she couldn't have cared less.

Closing the zine, she decided to stop writing for good. No one would miss her. Life went on, with or without "The Colorful Days of a High School Girl."

Meanwhile, MK became the indisputable top diarist. A few people attempted to copy her style, but no one ever got close. Next to hers, everyone could tell their own diaries were inferior goods.

ONE DAY, WITHOUT WARNING, *The Secret Diaries* was gone. Chie thought the zine's late delivery was only temporary, something due to a mailing or printing hiccup, but it wasn't. She tried calling the publisher, but the line was dead. Her subsequent payment bounced. She went to a few bookshops that used to stock it, but none of them seemed to know what had happened. A rumor circulated that the owner had been in serious debt and was being chased down by loan sharks. Another said a big publishing house had bought the business. But then, what kind of company would want to acquire a cheap zine publishing anonymous diary entries? It didn't come across as a sound investment.

Chie didn't really care about the details. She was a little sad, of course. The zine had brought her to Miwako. But now that they were friends, she didn't need it anymore. Chie was content knowing she was probably the only one who'd gotten to know the real MK, though she never could bring herself to tell Miwako the truth. She was too afraid to lose her.

Because of that, even until her death, Miwako Sumida remained ignorant of the fact that Chie Ohno knew her secret identity.

1 3

Field
of
Roses

The morning came faster in Kitsuyama than in Tokyo. No one needed an alarm clock. In the early hours, roosters woke the village.

Opening her eyes, Chie forgot where she was for a moment. The light bulb and paper shade were unfamiliar. *Ah, that's right, I'm in Miss Sugi's clinic.* Chie got up and yawned. The warm sun crept through the windows and filled the tatami room. She folded up her futon and pushed it back into the cabinet. Opening her bag, she took out a change of clothes and a towel.

Ryusei was already dressed when Chie came out of her room. He was pressing his thumb and forefinger against the bridge of his nose. His eyes looked bloodshot.

"You didn't sleep well?" she asked.

"I did, but not for long. I'm just not used to this place yet," he said. "I'll see you later."

"Uh-huh."

Stepping into the corridor, Chie took a good look at her surroundings. All the windows had already been opened. The wooden flooring was no longer cold. If anything, it felt warm on her bare feet. She looked out and saw a group of birds chirping and hunting for food among the grass patches. Some of the villagers, including children, were heading out. A few carried farming tools while others herded their cattle.

"Good morning," Miss Sugi said, coming out of one of the rooms. The sleeves of her mauve kimono were tied up with a tasuki. "Did you have a good rest?"

"Yes." It occurred to Chie that she should have woken up earlier to help out. "I'm sorry, I'll be ready soon."

"Take your time. You must be tired from yesterday's journey, and it's only your first day."

Chie excused herself and went to the bathroom. She caught her reflection in the mirror. Her long permed hair was a mess, all clumped together. How could she not have noticed yesterday? She laughed. *Look at what you've become after a single day of hiking.*

Except it hadn't been just a hike, more like a pilgrimage.

She took her clothes off and turned the tap on. Cold mountain water poured out. Chie closed her eyes and thought of Miwako Sumida. They had been so young and carefree, lying atop that water tank and staring at clouds. Those days felt so far away now, almost like she'd imagined them.

Chie reached for the soap and worked it into a lather.

If, at some point back then, she'd told Miwako that she knew about her identity as MK, would it have changed anything? Miwako would probably have been embarrassed that her cover was blown, and that Chie knew she was writing such strange stories.

No, Miwako wouldn't have reacted that way. She would have turned red. Not out of embarrassment, but anger. She would have seen it as an intrusion into her personal life, and wondered if that was why she and Chie had become friends. Yes, that was more like it.

But after her anger subsided, would they still have been all right? If so, would she have opened up and told Chie what had happened to her before it was too late?

Chie had promised herself she wouldn't cry after the funeral, but that morning, she couldn't help it. She let the bathwater wash away her tears. She knew she shouldn't take too long. Ryusei and Miss Sugi were waiting for her. But she didn't want them to see her like this.

Miwako, how could you leave me without a word?

MISS SUGI, RYUSEI, AND Chie had breakfast together in an open kitchen overlooking the mountain. Miss Sugi had prepared a meal of steamed rice with grilled ayu fish, miso soup, rolled omelet, and sliced pickles. Despite their simplicity, each of the dishes was fresh and flavorful. The rice was especially light and fluffy. It tasted so good you could eat it on its own.

After they finished eating, Ryusei asked Miss Sugi if she could guide them to the spot in the forest where Miwako had last been so they could leave flowers for her.

"Are you sure you want to do that? It can be very difficult emotionally," Miss Sugi said while collecting the dirty dishes.

"Please don't worry about that," Chie said, helping Miss Sugi with the dishes. "We came here precisely for this."

"All right."

Ryusei bowed his head. "I'm sorry to trouble you."

"It's no trouble at all," Miss Sugi said. "But unlike Tokyo, we've got no flower shop here. You'll have to gather flowers from the field yourselves."

"I'm sure we can manage."

The three of them left the clinic shortly afterward.

In the morning, the village felt completely different. Without the fog, the place wasn't so otherworldly. Chie spotted about twenty to thirty houses scattered loosely over the settlement. Some had animal pens, filled mostly with goats and chickens.

On the way to the forest, the three of them passed two women carrying baskets full of clothes on their backs. The groups bowed at each other.

"In the past few years, our number of residents has decreased," Miss Sugi said. "Some of the younger generation have moved to the city." Despite her traditional wooden sandals, she didn't have any difficulty leading them into the forest. Perhaps she went there frequently.

"Where are you from, Miss Sugi?" Chie asked. "You're not a local, are you?"

"I grew up in Osaka," she said.

"I wouldn't have guessed. You don't speak with the Kansai dialect."

She gave a slight smile. "That's because my family moved to Tokyo after my father's job relocation. He was also a doctor."

"Then what brings you here?"

"I like to think it's fate," Miss Sugi answered. She gestured to the field in front of them. "Usually there are lilies and irises there, but because it's already autumn, all that's left are wild roses." She pointed to the border of the open clearing, where large bramble bushes grew in a partially shaded area. "Take your pick."

Swathes of white and pink were streaked across the large shrubs. The flowers had bloomed beautifully in the cool weather. Chie walked up to them in awe. She had never seen roses so huge. She took a few steps into the field and crouched down in front of a white rose bush. Ryusei stood behind her.

She turned to him and asked, "Can you believe such beautiful things grow on their own in the wild?"

"Uh-huh," he mumbled, not paying attention. "Do you want the white ones?"

She nodded.

He went to pluck some.

"Be careful with the thorns," Miss Sugi said.

Too late. Ryusei had already pricked his finger.

"Are you all right?" Chie asked, taking the roses from his hands. "Let me do it."

"I'm fine." He sucked his thumb. Standing, he turned to Miss Sugi. "I think we've got enough."

"The site isn't far from here," the older woman said.

Ryusei and Chie followed Miss Sugi to another pathway that led them back into the forest. It was a continuation of the route they had used to come from the village. Along this path, the trees were ancient, their foliage lush. Huge roots covered with tiny mushrooms twisted and overlapped each other. Twigs were scattered on the floor of the forest, snapping and crunching under their feet.

"Were we somewhere around here yesterday?" Chie glanced at Ryusei.

"It's possible," Miss Sugi said. "After all, this forest covers a large portion of the mountain."

"It's so quiet. Do people come here often?"

"Sometimes, to chop wood, but not at this time of year." Miss Sugi touched one of the trunks. "It's too damp. You can feel it. We can't make fire with this."

"Are there any animals here? Apart from the usual insects and night critters," Ryusei asked, probably thinking about the cat he'd claimed to have heard.

"The villagers believe foxes used to roam the forest, but if you ask me, I think it's just a myth."

"What's the shrine for?" Chie asked. "Do people still use it?"

"It's for the goddess of the earth, but the public isn't allowed to enter. The place has become pretty rundown since the last miko unexpectedly passed away. It happened a long time ago, even before I arrived here. But the villagers still can't think of anyone to replace her."

"Was she ill?"

"No, she fell and broke her leg in the forest. Nobody realized she was missing until a few days later. She pretty much lived on her own. By the time the villagers found her, she was already dead. It was during the winter, so the cause was either thirst or hypothermia."

"That's so sad."

"Indeed. Poor girl. I heard she was still rather young." Miss Sugi stopped abruptly and took a deep breath. "We're here. This is where Miwako met her end."

Chie's chest tightened as she stared at the tree in front of her. The trunk was wide and had patches of moss near its base. White fabric was tied on to one of its lower branches.

Her throat went dry. "How did Miwako get up there? It's so tall."

"She brought a ladder," Miss Sugi said. "The villagers took it away when they retrieved her body, but they left the fabric there to mark the tree."

Chie knelt and put the white roses down, leaning them against the tree trunk. Clasping her hands together, she said a silent prayer.

Miwako, may you find peace, wherever you are.

Standing, she turned to Ryusei. He was still staring up at the fabric, dumbstruck.

"Ryusei," she called, but he didn't budge. "Ryusei," she repeated, louder this time.

Still staring at the tree, he said, "I'm sorry, but can you go back without me? I want to spend some time alone here."

"No," Chie said. "What if you get lost, like we did yesterday?"

"I'll be fine. I just need to follow the pathway back, right?"

"I'm not leaving you here," she insisted.

"I said I'll be fine," he said, sighing.

Chie hesitated, but Miss Sugi pulled her away. "We'll wait at the flower field."

Ryusei finally turned to them. "Thank you, and sorry to trouble you."

Miss Sugi and Chie returned to the path and traced their way back. When they were far enough from Ryusei, Miss Sugi asked, "He's the one Miwako liked, isn't he?"

"Did she say that?" Chie asked.

"She said that back in Tokyo, there was someone she liked."

Chie paused for a moment. "I guess it could have been him."

MIWAKO AND CHIE HAD good enough high school examination results that they could have gone to any university they wanted, but in the end, they chose Waseda. Chie couldn't remember if she or Miwako had suggested it. What she did remember was that the decision wasn't hard. One of them had brought it up, and the other simply agreed.

"It's a prestigious school. My parents would definitely approve," Chie remembered saying during one of their cloud-gazing sessions. "But isn't it pretty far from your house?"

"Actually, I've been thinking of living on my own," Miwako said.

Chie's eyes widened. "Woah, what's this? An act of rebellion?"

Miwako laughed. "Possibly, but I'd need to find a part-time job to cover my rent."

"Then let's find a job together before the new term starts."

The two of them found temporary work in a dessert café in Oshiage. By coincidence, a part-timer who had already been working there for quite some time was the same age as them and also heading to Waseda.

"I'm Sachiko," she said, boldly introducing herself by her first name. Petite with cropped hair, the girl had a cheerful disposition.

The addition of Sachiko Hayami to Miwako and Chie's friendship felt completely natural. The three of them worked the same shift. During their breaks, they talked about "girl stuff"—Sachiko's words—like the new dessert shop on the next block or the latest limited-edition accessories. Before long, they spent their days off together too.

Chie had thought she would find a third person intrusive, but she didn't. Sachiko was naturally sweet and easy to get along with. She was the kind of girl who would pick up a pen from the floor and put it on the table so no one would step on it. She was also clearly popular. Barely a week into their first term at Waseda, a few upperclassmen had come up to her and asked her out. But she turned them all down.

"You don't like him?" Chie asked after a particularly good-looking upperclassman walked away, looking dejected.

"That's not it," Sachiko said. "I don't really know anything about him. We've never spoken to each other before, so how can I like or dislike him?"

"So why did you turn him down? He has a pretty face."

"If I dated him, I'd need to spend time with him, wouldn't I? And I couldn't hang out with you and Miwako."

Chie laughed. "Come on, what kind of reasoning is that?"

Next to them, Miwako kept silent. Her eyes were glued to the romance novel in her hands.

"But it's true," Sachiko said. "I dated a classmate in high school, one I actually liked, and we were always together. It wasn't long before the girls in my class stopped invited me to their gatherings. I felt left out."

Chie understood what Sachiko meant, but she still thought her reasoning was strange. High school romance should triumph over hanging out with girlfriends. "You had your boyfriend to spend time with."

"Precisely. I told myself it was fine since I had him. But in the end, he went off to college somewhere abroad. He didn't even tell me about it until graduation day."

"How could he do that?"

She crossed her arms. "He wanted us to only have good memories together. Awful, isn't it? He was just using me as someone to spend time with in high school."

"But what about you?" Miwako asked after being quiet all this time. "Weren't you happy during those times too?"

"Of course those were happy years, but still." Sachiko shook her head. "Anyway, I have an idea. We can find three guys who are good friends, and then the three of us can date the three of them. That way, we can be together forever."

"Count me out," Miwako said. "I'm not dating anyone."

Sachiko pouted. "Come on, don't be like that."

"Have you considered what would happen if one of us broke up with their boyfriend? Would the other two also have to break up?"

"Ah, that's true," Sachiko muttered.

"Anyway, it wouldn't be easy to find three guys who are friends and like the three of us," Chie said, laughing. "I think we can forget it."

In a strange turn of events, Toshi, one of the upperclassmen who had already been turned down by Sachiko, asked her out again. This time, she told him her real reason for declining was that she hadn't wished to be distanced from Miwako and Chie.

"That's easy," Toshi said. "I've got two good friends who aren't seeing anyone. Why don't we set up an informal get-together? And we'll take it from there."

When Sachiko passed on the message, Chie thought it would be a disaster. The two guys were probably being dragged along by Toshi and wouldn't be interested in her or Miwako. Once they arrived, that seemed like the case, especially since one of them—the tall, good-looking guy, Ryusei Yanagi—was quiet the entire time.

What Chie hadn't expected was for Ryusei to leave the goukon with Miwako. Another thing she never would have foreseen was that she would end up dating Toshi herself, since he'd been after Sachiko, or that the third guy, Jin, would get together with Sachiko instead. So the three girls had ended up with their three dates.

It wasn't exactly true, of course, since Ryusei had never technically dated Miwako. She always turned him down flat, despite him relentlessly chasing after her.

And Miwako *had* known Ryusei's feelings and his sincerity. He, on the other hand, had no idea that Miwako had had feelings for him too. But Chie noticed Miwako behaved slightly differently when Ryusei was around. Just slightly, but it was still obvious to her. Miwako would look down at her book a little too much, tilt her head a little too obviously, fiddle with her watch a little too often. Whenever the other girls—apart from Sachiko and Chie—talked to Ryusei, Miwako would avert her eyes. Or was that just Chie's imagination? But other girls seemed to share the same thought.

Sometime last year, a group of girls had stopped Miwako and Chie in a quiet hallway while they were walking to class.

"We need to talk to her," one of them told Chie, glancing at Miwako. "Can you leave us alone?"

Chie sensed hostility in her tone. "What business do you have with my friend that I can't hear?"

152 | Clarissa Goenawan

"Don't be annoying," a tall girl with a ponytail said.

Another girl whispered, "Careful, she's Toshi's girlfriend."

Chie knew Toshi was well-liked, but she hadn't realized other girls were this afraid to upset him.

"We just need to ask her something," the first girl said, flashing a smile. "All in good fun."

"Then it shouldn't be a problem for me to stay."

The ponytail girl clicked her tongue but said nothing. Chie turned to Miwako, who seemed unaffected.

"What do you want to know?" Miwako asked.

The first girl crossed her arms. "What's your relationship with Ryusei? Are you seeing each other?"

"Why should I tell you?"

"Because Ryusei and I get along well, but some people think he's going out with you. I know it's just a rumor, but I would hate for people to say I was going around snatching other girls' boyfriends."

Miwako didn't answer.

"Come on, it's a yes or no question," the girl continued.

Yet Miwako remained silent.

"Hey." The ponytail girl grabbed Miwako's hand. "You should answer when someone asks you a question. It's only polite."

"Stop it," Chie said. "It's you who are—"

Before she could finish her sentence, someone came from behind and grabbed the ponytail girl's hand. "It's only polite not to touch others without their consent."

Chie didn't need to turn around to see who it was.

"If you have something to ask about me, you should come directly to me," Ryusei said. "Don't go harassing Miwako."

The first girl's face immediately turned red. She stormed off, and the rest of her group followed.

"Are you all right?" Ryusei asked Miwako.

"What was that?" She looked away. "I appreciate your help, but I'm capable of handling my own problems. I don't need you to save me."

Ryusei smiled. "I knew you would say that. You're so predictable."

"Something wrong with that?"

"No, nothing," he said, still smiling. "Just too predictable."

Miwako grabbed Chie's hand and they walked off, leaving Ryusei alone.

"You're hurting my wrist," Chie said when they were far enough from Ryusei.

Miwako let go of her hand. "I'm sorry."

"You know, maybe you should be more honest."

"About what?"

Chie took a deep breath. "You like him, don't you?"

Miwako put on a puzzled expression. "What are you talking about?"

"Don't play dumb. We've been friends for so long. I know you well enough to see that you like him."

Miwako crossed her arms.

"Why do you keep rejecting him? He really likes you. Why don't you give it a try? I don't understand what's holding you back."

Miwako was quiet for a moment before she said, "I would lose him."

Chie rolled her eyes. "What do you mean? If you don't do anything, of course you're going to lose him."

"I don't like telling you this, but there are things you don't know about me." Miwako shook her head. "Never mind, forget it."

"Hey, don't do that. What did you want to say?"

"Ryusei is an important friend. Not just to me, but to the rest of us. If I go out with him and things end badly, it will be awful for everyone."

"You're scared, aren't you?"

"Maybe," Miwako said after a pause. "But for now, Ryusei and I will remain friends."

Chie shrugged. "Suit yourself. This is your life, and you make your own decisions. But one day, it's going to be too late, and you're going to regret it."

She was so frustrated. Why couldn't Miwako just act on her feelings? If she liked Ryusei, she should tell him. What could possibly be worse than ignoring him like this?

But Chie knew she couldn't accuse Miwako of deception. She herself was still hiding what she knew about Miwako's former life as MK. They were best friends—or at least, Chie thought they were—but she couldn't tell Miwako that one simple thing. She, too, was being dishonest. Because she, too, was afraid of losing a friend, which was why she thought she understood Miwako.

As it turned out, she didn't.

14

It Takes
One
Hundred
and
Twenty-Eight
Steps

Around lunchtime, the local children arrived at the clinic. They didn't seem surprised to see Ryusei and Chie. If anything, they looked as if they were expecting these total strangers. The children greeted them, and several bravely introduced themselves.

Miss Sugi brought the dishes out and everyone sat on the porch in a big circle. She passed around bowls and chopsticks, and the children took turns scooping their food. To call them children, though, wasn't exactly right. A few looked like they were in their late teens.

"How long are you going to stay here, Miss?" asked a young girl seated next to Chie.

"Perhaps a couple of days," she said. "I haven't really decided."

The girl glanced at Ryusei. "What about him?"

"I'm not sure. You'll have to ask him yourself."

She nodded and walked over to Ryusei. Chie saw him leaning toward the young girl to answer, and the two of them laughed. A few other children joined in on their conversation. Chie felt a little left out, but she admired Ryusei for his easy way with the children. He was more relaxed here than in Tokyo. For some reason, back in the city, she felt he was constantly on his guard.

"Where are you from, Miss?" a boy asked, taking the space the girl had left.

"I came here from Tokyo," Chie said.

She waited for him to say something, but he was quiet.

"What's the matter?" she asked.

"No, it's just . . ." He looked down. "One of the other volunteers we had was also from Tokyo."

After this, he quickly moved to another seat. Chie knew whom the boy had meant.

Miss Sugi had cautioned Ryusei and Chie not to speak a word about Miwako to the children. They were probably still in shock, realizing for the first time the desperate actions a person was capable of.

"Chie," Miss Sugi called. "Can you help me bring out more rice?"

"Yes, of course," she said.

Walking to the kitchen, Chie took another glance at the children.

A few weeks ago, Miwako had probably stood in this same spot, looking at the young ones. What had she possibly been thinking? What made her travel so far from home? What was she seeking?

MIWAKO MUST HAVE SHOWN some signs of something being wrong before she left. Chie hated herself for not realizing it. After her friend's death, she replayed their last weeks together over and over. Finally, she concluded there had been no way for her to know. Miwako had kept her secrets to herself and had guarded them very closely.

One morning, about half a year ago, Sachiko had come to class alone.

"Miwako should be here already," she whispered as she sat in the empty seat next to Chie's. "What's taking her so long?"

"Weren't you with her earlier?" Chie asked.

"Uh-huh. But she needed to use the bathroom and told me not to wait for her. I had to return some books to the library, so I left."

Biting her lip, Chie thought of those girls who had confronted Miwako a few days earlier. Surely they wouldn't try to corner her again? But if she were alone in the bathroom when class started, no one would be there to help.

"Which bathroom was it?"

"The one near the basketball court."

Oh, no, not that one. That particular place was practically deserted during class hours. Chie closed her textbook and stood.

Sachiko glared. "Where are you going? The class is starting."

"I'm going to look for her."

Chie left the classroom and ran to the basketball court, not stopping until she reached the bathroom. She pushed the door open and shouted, "Miwako, are you here?"

No reply.

Chie looked at the stalls. Only one was occupied, but the whole place was dead quiet. *I'm overreacting*, she thought. But just as Chie was about to leave, she heard a gurgling sound. She turned back and knocked on the door of the occupied cubicle.

"Miwako?"

There was the sound of flushing water. Chie smelled something rancid.

"Are you sick?" Chie asked. "Open the door, please."

Still, no one answered.

"Miwako, please. I know you're in there."

The door opened and Miwako emerged from the cubicle, looking pale and exhausted.

"What happened?" Chie asked.

"Nasty food poisoning," she said. "I'm going home to rest."

"I'll go with you."

Miwako gave a thin smile. "You didn't bring your bag with you, did you? Are you going to go back to the classroom to get it and just walk out?"

Chie cursed silently.

"Don't worry about me. I'm fine."

"You should see a doctor," Chie said and laughed. "You look like a pregnant woman with morning sickness."

Miwako's eyes widened. Chie's blood went cold. Miwako quickly looked away, but it was too late.

Chie caught Miwako's arm. "Be honest. Are you pregnant?"

Miwako took a step back. Her mouth shut tightly.

Chie maintained her hold on Miwako, not wanting her to walk away. She took a deep breath and said, "We're friends, aren't we?"

Miwako lowered her head. Tears began to flow down her cheeks. They fell onto Chie's hand and onto the tiles.

"I don't know why I'm crying," she said, trembling. "I really don't."

Chie pulled Miwako into her arms and hugged her. "It's okay," she whispered, tightening her embrace. "It doesn't matter. You can cry. Of course you can cry."

Suddenly, everything made sense. Her diary entries, her refusal of Ryusei's advances. They had been friends for so long, yet Chie hadn't noticed her best friend's suffering. How could she not have?

I'm sorry, Miwako. I'm sorry you've had to go through this alone.

They stood there for a long time, holding each other, both sobbing. Miwako had such a strange cry—Chie could feel her heave and the tears falling onto her bare shoulders, but she didn't hear a sound.

WHEN MISS SUGI ASKED Ryusei and Chie to teach the children, Chie wasn't convinced she could. She didn't feel confident enough in what she'd retained from her high school classes.

"It's not difficult," Miss Sugi reassured her. "If you're not sure, you can always ask me. I'll be right inside the clinic."

It turned out Chie's hesitation was unfounded. The math problem in front of her was far too easy for a boy who looked like he was in his mid-teens.

"This is how you do it," Chie told the boy, crossing out matching parts on each side of the equation.

"Thank you," he muttered. "You make it seem so easy to understand."

Chie smiled. She left him on his own and went out to the porch to rest.

Observing the children even over just a short period, Chie had grown to admire them. They cared enough to come here for lessons after hours in the field, even though the clinic didn't have a proper school facility. Forget nice classrooms. The children simply studied in the shaded areas of the yard. They had neither tables nor chairs, and more than one child had to share a single tattered textbook.

Ryusei came over and sat next to Chie. She poured him a glass of water.

"Thanks," he said, finishing it in a few big gulps. He took the water pitcher and poured another. "Is it always this hot in the middle of the day?"

Chie shrugged. "I guess we've become too used to staying indoors."

"Spoiled, aren't we?"

She laughed.

"Miwako used to teach art here," Ryusei said. "One of the

kids told me, and I remembered her writing about it in her letter."

"Hey, Miss Sugi specifically told us not to mention her."

"I didn't bring her up. But then," he said, gesturing to the young girl who had spoken to him earlier, "that girl asked me if I was a friend of Miwako's, and I couldn't bring myself to say I didn't know her."

Chie pressed her lips together. She would have done the same.

"She went on and on about Miwako. How good she was at drawing cats. I wanted to tell her that was the only thing Miwako could draw well." Ryusei gave a dry laugh and stared into the distance. "The girl thought I was the guy Miwako liked back in Tokyo. I told her I wasn't him, but she wouldn't believe me. I didn't even know Miwako liked anyone."

Chie shook her head. *He's so dense.*

"You were so close to Miwako. Did you already know this?"

"Of course I knew."

"Why didn't you tell me?"

Chie was so frustrated with him—with both of them—that she began to laugh. *It was so obvious the two of you were suited for each other. The world's biggest idiots.*

Before Ryusei could ask any more questions, Chie stood and walked over to a group of children. As she started a conversation with them, she stole a glance at him. He looked like he wanted to chase after her and interrupt, but eventually, he just went back into the building.

A NOISE WOKE CHIE in the middle of the night. It was the sound of a screen door sliding. Chie got up, thinking someone was trying to sneak into her room. But then she realized the sound had come from Ryusei's room. Perhaps he was going to use the toilet. She reached for her watch to check the time. Half past midnight.

Chie's T-shirt was damp from sweat. She'd been freezing last night, so this afternoon she'd closed all the windows and layered on multiple blankets. But now her room was stuffy. Chie got up and opened her windows one by one.

She looked outside as a shadowy figure walked out of the building. She couldn't see clearly, but it could only be Ryusei. His tall profile was pretty recognizable. What was he doing, leaving on his own in the middle of the night? It was freezing outside. Maybe he couldn't sleep and had decided to take a walk.

In the mountains, the night sky was breathtakingly beautiful, bright and clear and sprinkled with hundreds of brilliant stars. If it weren't so cold outside, she would have loved to take a walk too.

Chie returned to her futon and lay down, but then a thought hit her. *What if Ryusei isn't just going out for a walk? What if he's planning to harm himself?* She got up again, just in time to see Ryusei walk into the forest. It gave her chills. *I need to find Miss Sugi.* But if she did, she would lose track of Ryusei.

Grabbing her coat, Chie ran to the front door. She hastily put on her shoes and chased after him. Ryusei had already gone down the pathway toward the forest. She shouted after him, but her voice couldn't reach him. Chie's heart beat faster. *Did he have anything with him? A rope or a stepladder?* She couldn't tell. He was practically out of sight now.

The forest seemed menacing again, its thick foliage blocking the moonlight. Chie couldn't tell what was in front of her. In the darkness, she stumbled over a tree root and fell, landing on damp, mossy soil. She got back up, heartbeat racing.

I'm scared. I want to go back.

No, this wasn't the right time for hesitation. Chie took a deep breath and shouted, "Ryusei, please wait!"

Her voice echoed in the dark. Chie paused and steadied herself. Could he hear her? Should she try shouting louder?

A bright light shon on Chie's face, blinding her. She squinted.

"Chie? Is that you?"

Shielding her eyes, she tried to say something, but she couldn't think properly.

"What are you doing here?" Ryusei came over to her. "You're shaking."

"You can't kill yourself," she said, grabbing his arms. "Miwako wouldn't want that."

He went quiet before bursting into laughter. "What made you think I was going to kill myself?"

She let go of his arms. "You went into the forest all by yourself in the middle of the night."

"I couldn't sleep, so I took a walk."

Chie narrowed her eyes. "All the way here? Really?"

He sighed. "You're right. There's something I need to do. I'm sorry I made you worry, but I'm not planning to do what Miwako did. I have someone who needs me to take care of her."

"Who is it?"

She didn't expect him to answer, but he did.

"My sister," he said. "I could never leave her on her own, especially knowing how much it hurts to lose someone important to you." He offered her a warm smile. "You shouldn't go into the forest without a flashlight. What if you'd gotten lost again?"

"But are you walking to . . . ?"

Ryusei nodded.

They continued to walk on the pathway until they reached the tree where Miwako had died. The white roses were still fresh, despite having been left there for nearly a day. Their petals remained unblemished, coated with a thin layer of dew.

Moonlight seeped through the leaves, falling on the roses and making it appear as if they were shining, lending them an almost ethereal beauty.

Chie averted her eyes. Both of them were quiet as the wind rustled through the dense foliage. The buzzing sounds of nocturnal insects crept all around them.

"It takes one hundred and twenty-eight steps to get here," Ryusei suddenly said.

She turned to him. "What?"

"One hundred and twenty-eight steps," he repeated. "I counted them all the way here from my bedroom door."

"Why would you do that?"

He shrugged. "Whenever I feel upset or uneasy, I start to count something. Anything. It doesn't need to be something significant; it just has to be countable. It calms me down." He paused and scratched the back of his head. "Kind of weird, right?"

Chie shook her head in response. "Everyone has their own way of coping with life. When did that habit start?"

"When I was about seven. There was a tragedy in the family."

"Ah." She didn't ask anything further, not wanting to probe into his private life.

Crouching down, Ryusei took out a flat, rectangular tin box from his jacket and placed it on the ground.

"What's inside?" Chie asked.

"Miwako's letters," he said. "I thought it would be appropriate to bury them here, even if I still don't quite understand what she was going through."

She felt a lump in her throat. "I'm sorry."

He chuckled. "What are you sorry for?" Using his bare hands, he started to dig a shallow hole in the damp soil. "I should be the one who's apologizing for dragging you here."

Ryusei reached for the tin box and unlatched its catch. The stack of neatly folded letters was inside. Chie immediately recognized the handwriting on them as Miwako's, each of the characters small and round and unnaturally uniform.

Chie put her hand on his shoulder. "You really loved her, didn't you? I wish things could have turned out differently."

"It doesn't matter anymore."

"Don't say that." She took the box from Ryusei's hands and placed it on the ground. "But I do think now is a good time to bid farewell to these letters." She was about to close the box when she realized there had been five of them inside. "I thought you said she only wrote four letters to you. Three from Kitsuyama and the one you received from her mother."

"Ah, yeah." He singled out one of the letters and passed it to Chie. "Miss Sugi gave this to me earlier. Miwako had left it with her for safekeeping."

She took it from him. "Why didn't she give it to you right when we arrived at her place?"

"According to Miss Sugi, Miwako didn't leave a name, just some cryptic descriptions. She couldn't be sure it had been intended for me until today."

Chie recalled the conversation she had with Miss Sugi, when the older woman asked if Ryusei was the one Miwako had liked. She unfolded the letter in a hurry, wondering what kind of final message she had left.

Unlike her letters to Ryusei, this one wasn't addressed to anyone in particular.

> *I'm sorry I couldn't keep my promise.*
> *I'm sorry I've let you down.*
> *I'm sorry for giving up.*

We could have talked. I could have been more honest about my feelings, my struggles, the past I loathe so much. But I chose to keep all of that hidden. I pushed you away when you tried to reach out to me. I put up the wall between us. I lied to you, pretending everything was okay. I thought what I needed was time, but what I really needed was courage. The longer I waited, the more difficult it was for me to change course. I made a mistake and sank too deep.

Remember that time you told me your plans for after graduation? Sometimes I imagine myself sitting in a large audience, watching you onstage, delivering a company speech as I beam with pride. Other times, I see us curled up on a sofa, reading with our legs entwined, Tama napping in between.

In my mind, the windows are always open, and the sky is bright and blue.

And we are happy.

This picture has blurred and faded in the past few months, no matter how desperately I try to recall it. Even my memories of us from the past are receding—you and me leaving Ikeda bookshop, purchases in hand. These have been replaced by something else.

I'm sorry for everything I could have done but didn't.

I hope you don't fault yourself for not knowing. It was I who deceived you.

"I've failed her," Ryusei told Chie. "Despite coming all the way here, I can't figure out what she was trying to tell me. Instead of getting closer to the truth, I've become more confused. I don't even know if this letter was meant for me."

Chie creased her brow. "Of course it was."

"She was in love with someone else."

"Ryusei." Chie sighed. "You're so dense. It was always you."

"You don't need to say that to make me feel better."

"Why would I lie about something like that?"

He paused.

"Miwako was afraid," she continued.

"Of what?" He shook his head. "Did she think I would hurt her?"

"She was afraid you would leave her as soon as you found out the truth."

He looked right at her. "What do you mean?"

1 5

The Kobayashi Women's Clinic

Two days after Chie learned of Miwako's pregnancy, they went together to Kuromachi by train. Even though there were plenty of women's clinics in Tokyo that performed the procedure, Miwako chose to travel to another city, probably to ensure she wouldn't come across an acquaintance.

For the entire train ride, Miwako clung tightly to the hem of her white cardigan. Whenever Chie asked if she was all right, she would simply nod.

"I'm okay," Miwako had told Chie the other day in the bathroom by the basketball court. "I've made an appointment. Everything will be fine."

"If that's what you've decided, I'll come with you."

Miwako smiled. "I appreciate your offer, but really, I can handle this on my own."

Chie shook her head. "I don't want you going through this alone. Please, let me accompany you. It's the least I can do as a friend."

Yet, despite her earlier insistence, Chie wasn't sure if her presence was actually making Miwako feel better. For one, she wasn't sure what to say or do to comfort her. Her mind had gone blank.

A few hours passed before they arrived at the Kuromachi train station. Miwako told Chie they had to transfer to a bus. Chie remembered nodding silently at Miwako. No words seemed right at that time.

The bus ride was nauseating, following a long, winding road. Miwako kept sucking on mint candies and held a plastic bag in her hand in case she needed to throw up. That didn't happen, but when they finally got off the bus, her face was completely drained of color. Seeing how ill Miwako looked, Chie was shaken.

"We need to cross the road," Miwako said, brushing her hair behind her ear.

Chie mumbled in agreement and followed her. They had alighted in a quiet suburban neighborhood. The residential area consisted of small clusters of two-story houses. Unlike in Tokyo, the gaps between buildings were sizeable, each filled with either a garden lot or a parking space for one or two cars.

As the two of them walked, they could hear chatter coming from the houses. One had its radio turned up a little too loud. A nostalgic folk song traveled through the neighborhood, lamenting about love and fate.

Turning onto a smaller alley, Chie inhaled the thick fragrance of curry from one of the homes. She glanced over at Miwako, who had covered her nose with a tissue. Not wanting to make her feel worse, Chie pretended not to notice. Hopefully the clinic wasn't too far ahead.

A postman on a red bicycle passed by. Miwako turned onto another alley. Toward the end stood a small clinic with a sign that read KOBAYASHI WOMEN'S CLINIC. Chie pushed open the glass door, and a middle-aged nurse greeted them.

"Good morning," she said. "How can I help you?"

"I'm Kojima," Miwako said, passing her patient's card to the nurse. "I have an appointment with Doctor Kobayashi at half past eleven."

Not Sumida, Chie noted.

The nurse glanced at her appointment book. She looked up at Miwako and smiled. "Please take a seat, Miss Kojima. I need you to fill out some forms."

Miwako and Chie sat on a white U-shaped sofa. The nurse passed Miwako a red clipboard with a few sheets of paper attached to it. Chie could easily guess their contents. Her basic information, a health questionnaire, and of course, the consent form.

Chie wondered who the father was and the circumstances of all this, but she couldn't bring herself to ask Miwako. At least, not now. One thing was for sure: Miwako hadn't wanted him here.

The poster on the wall showed the development of a fetus. One week, two weeks, three weeks . . . After nine weeks, a fetus was nearly an inch long and weighed a fraction of an ounce. It was about the size of a grape. Its heart was finished dividing into four chambers and its valves were starting to form. From the illustration, the fetus looked nothing like a human baby, though Chie recognized the shape of an ear and ten tiny fingers.

"Miss Kojima, have you finished filling out the forms?" the nurse asked.

Miwako nodded.

The nurse passed her a tiny plastic cup. It had been marked with the initials MK using a black marker.

"I need a urine sample. When you're done, you can leave the cup in the tray in front of the bathroom. After that, please go to the second floor. Doctor Kobayashi will attend to you soon." The nurse turned to Chie. "I'm sorry, but you can't accompany her upstairs. The procedure will take about two to three hours. You may want to take a walk, but to be honest, there isn't much to see in this neighborhood."

"It's all right," Chie said. "I'll wait here."

"Thanks," Miwako whispered.

She disappeared into the back room, and Chie was left alone in the waiting room with the nurse. Something about the clinic troubled her. Was it the glaring light strips, or maybe the sterile all-white interior? It could even be just her state of mind. Chie took a deep breath to compose herself. The least she could do for Miwako was remain calm.

The nurse went upstairs shortly after, leaving Chie alone. She regretted not bringing a book, but with recent events, it hadn't even crossed her mind. Bored, she glanced at the stack of magazines on the coffee table. Every single one was a parenting magazine. She reached for the one on top.

The magazine was full of photographs of smiling young mothers and laughing toddlers with matching clothes. Most probably weren't real-life parent-child pairs. Chie scanned the headlines: "Healthy Eating for Expectant Mothers," "The Ultimate Guide to Surviving the First Year," "Ten Things Every Smart Parent Needs to Have." One article was about babies who had defied the odds, either because they'd been born too early or were sickly, yet managed to survive.

Chie closed the magazine and put it back on top of the pile. She should go outside and take a walk around the complex. There might not be anything to see, but getting some air was better than being cooped up here, thinking about Miwako and what she was going through at that moment.

But Chie's legs felt heavy. She couldn't bring herself to move. Crossing her arms, she sat still like a statue. Gradually, she lost track of time. She didn't know how long she had been sitting there when the nurse returned.

The procedure was over, but Miwako had to lie down for a while.

"Just to be sure there are no complications," the nurse said with a reassuring smile.

She went back upstairs after that, and Chie was on her own again. A white clock was perched on top of the reception counter, its second hand seeming to tick a little too slowly, as though time moved differently in this small town.

Chie took a deep breath. When was the last time she'd sat for hours, waiting for someone? Perhaps never. At least, not that she could remember. She was usually the one who showed up late and made others wait.

"Chie?" Miwako's voice interrupted her thoughts.

She stood up. "How are you feeling?"

"I'm fine. Sorry you had to wait so long."

"Don't worry about that."

They left after the nurse gave Miwako some painkillers.

"You might develop a fever, and there might be a little bit of bleeding. Those are normal; there's nothing to worry about," the woman said. "But if there's a lot of blood or the pain becomes unbearable, please call the clinic right away."

And that was all. In three short hours, Miwako's pregnancy was terminated.

Miwako and Chie took the bus back to Kuromachi station before boarding the train back to Tokyo. After leaving the clinic, neither of them uttered a word. They sat in silence, each drowning in her thoughts.

THAT CHAPTER IN MIWAKO'S life had always felt distant to Chie. As if it didn't belong there, or it had never happened. But

Chie knew it was all true. Miwako Sumida had been pregnant. And she'd chosen to end that pregnancy at a small women's clinic in the quiet suburb of Kuromachi.

"Do you know who the father was?" Ryusei asked.

Chie shook her head. "She wouldn't tell me. I do know he passed away shortly before Miwako left Tokyo."

"She didn't kill him, did she?"

"You know Miwako wasn't capable of killing anyone," Chie said. "Do you believe in karma?"

"Maybe."

"Miwako told me he died in a bad traffic accident. His body was burned beyond recognition. It was probably his punishment."

Chie knew they shouldn't be speaking ill of a person who'd passed away, but she couldn't accept Miwako's suffering.

"He forced himself on her," Chie said.

Ryusei looked at her. "Did she tell you that?"

"Not necessarily," she mumbled. Chie couldn't explain that she had inferred this from MK's diary entries. "But we both knew she wouldn't have hidden this otherwise."

He nodded slowly. "I wonder why she didn't go to the police. Was she trying to protect him?"

"Before his death, she told me she was planning to tell everyone the truth. I even asked her if there was anything I could do to help, but she told me that she had to handle it on her own terms."

"When was this?"

"Two months before she left Tokyo," Chie said. "Just a few weeks later, she called and told me on the phone that she had lost her will to fight. 'It's over,' she said. 'There's nothing to be gained from speaking out now.' I told her that wasn't true, but she wouldn't listen. It was during that last conversation that she told me he had died."

"Do you think his death had to do with her suicide? Was it why she came here?"

"I don't know. She didn't say much." Chie sighed. "When I learned from her mother that she was in Kitsuyama, I wanted to come and see her, but she insisted she needed to be alone. Even now, I still think about it. If I had ignored her wishes, maybe she would still be here."

"There's no way to know that."

Chie bit her lip, fighting back tears.

"What if we had come here and things had ended the same way?" Ryusei said. "Then we would be asking ourselves, 'If we had just listened to her, would things have turned out better?' A lot of different paths can lead to the same place."

Closing her eyes, Chie pictured a garden maze. There were plenty of turns in it, but there was ultimately only one ending. One's choices along the way were irrelevant.

Lightning flashed, followed by thunder in the distance. The wind blew harder, causing tree leaves to scrape against one another.

Ryusei furrowed his brow. "It's going to rain. We need to go back."

Before they could take another step, Chie felt heavy droplets of water on her arms.

"Let's go," he said. "We've got to hurry."

Ryusei grabbed Chie's hand, and they ran back to the village. In a matter of minutes, it was pouring. Despite the dense forest, both of them were wet. Bright flashes pierced the tiny gaps between the leaves. The echoing thunder sounded so near.

Chie stepped on a mossy trunk and fell to the cold, mushy ground.

"Are you all right?" Ryusei asked, pulling her up.

She nodded. "I'm fine."

Another roll of thunder crashed down louder and clearer than the previous ones. She was about to keep running when she noticed Ryusei wasn't moving. His expression had changed. He had the same look he'd had on the journey up when he'd insisted he'd heard a cat.

"What is it?" Chie asked nervously.

Instead of answering, he ran back into the forest.

"Where are you going? The village is that way!" Chie shouted, but Ryusei didn't stop. Not wanting to abandon him and return alone, she chased after him.

Something is happening. And for some reason, Ryusei could sense it.

He stopped abruptly, and Chie saw another bright light.

No, not just a light. She held her breath. It was fire. The tree Miwako Sumida had hanged herself from was engulfed in flames.

EVEN THOUGH THE WHITE fabric had already been burnt to ashes, Chie recognized the tree. Ashen black roses were scattered at its foot. Despite the rain, the fire rose high in the dark forest.

This isn't the time to stand here and stare. If we don't put the fire out now, it will spread. The whole forest will be destroyed.

Chie turned to Ryusei, but he was in a daze. The intensity she had seen in his gaze earlier was gone. He was just staring at the burning tree now, eyes empty.

In the distance, a bell started ringing, reverberating through the rain. Someone shouted, "Fire! Fire!"

Chie heard approaching footsteps and loud noises. *I should get away from the fire.* But her fear paralyzed her. She stood before the tree, rooted in place again.

"What are you doing?" someone shouted, pulling Chie away to a safer spot.

The villagers arrived with big buckets of water. They doused the tree, but the fire continued to blaze. Ryusei stood still, unreactive, as people pushed him farther and farther from the tree.

Chie reached for his hand. "Ryusei, let's go now. Please."

He turned to face her, but he didn't budge. Chie swallowed hard. He wasn't himself. His body was there, but his mind was somewhere far away. She had no idea what to do. She felt like she was about to lose him.

Someone stepped in front of Chie and threw a bucket of water at Ryusei's face.

Chie gasped.

"Get out of here," Miss Sugi shouted at Ryusei. "You're blocking the way!"

He finally snapped out of it and swiftly walked off. Chie wanted to go after him, but Miss Sugi stopped her.

"Let him be. He needs to cool down."

"But—"

"It's all right. Leave him by himself for now."

Hesitant, Chie complied.

The tree was still burning despite the rain and the buckets of water being thrown onto it. Oddly, while the fire wouldn't die down, it wasn't spreading either. The tree continued to burn, the villagers' efforts seeming to have no effect at all.

The fire rose like a wild beast, ravaging life from the tree with its insatiable hunger. This scene of sheer destruction was one Chie would never forget.

WHAT FOLLOWED WAS A blur. A man passed Chie a large pail. She followed suit with the rest of the crowd, scooping water from the river and coming back to throw it onto the tree while the rain continued to pour. To and fro, countless times. No one stopped until dawn broke and the fire was finally put out.

By the time the sun came up, the rain had stopped. Everyone was drenched and covered in ash and mud. Despite this, the villagers were in high spirits. They laughed and patted one another's backs, saying, "Good job, well done. You worked hard." Seeing this, Chie felt an immense sense of satisfaction.

In the end, the only casualty was that one tree. What was left was a blackened, hollow monument. Chie thought the whole episode must be a message from Miwako. But what was she trying to say?

She inched closer and touched the burnt trunk. It was then that she noticed a shallow hole in the ground. The tin box containing Miwako's letters was gone.

Entering the warehouse, she found an unfamiliar man crouching in front of Tama.

"WHO ARE YOU?" FUMI shouted. "What are you doing here?"

The stranger turned to her. Fumi took a good look at his face. Young, probably early or mid-twenties, definitely younger than her. Wearing a blue gingham shirt over a white T-shirt and a pair of faded jeans, he looked like a university student.

"I just asked you what you're doing here." She continued to raise her voice. "You're trespassing on private property."

He raised both his hands and grinned. "Miss, do I look like a suspicious person? Don't be so aggressive."

"You're on my property without permission. You're obviously suspicious."

"Hey, come on." He laughed, a pair of dimples forming on his cheeks. He held out a key to the partitioned office, identical to hers. "My name is Eiji. I'm looking for Kenji."

"Ah, you should've said so earlier," Fumi said, setting her plastic bags down and taking out a can of cat food. "Kenji is away on a long trip. To be honest, I don't know where he is or when he'll be back. It's been several years."

The young man paused, seemingly deep in thoughts. "In that case, I'll stay here and wait for him."

Fumi furrowed her brow. "Excuse me, what did you just say?"

"I'm going to stay here and wait for Kenji until he returns." Eiji flashed Fumi a big smile. He gestured to Tama, who was enjoying her dinner. "Is this the resident cat?"

"Yes."

"What's her name?"

"Tama."

"How old is she?"

"Wait, wait." Fumi sighed and crossed her arms. "Let's get one thing clear. You can't stay here. This is *my* studio. Kenji entrusted it to me to do my work, and I'm not having some stranger in my workplace." Fumi noticed the boy had brought a huge rucksack, which sat near his feet. "Where are you from, anyway? Are you on vacation or something?"

"On vacation, huh?" He laughed. "You could say that."

"I'm sorry, Eiji, but you need to leave. I've got a lot of work to do."

"Hey, don't be like that. I have nowhere to go, and I've got no cash."

"What do you mean? You came to Tokyo without any money?"

He nodded. "I've got enough for instant noodles, but that's about it."

Fumi gritted her teeth. Was he for real?

"Kenji said I could crash at his place whenever I wanted, for as long as I wanted," the young man said.

Well, too bad. None of her business. "As you can clearly see, the man isn't here. Why don't you go back to wherever you came from?"

"I can't do that," he said, pausing. "I'm running away from home, so I've got nowhere to return to."

She frowned. "Why did you run away? Don't you have another friend you can go to?"

Instead of answering, Eiji yawned. "I'm so tired. Can I sleep on the floor, just for the night?"

FUMI HAD NO IDEA why she'd led this stranger back to her apartment. She had never brought anyone there before, not even Kenji. The next thing she knew, Eiji was standing by the door while she set up a makeshift bed for him on the sofa. If her brother were there, he would have been chiding her for giving in to yet another jerk.

"I like your apartment," Eiji said, glancing around. "It's simple, but very comfortable. Did you decorate it yourself?"

She glared at him. "If you keep talking, I'll throw you onto the street."

He laughed. He had a smile she would've found charming if he hadn't been testing her patience.

"Hey, tell me your name," he said.

"What for?"

"So I know how to address you."

"There's no need. You're leaving tomorrow anyway, first thing in the morning."

"Yes, but until then, I want to speak to you properly. Or I could just call you 'pretty girl.'"

"Call me that, and you'll spend the night sleeping on a park bench with a black eye," Fumi said. She wasn't sure whether to laugh or cringe at his feeble attempt to flatter her. "But if you insist, you can call me Fumi."

"Can I call you Fumi-nee?"

"Up to you."

"I'll call you Fumi-nee. You seem like the nice older sister type. I always wanted a sister," Eiji said. "Do you live here by yourself?"

"My brother lives with me."

"Where is he?"

"He's been staying elsewhere. He should be back any day now."

"But for now, you're here all by yourself?"

"Like I said, he'll be back any day now." She carried the sofa's cushions to Ryusei's room and put them on his bed.

"A woman living alone," Eiji mumbled. "Aren't you afraid I might attack you?"

Fumi sucked in her breath. This guy was messing with her. "That's enough. Get out. The door's unlocked."

"Hey, I was just teasing you," he said. "I'm sorry, it was a bad joke. But please, let me stay the night. I won't bother you."

She clicked her tongue.

"Okay, maybe a couple of nights. Please?"

Fumi narrowed her eyes and crossed her arms. "Seriously? Don't waste your time. Like I told you, my brother lives with me. It's not my place to give you permission to stay here."

"Of course it is. This is your apartment. It's entirely up to you. Come on, at least let me stay here until your brother returns. I promise to leave by then."

She frowned. "And if I say no?"

He licked his lip, seemingly hesitating. "I really don't want to resort to this, but the studio doesn't belong to you, Fumi-nee, and I'm pretty sure you don't have any legally valid proof that Kenji entrusted it to you."

"That's ridiculous." Fumi felt anger surge up inside her.

"It would just be your word against mine, and in the eyes of law, Kenji's promise means nothing if you can't prove he made it. Look, I'm not trying to blackmail you. I have no intention to report you to the police for . . . what did you call it earlier? Ah, yes, trespassing on private property."

She crossed her arms. "Do you really expect me to let you stay after you just threatened me like that?"

He shrugged. "I have no choice, you know. How was I supposed to know Kenji wouldn't be there? I was planning to crash at his place."

Fumi took a deep breath.

"You can just think of me as a pet, one you don't need to feed. I won't trouble you, and I'll try my best to be helpful," Eiji said.

"You're more of a pest than a pet," she muttered.

"If you're that uncomfortable with me being here, I'll go back to the warehouse. Is that better? I can sleep on the floor. I promise not to touch any of your things."

No, that wouldn't do. The studio's concrete flooring was so hard and cold, anyone would get sick spending the night there. She knew letting Eiji stay in her apartment was a bad idea, and she could almost hear Ryusei's voice chiding her, but . . .

"If you're so tired, why are you still standing by the door?" Fumi eventually said.

Eiji's eyes lit up. "You're letting me stay?"

"Only for a few days," she said, too quickly. "Until you get a job and find proper accommodations."

Fumi couldn't tell if Eiji even heard her. He was busy settling onto the couch like an excited puppy.

"Do you need a blanket?" she asked. "I can lend you one."

"Nah, I like the night breeze," he said. "What about you? What do you usually do at this hour? Are you an early sleeper?"

Fumi glanced at her watch. Still eight in the evening. Her shift started at ten. She should be able to nap for a bit, but she had to complete some sketches for a commissioned painting.

"You can rest." She rubbed her neck. "I'm not tired."

"You're lying," Eiji said.

"What do you mean?"

"You haven't realized it?" He mimicked her gesture. "Whenever you're hiding something or talking about something that makes you uncomfortable, you touch your neck."

Fumi pulled her hand down. How had he figured that out so fast? They had just met.

"I'm going to sleep," he said, curling up with his back to her. "If you're tired, you should rest. It's not good to push yourself all the time. You need to listen to your body more."

She hated to admit it, but he was right. She ought to start taking better care of her health.

THE FIRST NIGHT EIJI stayed over at Fumi's apartment, she had a dream about Miwako. It was of something that had happened a year ago.

Fumi was entering the studio when she saw Miwako crouching in front of the two run-down bicycles.

"What are you doing?" Fumi whispered over Miwako's shoulder.

"Nothing." Surprised, she abruptly turned around and stood, hiding a sketchbook behind her back. "You shouldn't sneak up on people. I thought you were a ghost."

Fumi laughed. "You're the one who was off in your own world. What were you doing?"

She shook her head. "Nothing."

Right. Fumi walked around Miwako and pointed at the sketchbook. "What's that?"

"Hey!"

Fumi snatched the book out of Miwako's hands despite her protests. Flipping through the pages, she saw pencil sketches of varied subjects. Cats, birds, some still lifes, and on the last page, a stiff outline of two bicycles, still half-done. All the images were crooked, and their proportions or angles were odd.

"No wonder you were hiding this," Fumi said, chuckling.

Miwako grabbed the book back. "I knew this would happen."

Fumi laughed and leaned toward Miwako. "Should I take you under my wing? It's about time for me to have an apprentice."

Miwako's eyes widened. "Are you serious?"

"You don't want to?"

"Of course I do," she said. "But wouldn't that be bothersome for you?"

"I wouldn't be offering to teach you if it were a bother," she said, winking. "The thing is, I'm very strict. You're going to have to work really, really hard, and I mean that."

"That's not a problem. I'll work hard. When can we start?"

Fumi had never seen Miwako so eager, and somehow the girl's enthusiasm infected her. "How about now?"

Miwako followed Fumi to the partitioned office, and they settled at the table. Fumi flipped open the drawing book to a new blank page and handed Miwako a black pen.

"I want you to draw straight horizontal lines from right to left. Make sure they don't touch each other," she said. "Fill the entire page. Try to leave the smallest space possible between the lines."

Miwako seemed puzzled. "I can't draw a straight line."

"Just try your best. It's to train you to draw the lines you intend to. Once the entire page is full, do the same thing on the next page, but with vertical lines instead of horizontal ones."

Miwako frowned, but she did as she was instructed. Fumi watched her struggle to keep the lines straight.

"Can I use a pencil instead?" Miwako asked.

Fumi shook her head. "I don't want you erasing the lines. I gave you a pen for a reason. It's good practice to sketch with a pen."

"You really are strict, aren't you?"

Fumi's lips curled up. "You had fair warning."

Miwako laughed, her face inches away from the paper. She had terrible posture. Fumi was about to lecture her about it when she noticed something. It was only a faint outline, but she saw a man standing behind Miwako.

The man looked like your typical middle-aged office worker—he was in a crisp white shirt, striped tie, dark-gray suit, and matching trousers. He wore a pair of thick-rimmed glasses identical to Miwako's. There were distinct similarities between his features and hers—they had a similar high nose bridge and small lips.

"Miwako," Fumi said. "Did someone close to you die recently?"

She shook her head. "No. Why?"

"It's just . . ." Fumi rubbed her neck. "Nothing, it's nothing. Don't worry about it."

Fumi forced a smile, but she could clearly see a man standing there, barely a couple feet behind Miwako. He didn't seem angry. If anything, his face was gentle. He looked completely serene. Fumi wondered if she should ask Miwako again, but she didn't want to frighten her. People never understood what she saw.

"Where did you buy your glasses?" Fumi asked Miwako.

She didn't reply right away. After a brief silence, she finally said, "I didn't buy them. They're a memento from my father. He passed away a long time ago."

"How long ago?"

"Why do you ask?"

"Never mind," Fumi said, rubbing her neck again. "I'm sorry for bringing up something so upsetting."

"No, it's not upsetting. I'm just curious as to why you wanted to know."

"Sorry, I didn't mean to meddle in your personal affairs."

"I never said you were doing that that. It surprised me a little, that's all," Miwako said, putting down the pen. "My father was diagnosed with terminal cancer when I was ten. He was a strong man, and he did the best he could, but in the end, the illness got the best of him."

Fumi felt a lump in her throat. She didn't know Miwako had lost a parent too.

"My father got the glasses from my grandfather, and in turn, he left them to me. I got an eyeglass shop to change the lenses to non-prescription ones so I could use them. I like to think that wherever I go, I'll have a piece of him with me. Sort of like a lucky charm." Chuckling, Miwako turned to Fumi. "I know it sounds silly."

Fumi shook her head. "It sounds nice. He must have been a good father."

"Yes, he was," she said. "I wish we'd had more time together, but I've learned to accept fate."

Fumi paused and narrowed her eyes. She'd heard those words before. Hadn't Miwako said them not too long ago? She felt as if they'd already had this conversation, but why was she experiencing it again? This could only be a dream. Yes, after all, Miwako Sumida was dead. Fumi sighed. How could she forget? She had gone with Ryu to Miwako's wake.

She turned to Miwako. The girl seemed so real, so alive.

"What's wrong, Fumi-nee?" Miwako asked. "You're staring."

"Ah, sorry." All of a sudden, the cat popped into her mind. "Did you ever find Tama?"

Miwako shook her head. "I thought she was with you."

"Oh, you're right," Fumi said, vaguely recalling it. How could she have forgotten that too?

"How is Ryusei? You told me he went somewhere, didn't you?"

"Did I?" Fumi was becoming confused. "Yes, Ryu left the city, but he wouldn't tell me where he went. He's been gone for more than two weeks."

Miwako stared straight ahead. "Do you think he'll be okay?"

"Of course," Fumi said. "Don't worry about him—or about us."

"Okay."

"You know, Miwako, there was something I always wanted to tell you."

"Yes?"

"It's about your father. I didn't want to say anything then because it's a violation of my personal rules. The living shouldn't meddle with the dead. But since you're no longer around, I think I can ask you now." Fumi paused. "You said your father died peacefully due to illness, and that you've come to terms with his death. Is that true?"

"Yes, it is."

"If that's the case, then why does he follow you?"

Miwako's eyes widened. "What do you mean?"

"Actually, I—" Fumi flinched when she felt something furry brush against her legs. Looking down, she saw Tama staring up at her.

"Tama!" Miwako said. "I can't believe she's actually here."

"Yes. What a smart girl."

Fumi crouched down and stroked Tama's fur. The cat purred and curled up her tail. Before Fumi could continue her conversation with Miwako, she had woken up.

Sneakers,
High
Heels,
and
Milk
Pudding

It wasn't Tama who was staring at Fumi when she awoke. It was Eiji, standing near her desk by the window.

"I'm sorry for interrupting your sleep," he said, "but I thought you might catch a cold with your window open. I was about to close it. I didn't mean to wake you up."

Still confused by the dream, Fumi took a few seconds to process what Eiji had said.

The pink curtains at her window flapped around wildly. Lightning flashed and thunder rumbled. The table where Fumi had fallen asleep was full of sketches. Scattered by the wind, some of them had fallen to the floor.

"Ah, I knocked just now, but you didn't answer, and the door wasn't locked," he continued.

"I don't get sick that easily." Fumi got up and walked past him, closing the window herself before it started to rain and her sketches got wet. "Please don't come in here again without permission. It's creepy."

Eiji was quiet. Fumi realized she was being harsh, but she needed to set proper boundaries.

"I did say you could stay here for a while, but you can't just walk into my brother's room or mine," she said. "Especially mine. This is the first and last warning. If I learn that you've done this again, you're out. Got it?"

"Yes, boss."

"I've got to go now." Fumi stretched. Her limbs were stiff. Looking at her watch, she realized it was ten-thirty. She was already late for work. "I don't think my brother will return anytime soon, but if he does show up, don't panic. Ask him to call me."

"Where are you going at this hour?"

"To work."

"It's so late. What kind of work do you do?"

"None of your business," Fumi said, pointing to the door. "Now, if you would please excuse me, I need to get changed."

Eiji left as directed and she slammed the door. She couldn't believe he was so nosy. Seriously, what was the only kind of work one possibly did at this time of the night?

Sighing, Fumi opened her cupboard to pick a dress. Was it shallow to admit one of the main reasons she'd chosen hostessing— apart from the easy money—was because she loved the opportunity to dress up? Her painting gigs required her to be in old T-shirts and jeans most of the time, even though she preferred to wear pretty dresses and makeup.

Of course, there also wasn't much choice for Fumi Yanagi. It wasn't like she could just work in a standard corporate office.

Fumi singled out a blush-colored dress and a beige coat. Laying them on her bed, she took out a pair of dainty, dangling earrings and a matching necklace. After that, she checked her nails. The polish on her left pinky was chipped. She cringed. She couldn't afford to waste much time fixing it since she had overslept, but she reached for a bottle of polish and quickly ran the brush over the gap. No one would pay close attention to her nails in the dim lighting of the bar, but she still wanted to look as perfect as possible. She blew on the fresh polish in a bid to make it dry faster.

Her brother had been telling her to quit hostessing for some time now.

"It's unhealthy," Ryu said. "They make you drink too much, and the hours mess up your sleep schedule. Are you trying to die young?"

"Stop that," she said. "I won't die before you're married, which won't happen anytime soon if you keep chasing after Miwako."

"Shut up."

Fumi always won an argument with Ryu when she brought up Miwako. Her brother would become too flustered to retort. Sometimes she felt sorry for him. Other times she just felt like teasing him, which happened more often. He was so innocent in his awkward moments, reminding her of how he'd been as a child. Ryu had really depended on her back then.

And Miwako . . . why had she been in that dream?

Fumi had long suspected a connection between the unconscious mind and the soul, but it wasn't like there was anyone to discuss her hypotheses with. Their father was dead now, and she'd never met anyone else with the same curse. She still had so many questions for him. But no matter how many times Fumi called for him, she couldn't catch even a glimpse of his spirit.

Eiji turned to Fumi and whistled. "Aren't you dressed up, Fumi-nee? You look gorgeous."

Ignoring him, she saw Eiji was wearing his sneakers. "Are you going out too?"

"Yes, I'll walk you to wherever you're going."

This surprised her, but she kept her expression in check. "You don't need to. I go to work on my own all the time."

"Your brother must be useless, then," he said. "I would never let a girl walk around by herself at this hour."

Fumi laughed. She knew she should reprimand Eiji for criticizing Ryu, but the whole attempt at chivalry was hilarious coming from a youngster who had just attempted to blackmail her. "Thanks for offering, but I'm fine, really. And didn't you say you were tired?"

"Not anymore. I had a nap too, so I'm fully recharged." He looked out of the window. "Guess we got lucky. Doesn't look like it'll rain after all."

He seemed set on accompanying her, so she said nothing. She walked out in her silver-sequined heels, Eiji following behind. With Fumi in these shoes, he was significantly shorter than her. Her puffed-up hairdo emphasized their height difference, though he didn't seem to mind. He seemed at ease walking next to her, unlike most men she knew.

"Where are we going?" Eiji asked.

"Shinjuku," Fumi said. "Ever been there?"

"Uh-huh."

"I bet you've never been to the part I'm going to."

He chuckled. "Really? You seem sure about that."

She waited for him to say something more, but he had gone quiet. Fumi eventually asked, "You're not going to guess what I do for a living?"

Eiji shrugged. "You said it was none of my business."

"True, but you're going to find out anyway if you keep following me."

"Do you want me to stop here?"

She couldn't answer. It was nice to have someone to chat with on the way to the train station, but she didn't want him to find out she was a hostess.

"It's fine," Eiji said. "I'll walk you to the station and head back."

Fumi nodded. It was uncommon for someone as young as him to

be so sensitive and understanding. Somehow, she felt comfortable around Eiji. But if he continued to stay at her place, sooner or later, he would learn about her job, maybe even her curse. What would he think of her then? Would he react with sympathy or disgust?

"You're always overthinking something, aren't you?" Eiji asked.

She clicked her tongue. "You're imagining that."

"Your face tells me everything. You're so easy to read, do you know that?" he said. "If you have something to say, I'll listen."

Fumi shook her head. "Like I said, it's all in your mind."

Eiji shrugged and continued to walk. "Just now, were you having a bad dream? When you fell asleep at the table, you kept on mumbling something, and you were sweating."

"Was I?"

"Yeah."

She paused. "I did have a dream."

"Was it bad?"

"Not really," she said, "just strange."

"Most dreams are strange, aren't they? Do you want to talk about it?"

"Maybe next time." She turned to face him. "The train station is just around the corner. Thanks for walking me here."

"Ah, right." He waved at her. "Take care, Fumi-nee, and don't drink too much."

Her heart skipped a beat. Had he just said that? She had been naïve earlier. Anyone could guess what kind of job she would be doing late at night, especially all dressed up like this. Waving back at Eiji, Fumi Yanagi forced herself to smile.

DESPITE RUSHING ALL THE way to the bar, Fumi reached her workplace over an hour late. Mama-san glared at her when she entered.

"It's unlike you to be late, Fumi-chan," she said in a flat tone. Normally Mama-san shouted at the girls when they were late, but Fumi was her favorite. She had the biggest number of regular customers among the girls, and most of the time, she brought the highest revenue too.

"I'm sorry," Fumi said, catching her breath. "Did I miss anything?"

"Mr. Takahashi is looking for you. Don't make him wait any longer."

Fumi nodded and excused herself to the dressing room. After putting down her belongings and touching up her makeup, she went to the bar.

She opened the door and stood in the corner for a couple of seconds, waiting for her eyes to fully adjust to the dim lighting. Mr. Takahashi sat on the scarlet circular sofa next to Sanae, one of the newer hostesses.

"Good evening," she greeted him. "I'm sorry to have kept you waiting."

"Ah, Miss Fumi." The scrawny middle-aged man threw her a gleeful smile. "It's rare for you to be late, isn't it?"

"Yes, there was something I needed to take care of at home," she said, discreetly gesturing for Sanae to leave them alone.

"I hope nothing bad happened," the older man said.

"Oh, no, don't worry about that." She laughed, wiping the condensation off Mr. Takahashi's glass and topping it up with watered-down whiskey. "A stray cat followed me home and refused to leave. I had no choice but to let him stay."

"He must be charmed by your beauty," he said.

Fumi smiled. "You always say the nicest things, Mr. Takahashi. May I join you for a drink?"

"Of course. You never need to ask, Miss Fumi. You're too polite."

She mustered another smile.

In her line of business, smiling was essential. If you had nothing to say, smile. If people said something nice, smile. For most things, you just had to smile, but all the smiling wore her down. Wasn't there anything beyond smiling and looking pretty?

Mr. Takahashi began to tell Fumi about his day at work. He was an auditor at a large, publicly listed firm. He worked long hours and was the second longest-serving employee in his department, but he harbored a certain bitterness. He had been waiting for his promotion for years, but it wasn't about to happen unless the chief auditor retired, and the old man was a stubborn workaholic.

"The chief left the office so late again," Mr. Takahashi lamented. "I'm tired of waiting for him day after day."

Fumi nodded sympathetically. "That must have been unpleasant."

"I told my wife I'd take her out for dinner. Tonight is our thirty-fourth wedding anniversary. I hate to break my promise, but sometimes these things are beyond my control."

"Don't worry. She'll understand. After all, you work for the sake of your family."

He took a sip of his drink. "I'm not sure about that, Miss Fumi. She must be mad at me right now."

Fumi wanted to tell Mr. Takahashi his wife would be less upset if he were at home apologizing to her instead of out drinking with a bar hostess. Of course, she shouldn't tell him that. She was paid to listen and appear to empathize with him, but for once, she couldn't let go of the niggling feeling in her chest.

"Mr. Takahashi, why don't you go home and explain the situation to your wife?" Fumi asked against her better judgment.

"I don't want to." He shook his head. "She'll nag me. You couldn't possibly understand a woman's feelings."

His words pierced her. He probably hadn't meant them to. No, she was sure he didn't realize how his comment hurt her, though that didn't mean it didn't.

"Don't worry, Miss Fumi," he continued. "It's better for me to stay here until she's gone to bed. Tomorrow, her anger will surely have subsided."

"But what if she's waiting up for you at home?"

Mr. Takahashi laughed. "That old woman? She won't. We've been married for so long, she no longer cares about me. She'll already be asleep if I catch the last train home."

Fumi knew this was a losing battle. "Is that so? In that case, I'll drink with you until it's time for you to go."

"Yes, please."

She topped up Mr. Takahashi's drink and listened to more of his stories, wiping the glass every now and then and nodding politely at appropriate times.

The bar was rather quiet that night. There were only two big groups of guests plus a few regulars. Fumi spotted one newcomer, a bald man in a worn-out business suit who sat next to Sanae. He placed his tattered briefcase on his lap, seemingly uncomfortable here. Hopefully, the new girls hadn't forced him in. The ones the bar had just hired to solicit on the street could be quite aggressive at times.

The bar wasn't so big in the first place—at any given time, there were never more than ten girls working. But what they lacked in numbers, they made up for by catering to certain tastes. Though nowadays, men were getting more and more adventurous, so it was no surprise to see more bars like theirs, employing women who hadn't been born in the right bodies.

Fumi's fellow hostesses had chosen to work at the bar for many reasons. Most were saving up for operations or supporting good-for-nothing partners. A few were saddled with mounting debts and being hounded by the yakuza, but there were sadder stories. Some had families who had kicked them out because of who they were. And Fumi was sure there were also those who, like her, were just there to be appreciated as girls. But they were all kidding themselves. No matter how beautiful they looked, how elegantly they behaved, their clients never saw them as real women.

"Miss Fumi."

She leaned in toward Mr. Takahashi, hoping he hadn't realized her mind had been somewhere else. "Yes?"

"Do you think I should go home now?"

Fumi paused. He was probably hoping for her to give him an excuse to stay by telling him it was all right to spend time with her over his angry wife, but there was no way she could do that.

"Yes, I think so. Your wife might be waiting for you."

Mr. Takahashi put down his glass. "Only you would tell me that."

The edges of Fumi's mouth lifted. She was so used to putting on this polite smile that she did it reflexively whenever she had nothing to say.

"Actually, I know my wife is still awake, waiting for me. She's most likely watching television in the living room, trying to rein in her anger." He looked down. "I don't want to face her. This isn't the first time I've gone back on my word. I've disappointed her so many times."

Fumi reached for Mr. Takahashi's hand. "Apologize to her and tell her about the situation at work. I'm sure she'll appreciate your honesty."

The middle-aged man kept his head low.

"Do you know her favorite snack?" Fumi asked.

He looked up. "She likes milk pudding."

"You should be able to buy that from the 24-hour convenience store down the road."

Mr. Takahashi glanced at his watch. "It's past midnight, so it's no longer our anniversary."

"It doesn't matter," Fumi said, trying to suppress her impatience. "Better late than never."

He paused. "You're right."

Finally. Fumi breathed a sigh of relief.

Mr. Takahashi stood, and Fumi took his arm. They walked together to the front door. His head was the same height as her shoulders. *I really shouldn't wear these heels*, she thought. Out front, Mr. Takahashi waved at her and she bowed to him. She stood in the doorway and waited there until she couldn't see him anymore.

"Was there something wrong?" Mama-san asked. "Mr. Takahashi left early. He usually stays so long, we have to keep reminding him we're closing."

Turning to face her, Fumi gave a thin smile. "He needs to be somewhere. Guess I won't be getting much business tonight."

"Ah, about that . . ." Mama-san's face lit up. "A first-time customer saw you and expressed his interest."

"The man with the briefcase?"

"Yes, the bald one. He looks so nervous. He doesn't seem like someone who usually comes to these bars. I wonder what he's doing here."

"People have all sorts of objectives," Fumi said.

And it was never her business to know unless they wanted her to.

Lingering
Regrets
and
Pain

Slightly buzzed, Fumi rummaged through her handbag and took out a bunch of keys. Which one opened the front door? Ah, there. Got it. She tried to insert the key but dropped the whole set on the floor. The loud clanking noise echoed in the quiet night. Fumi cursed and picked them up.

She opened the door. The apartment was dark and silent. Well, what had she expected? Someone waiting up for her? Fumi reached for the switch and turned on a lamp. Light flooded the room.

Eiji peeked out over the top of the sofa. "Welcome home."

Fumi almost apologized to Eiji for waking him up, but she reminded herself she didn't need to. This was her house.

"How was work?" he asked.

"Same as always," she said, putting down her handbag. "Nothing really changes there."

"You must be tired."

She answered with a shrug.

"Why don't you treat yourself to a late-night dessert?" he asked. "There's a milk pudding in the fridge."

Her eyes widened. "A milk pudding?"

"Yes, in a plastic bag. You'd better eat it now. It expires tomorrow." Eiji glanced at the clock. "Oops, it's already way past midnight. But I doubt a couple of hours makes much of a difference."

Fumi went to the kitchen and opened the fridge. There was a small white plastic bag she hadn't noticed. Opening it, she found a milk pudding she didn't remember buying. Could it be Ryu's? But he didn't usually eat sweets.

Eiji looked over her shoulder. "You forgot about it, didn't you?"

"I wasn't the one who bought it," Fumi said. "Maybe my brother got it for me but forgot to tell me."

"Good thing I reminded you, then. It might've gone to waste."

"Yes, thank you." She peeled open the seal. "But if you think that I'll let you stay longer just because you're being nice, you're mistaken."

"Hey, that's not fair. I'm not angling for anything." Eiji laughed.

Fumi rolled her eyes and dug into the pudding. It was so soft, melting instantly on her tongue. "Why don't you tell me what's on your mind, then?"

"Maybe another time," he said, lying down on the sofa. "It's already late. You should sleep."

Fumi took another spoonful of the dessert. She didn't want to admit it, but it was nice to have someone else in the house when Ryu wasn't around. Since he'd left, the apartment had felt too big, too quiet. Too lonely.

She still couldn't believe it when a week ago, her brother had told her he was taking a long trip by himself. Prior to that, apart from school trips, he wouldn't leave Tokyo without her.

"Where are you planning on going?" she asked Ryusei.

He shrugged. "Anywhere but here."

She caressed her neck. "Is this because of Miwako?"

Ryusei avoided her eyes. "Sorry I can't keep my promise about Tama, but I'll stock up on canned food for her."

I'm not worried about that, Fumi wanted to say, but no words came out. She couldn't stop him, knowing how much he was hurting after Miwako's suicide. And she wasn't sure how to explain her unease at being alone.

"I take it that you're not going to tell me where you're going or how long you'll be away?" she said, trying to remain calm.

He nodded. "I'll be back before Tama's food runs out, and before Waseda kicks me out."

"Oh, that's a relief."

But not quite, since the next day, Ryu bought enough canned food for Tama to last an entire season. How long was he seriously planning to travel? Still, Fumi didn't stop him. She couldn't. When it came to Ryu, she couldn't bring herself to be selfish.

"Fumi-nee?" Eiji's voice roused her from her thoughts. "Good night."

"Good night," she said, scooping up the last spoonful of milk pudding. She could taste a hint of vanilla. If only life were as sweet as her dessert.

As the days went by, Fumi got used to having Eiji around. His presence was comforting, even though he was only there because he didn't have a ton of money or anywhere else to go. But it soon became obvious he wasn't even looking for a job.

Eiji lingered in the apartment day and night. Fumi had no idea how much money he actually had, but he would probably only leave when he ran out of cash.

"Move," she said, running the vacuum cleaner near his legs.

Eiji got up on the sofa, which had become his personal island. "Are you not working today, Fumi-nee?"

"There's not much to do right now in the studio," she said. "After I'm done cleaning, do you want to go out? I can show you around the neighborhood. You seem to be home all the time. Shouldn't you be out sightseeing?"

"You make it sound like I'm a country bumpkin."

"Aren't you?"

He laughed. "You don't need to say it out loud."

"I'm not going to force you if you'd prefer to be at home."

"I'd prefer to be at home," he said. "Why don't we just spend some time together?"

"Where did you steal that cheesy line? From a romantic drama?" she asked, teasing him. She turned to Eiji. "So tell me, what do you want to do?"

He shrugged. "I don't know. Watch a movie?"

She rubbed her neck. "I don't like movies."

"There. You did it again."

"What?"

"Touched your neck." Eiji chuckled. "So you do like movies."

"Shut up." Fumi put down her hand. She hated when he called her bluff.

"Let me guess," he said, laying down on his stomach. "You love romantic movies with sappy endings, but you're afraid I'm going to laugh at you when you cry."

Fumi had no comeback, since Eiji was one hundred percent correct. "What kind of movies do you like, anyway?" she asked.

"I don't usually watch movies."

"There's no movie theater in your hometown?"

"I prefer books."

"Oh."

Eiji had no reason to lie, but Fumi found it hard to imagine a young man like him would choose books over movies. Fumi wasn't a book person, unlike Ryu.

"Do you want to go do karaoke?" Fumi turned off the vacuum cleaner after she had finished the whole apartment. "Or what about board games? I'm sure there are a few in my brother's room. His friends come over every once in a while to play."

Eiji was quiet.

"Or do you want to look at some photo albums?" she suggested. "I've got a lot of pretty friends."

He jumped from the sofa. "Let's do that."

Shortly after she had suggested the idea, Fumi wondered if it was wise to show him old photos. What if he realized something was off? But whether it was her identity or her night job, he was bound to learn sooner or later—his intuition was so sharp. If this was going to make him uncomfortable, it would be better for that to happen now.

"Why are you spacing out, Fumi-nee?" he asked.

"Be patient." She pulled a bunch of photo albums from a shelf and put them on the floor. She started with the vacation pictures with the girls from the bar. "These women are my colleagues. We took these photos last summer, when the lady boss brought us to Kyoto. We stayed at a ryokan."

"I've never been to Kyoto," Eiji said. "Or to a ryokan."

"It wasn't as luxurious as the ones you see on TV, but there was a nice open-air onsen, and the food was heavenly. We had seasonal nine-course kaiseki dinners. The sashimi was so fresh. We also had high-grade Wagyu beef. The meat was so tender I could split it with my chopsticks." Fumi sighed. "I hope I can go there again one day."

Eiji scanned through the pages, seemingly paying no attention to what Fumi had said. "You do have a lot of good-looking friends, Fumi-nee, but you're still the most beautiful."

Fumi rolled her eyes. "Haven't you learned? Flattery will get you nowhere."

"That wasn't my intention. I'm just telling the truth," he said. "But why do I feel like you're overly concerned about me looking at these? If you don't want to show me, you don't need to."

"It's not that," she said, brushing her hair behind her ear.

He looked into her eyes. "If there's something you want to share with me, I'll listen."

Fumi was moved by this, but she could practically hear Ryu lecturing her on protecting herself.

"If you don't want to talk, then don't," Eiji said. "It's fine to keep things to yourself."

She took a deep breath. "You probably already know I work as a bar hostess."

"Yes, I guessed as much," he said. "You're gorgeous, you dress up really prettily, and you work at night. When you left the house that first time, I thought you looked like a modern-day Cinderella."

If he was teasing, it didn't show. He said it like what she had just told him was an ordinary statement. As if she worked as an office lady or a shop assistant.

"Fumi-nee, you work very hard. You should be proud of yourself."

Hearing that, something inside her stirred, warm and glowing.

Eiji looked at another album. The photograph on the cover was of Ryusei and Fumi, both smiling. Behind them, herds of spotted deer roamed freely.

"That's your brother, right?" Eiji asked.

Fumi sat next to him and flipped open the pages. "Yes, his name is Ryusei. We went together to Todaiji Temple after he got into his first-choice university. Waseda, can you believe it?" Even now, Fumi's heart still beamed with pride whenever she recalled that particular trip. "My brother and I took the train from Tokyo to Nara, and we stayed there a couple of days for sightseeing."

"The two of you really look alike."

She nodded. "A lot of people say that."

Looking at the photograph of grinning Ryu brought Fumi pain. She hadn't seen him smile like that since Miwako's death. A few times when he thought he was alone, she'd caught him staring silently into the distance.

"Fumi-nee, you mentioned your brother didn't say where he was headed. Do you think he went back to Todaiji Temple?" Eiji asked.

"Perhaps," Fumi said. "But no matter how you beg, the gods won't bring back the dead."

"You sound so sure, like you're speaking from experience."

"I am," she said. "When I was young, I used to ask the impossible from the gods at the shrine by our house. But I eventually grew out of it."

Eiji said nothing.

"My brother is chasing his past. He needs to let go and move on."

Eiji didn't say a word. Had she revealed too much?

As they continued to flip through the pages, a photograph fell from the album. An old family picture, one of the few photographs Fumi still had of their late parents. Taken in front of their home—a shrine—it was of her father in a white Shinto priest robe. Her mother looked serene in her elegant mauve kimono, cradling baby Ryu in her arms. In front of them was Fumi, still dressed as a boy.

Fumi held in a breath and put the photograph back between the pages. After that, they went back to perusing the rest of the photos. For a moment, she contemplated saying something. Had

Eiji noticed? Either way, she decided not to say anything. She hated difficult conversations.

"Isn't this the orphanage?" Eiji pointed to a photograph. "Was this taken at Christmas?"

Fumi turned to look at the photograph. "No, not Christmas."

She and Ryu were posing with the orphanage's pastor and a few volunteers. The children, each holding a present, were all around them.

"After that visit to Todaiji Temple, we brought back some souvenirs from Nara. I thought the kids might like to receive them as presents, so I wrapped them."

Eiji nodded. "They look happy."

"Yes, they were ecstatic," she said and paused. "How did you know about the orphanage?"

"Oh, Kenji must have mentioned it."

Fumi began to feel uneasy. Pointing to the adults in the photograph, she said, "This is the pastor who runs the orphanage, and these are the volunteers."

"They look like university students."

It took her a few seconds before she answered, "Most of them are."

Fumi excused herself to the bathroom. Closing the door behind her, she took a deep breath. There was no mistake. Eiji was lying. He didn't know Kenji. He had never even met him. She had no idea how he'd learned the studio belonged to Kenji, but for sure, he hadn't recognized him, clearly standing amidst the volunteers in the photograph.

What do I do now? Why did I let him in here? Was it because I needed a friend?

20

She
Glowed
Under
the
Sun

Lying on her bed, Fumi thought of Ruri, her only friend from childhood, when she had still been living as a boy named Fumio Yanagi.

Fumio was thirteen when he first saw Ruri. They met during the school break.

That day, Fumio was sweeping the backyard. The cold weather had grown milder, and more people were coming to the shrine because of the holiday season. Ruri came out of nowhere, peeping out from the bushes and startling him.

"Visitors need to come in through the main entrance," he said, pointing to it.

He thought she had gotten lost, but the girl only stared at him in silence. Sighing, he continued to sweep. What a weird girl.

The girl eventually came out from the bushes and squatted near Fumio. He was uncomfortable being stared at, but didn't say anything out of politeness. Surely the girl's parents would come to pick her up soon. But by the time he'd finished sweeping the entire yard, she was still there.

The days were short, and the sky was getting dark. A flock of birds fled from the trees, disappearing to the other side of the shrine.

"You should go home soon," Fumio told the girl. "It's getting late. Your parents will be anxious."

She kept quiet. Was she deaf? Even so, she shouldn't be ignoring him. Fumio walked away, leaving her on her own. At first, he was worried. What if her parents couldn't find her? But then his mother called him for hot pot dinner, and he quickly forgot about the girl.

The next morning, he saw her again. This time she sat on the staircase at the porch behind the shrine.

"Good morning," Fumio said, but she still didn't respond. "I guess you're deaf and mute?"

She let out an exasperated sigh. "I'm not deaf or mute."

"Then why didn't you answer me yesterday?" He picked up his broom. "And you need to move aside. I need to sweep the staircase."

The girl stood and jumped down to the backyard. "I was confused. No one has spoken to me in a while."

He took another look at her. Wearing a white frilly dress, she looked just like any other girl in his class. Her bangs were swept to the left and secured with a flower clip. Her shoes looked worn. She wasn't wearing any socks, despite the chilly weather. But by all measures, she looked fairly normal.

"I'm Ruri," the girl said. "Do you want to be my friend?"

"Friend?" Fumio blurted out.

"Yes. Can we be friends?"

He quickly nodded. No one had ever asked him that.

"Good. Now, tell me your name."

"I'm Fumio Yanagi."

"Can I call you Fumio?"

He nodded again. He didn't tell her she was the first person—apart from his family—to call him by his first name.

"Do you live here?" she asked.

Fumio started sweeping. "Yes, my father's the priest here."

"Does that mean you're going to be a priest too?"

He shrugged. "Probably."

"You don't look like you want to."

"Maybe not."

Fumio knew he should have given her longer, more interesting answers and perhaps tried to ask some questions in return, but he was too nervous. He wasn't used to conversations like this.

Ruri continued to ask questions. "Aren't you supposed to be at school?"

He paused. "We're on break now. School is closed."

"Oh." She looked down. "I didn't know."

"You don't go to school?"

The girl shook her head. "My parents said I don't need to. They said I can study anywhere, even at home."

"You're so lucky. Mine won't let me skip school, no matter how much I beg."

Ruri looked at Fumio as if she was wondering why he would say a thing like that.

"You're not missing much," he continued. "Trust me."

She sighed. "I always wanted to go to school. I want to make friends."

Fumio tightened his grip on the broom. "School isn't the place to make friends."

"You don't have friends?"

"Not really," he said, wiping the sweat off his forehead. "I don't have many friends at school." Or rather, any.

"Is that so," she mumbled, then looked down. "What happened to your arm?"

Looking down, Fumio saw the blue-black marks on his right

arm. Flustered, he covered them with his sleeve. "I fell down. Stop being so nosy!" He hadn't meant to shout, but his voice came out that way.

Ruri's eyes went wide. "Sorry," she said.

Fumio felt bad for raising his voice at her, but he didn't want her to know what had happened to him. Even years later, when Fumi Yanagi thought of those early days at school, a shiver ran down her spine.

At that time, Fumio didn't know that there were boys like him, ones who felt that they had been born the wrong gender. In his small neighborhood school, he was always alone. Others noticed he was different. They labeled him weird, awkward, incapable of fitting in, and whispered behind his back.

A group of six girls ruled Fumio's class in high school, led by the skinniest and meanest among them, who always sported a designer bag. They would routinely single out a victim from their class, so all the students knew not to get into trouble with any of the girls.

Last year, they'd focused their energy on a quiet loner, though no one knew why. The group's constant and vicious intimidation forced the girl out of the school. Rumor was that she had moved to another city after a failed suicide attempt. Everyone was afraid of them from then on.

Though Fumio had never spoken a word to any of these girls, the group soon chose him as their next target.

They bullied him every day, scribbling on his desk or tearing pages from his books during recess. When the skinny girl was in a bad mood, she would call Fumio to the rooftop after school. Armed with brooms and sticks, the six of them would beat him. On the few occasions when Fumio refused to follow the group upstairs, they beat him even harder in front of their classmates outside the school doors.

A few students laughed, though most averted their eyes, pretending not to see anything. No one dared to help. They didn't want to be the next target.

On the rooftop, the girls often forced Fumio to strip down to his underwear. They hit him and kicked him before writing profanities on his bare skin with permanent markers. They laughed and mocked him until they grew tired, then left him on his own, sprawled on the ground.

After all of them left one day, Fumio slowly got up and gathered his clothes one by one. He prayed that everything would soon be over.

At times like this, he would look up at the clear, blue sky. How nice it would be to go up there. Then he looked down to the field, where the baseball team was playing a game. Not far off from them, the track and field team was doing their daily run.

Fumio grabbed the railing on the edge of the roof. The bar's metal was warm, baked by the afternoon sun. What would happen if he just . . . jumped? Then he wouldn't need to endure this pain any longer. But he couldn't bring himself to make the leap. When he looked down over that railing, he froze, legs rooted to the ground.

Hanging his head, Fumio dragged himself home and slipped into the bathroom. He took his clothes off and stared at his reflection in the mirror. The black marker stood out sharply against his pale skin. He had to rub these off before his family saw.

Turning on the tap, he grabbed a wet sponge and scrubbed his skin so hard, it turned raw and red. His vision blurred with tears.

This will stop soon, he told himself over and over, clenching his teeth. *They'll eventually get bored and leave me alone*. He wept silently in a wooden bath overflowing with hot water.

Those days, Fumio hated going to school. He really didn't know what he had ever done to offend those girls.

Their leader, the one who usually initiated the beating, always looked at him with disgust in her eyes. Fumio had never spoken to her prior to the day she had first called him up to the rooftop. He replayed his interactions with the rest of them over and over, wondering what he had done to deserve this treatment, but couldn't think of an answer.

At least he didn't need to interact with those girls during the term break, but it was only temporary relief.

"Can you wait here?" Fumio asked Ruri after he'd finished sweeping. "I need to go inside for a while."

She nodded, and he went into the building. He fetched a pail of water and a washcloth. When he returned, she was leaning against the wooden pillar. Her skin was fair, almost glowing under the sun.

Ruri turned to Fumio. "You're back."

He put down his stuff. "I still need to mop the platform." He dipped the cloth into the water and wrung it out. "Do you live around here?"

"Yes, my house is just a few blocks away." She tilted her head. "Am I disturbing you?"

He shook his head. "No. But aren't your parents worried? You've been away from them for a while."

"They aren't," she said, speaking softly. "They're used to it already."

Fumio wondered if Ruri had family issues. Maybe her parents were busy with work and left her alone all the time. He wanted to ask, but he knew better than to meddle in other people's affairs.

"You should go home soon," Fumio said, spreading the wash-cloth. "It's almost lunchtime."

"I'll wait until you're done," Ruri insisted.

Fumio shrugged. He knelt down and pushed the cloth from one end to the other. Ruri stood in the same spot the whole time, looking at the sky. What was she thinking? But he didn't ask. Perhaps she wasn't normal, like him, just better at concealing it.

Fumio Yanagi had never been good at blending in. Each time he was assigned to a new class, he tried his best to engage with his classmates. *Act normal. Look normal. Pretend you're completely ordinary.* But somehow, they knew he was putting up a front, and he always ended up alone. At least, until those six girls had turned their attention to him. He would have preferred to remain by himself, but it wasn't like he had a choice.

The wind rustled the trees. The branches swayed, and more dried leaves fell onto the ground. Fumio would have to sweep again in the afternoon. He looked over at Ruri. She was still gazing at the sky, the wind having messed up her hair. Stray strands covered her face, but she didn't seem bothered by them. She turned to Fumio.

"Can I come back later?" she asked.

He nodded. "The shrine is open to the public every day. Anyone can come in." What a silly answer, but he'd been unable to think of anything better to say.

They parted ways after Fumio finished his first cleaning shift.

And Ruri did return later that day, and the day after, and the day after that. She came to the shrine every day, standing around as Fumio did his chores. Even though they didn't talk much, he enjoyed her company. He secretly wished his school break would never end.

POURING CHOPPED ONIONS INTO the pan, Fumi heard footsteps behind her. *Eiji's up*, she thought, feeling tense.

"That smells good, Fumi-nee," he said. "What are you making?"

"Just soft-boiled eggs with vegetables," she said. "Why don't you wash up? Then we can have breakfast together."

He yawned. "I'm not hungry. I had a big dinner last night."

"But I already cooked for you."

"I'm sorry, I really don't have an appetite."

She clicked her tongue. "Fine then. I'll have your portion. Don't come crawling to me when you get hungry later."

Fumi took a plate, putting ketchup and mayonnaise on the side. Settling at the dining table, she grazed the steaming soft-boiled eggs with her knife. Their yolk spilled onto the plate.

"I love runny eggs," Fumi said, scooping up a bite.

Eiji looked over at her from the sofa.

"Are you sure you don't want breakfast? I never see you eat," she said.

"I eat when you're at work," he said. "I'm not much of a breakfast person, but thank you for thinking of me. I appreciate it."

Eiji rested his head on the arm of the sofa. Fumi took another good look at him. He was definitely much younger than her, perhaps around Ryu's age. He wasn't tan, so he was probably a city kid. He didn't have an accent, so it was hard to tell which prefecture he came from. He sounded like just about any other Tokyo youth.

"How did you meet Kenji?" Fumi asked.

"He's a friend of a friend," Eiji said. "Are you not working today, Fumi-nee?"

She saw right through his attempt to change the topic. "No, I'm free today. Why don't you tell me a bit about your and Kenji's mutual friend?"

He tilted his head. "Why?"

"No particular reason. I have some time, and you almost never talk about yourself. So tell me your story. I'm listening."

"Oh, really?" He smiled, showing off his dimples. "Why do I feel like it's you who wants to say something?"

"What do you mean?"

He gestured at her plate. "You barely ate your breakfast."

Only then did Fumi realize she had been absentmindedly holding her cutlery above her plate. Putting it down, she looked straight into his eyes.

"The game's up," she said. "I know you're not a friend of Kenji's."

There was a swift but tiny change in Eiji's expression. He hid it well, almost like he'd been expecting it. "What are you talking about?"

"You've never met Kenji. You didn't recognize him in one of those photographs yesterday, even when I pointed right at him."

Eiji went silent for a moment. "The photograph of the orphanage, wasn't it? He must have been one of the volunteers."

"You're quick." Fumi picked up her spoon and took another scoop of egg. "What should I do now? Kick you out?"

"This is your apartment. The choice is yours."

"Are you not even going to try to explain yourself?"

He laughed. "What is there to explain? My cover's blown, that's all. Yes, I've only heard of Kenji. I've never met him. You figured it out, Fumi-nee. Have you ever considered a career as a private investigator?"

Fumi was surprised at Eiji's lack of protest. Or rather, disappointed.

"You shouldn't confront a man when you're alone, Fumi-nee," Eiji said. "What if I reacted violently?"

She lifted her head. "You should know by now that I'm not like other women. I'm not intimidated by you."

"Yes, you're right. You're not the average woman."

Fumi felt a familiar ache. She thought she'd gotten used to it, but she hadn't.

"You're a superwoman, right?" he continued. "You hold two jobs and take care of the house all by yourself. You still have time to keep a pet . . . Wait, two pets."

She rubbed the nape of her neck.

"You're an awesome woman, Fumi-nee, and I'm sorry for lying to you and taking advantage of your kindness. But trust me, when I say that I think of you as a friend, I really mean it."

Hearing those words made Fumi flushed. Her cheeks felt warm. Not wanting Eiji to see her reaction, she stood and grabbed her handbag.

"Where are you going, Fumi-nee?" he asked.

"Work," she answered without looking at him.

"I thought you said you didn't have work today?"

Fumi reached for the doorknob. "I changed my mind."

**New Love
Is the
Best Cure
for a
Broken
Heart**

Fumi stopped in front of a convenience store. Colorful posters advertising promotions covered the glass panels. She pushed open the door. In a daze, she wandered to the sweets aisle. Rows of bubble gum, candies, chocolates, and crackers were lined up neatly on the shelves, some decorated with images of famous cartoon characters. Each package burst with color, vying for her attention.

Why was she here?

A moment ago, she had planned to confront Eiji and kick him out. Instead, she found herself running away. She turned to the refrigerated drinks section, running her fingers along the bottled soda, canned coffee, and boxes of fruit juices. Then she stopped at the milk pudding. Fumi started to chuckle, though she didn't know why. *Get ahold of yourself, Fumi*, she thought. But she couldn't stop. She laughed until she started to tear up.

"Are you all right, Miss?"

The store assistant, a girl who looked like she was still in her teens, stared at her.

"I'm fine," Fumi said. "Just remembered something silly. I hope I didn't scare you."

The girl smiled politely. "Of course not."

Clearly a lie. She'd been looking at Fumi like she'd lost her mind.

"Would you like a basket for your purchase?" the girl offered.

"No, I just . . ." Fumi reached for two packs of milk pudding. "I've got what I want."

She went to the cashier and paid. Leaving the convenience store, Fumi felt the weight of the pudding in the plastic bag. It swung slightly in her hand with every step she took. She deliberately slowed down her steps, wondering if she should go back home or perhaps to the studio. If she were to stop at the warehouse, she should have brought Tama's canned food with her. Probably home, then. But she didn't know what she would do if Eiji was still there.

"Fumi-nee!"

Hearing Eiji's familiar voice, Fumi looked up and saw him running toward her.

"Do you always storm out like that?" he asked.

She stared at him, eyes wide.

He stopped in front of her, trying to catch his breath. "What's that in the plastic bag?"

"Milk pudding," she said, looking elsewhere. She didn't want him to realize how surprised she was. "I bought two. You can have one."

He laughed. "I can't believe this is the first thing you're saying to me after what happened."

"Me neither," she said, smiling. "I should've chased you out."

"Yes, you should've." He paused. "What made you change your mind?"

She looked into his eyes, seeking an answer but finding none. What she did find was a tiny scar on the bridge of his nose she hadn't noticed before. How had Eiji gotten that? Had he fallen down? There was so much about him she didn't know.

A gust of wind blew, sending dry leaves onto the ground. In a park not far from where they stood, children were shouting, but their words jumbled together, and she couldn't catch what they were saying. A car passed by, a gleaming black Honda sedan.

"Miss, can you throw the ball back?" a kid with a baseball glove shouted from the edge of the park.

The ball had landed on the pavement right in front of Eiji. She waited for him to pick it up, but he just stood there. Puzzled, she reached for the ball and gave it her best throw back to the field. It went farther than she had expected.

"Not bad, Fumi-nee," Eiji said.

"You would've done better," she said. "I've never been good at sports."

"Maybe." He paused for a few seconds before he said, "But the kid asked you, not me." Eiji smiled. "Let's go home."

She furrowed her brow. "Why the rush? The weather's so nice."

He leaned forward. "You do know that you're wearing house slippers, don't you?"

Fumi looked down at her feet. She turned red. In her moment of fury and embarrassment, she'd left the house without putting on a proper pair of shoes.

"I'm surprised no one has called the police yet," Eiji said, suppressing a laugh. "Are you always this disoriented, Fumi-nee?"

"Stop that," she said, glaring. She tried to laugh it off, but all that came out was a pathetic snicker. Was it Ryu's absence that was messing her up like this?

"How old are you?" Fumi asked Eiji.

"Twenty-one."

"Ah, the same age as my brother," she said, walking in the direction of her apartment.

"Still no news from him?"

She shook her head and kicked at the gravel in front of her.

"It doesn't matter," Eiji said. "I'm sure your brother is fine wherever he is."

"I know," she mumbled and turned to him. "He needs to meet someone new. Did you know that new love is the best cure for a broken heart?"

He was quiet for a moment before responding. "Is that so?"

"Uh-huh." For a second, Fumi thought Eiji had sounded a little odd, but maybe that was just her imagination. Trying to liven up the mood, she asked, "Have you ever been to Yokohama? Let's go there one of these weekends. A change of scenery is always refreshing."

"Why Yokohama?"

"It's not too far. We can drive there. And I have a license, so we could rent a car for a day trip."

"That sounds nice, but I prefer to stay at home."

"Don't you get bored?"

He laughed, but it was obvious he was forcing it. They turned onto an alleyway. Three boys smoking in their high school uniforms took up the entire span of the pathway. All of them sported flashy hairdos and untucked shirts.

Fumi wanted to change direction to avoid trouble, but she was too late. The boys were already watching them closely. She tried to avoid eye contact and walk normally. But as she passed by, one of them whistled at her.

"Doing some shopping, miss?"

Fumi continued to walk.

"Hey, it's rude to ignore people," one of them chipped in. "You're pretty. How about we accompany you?"

"Stop it. I'm with my boyfriend," Fumi said, maintaining her usual calmness.

"Where's your boyfriend? I don't see him anywhere."

Fumi turned to Eiji, but to her surprise, he had shoved his hands into his pockets and walked away. She swore silently and gritted her teeth. The three delinquents looked in his direction with puzzled expressions. One of them laughed and grabbed Fumi's hand.

"Let go of me," she hissed. One against three. Fumi felt she had no chance, but she wasn't going to let them have their way.

"Be gentle, you're scaring her," one of the boys said in a mocking tone. "Hey, miss, what's that in the plastic bag?"

Pulling her hand back, Fumi used all her strength to slam the plastic bag at the boy nearest to her. She hit him square in the face, and he groaned in pain. Fumi used the opportunity to get past him. She ran without stopping. Loud curses and footsteps followed. Where was Eiji? Why had he abandoned her?

Seeing a park, she ran into it without much thought. There must be a policeman patrolling the area. Or maybe not. Why was it always so quiet whenever someone needed help? And whenever they wanted to be left alone, there was a crowd.

Fumi saw a public bathroom and entered the handicapped stall. Locking the door, she breathed heavily. Her pursuers' footsteps got closer. Why were these young men so persistent?

"Where'd she go?" one of them shouted.

"Should be inside one of the stalls," the other one said. "Why don't you go in and check?"

"What if someone else is inside?"

"It would just be a woman. What are you so scared of?"

Fumi heard a grunt, then the sound of door opening and closing, one after another. She crouched down in the corner, trying to make herself as small as possible.

"There's no one here."

"Don't tell me she's hiding in the men's room."

"Why don't you check?"

"We shouldn't go there. This is Higashi High's turf. They smoke joints in this park."

"Did anyone actually see her go into the bathroom?"

A brief silence ensued.

"Let's give it up."

"But she wrecked my face!"

"Your face was wrecked before she hit you."

There was laughter, followed by more curses and fading footsteps. Fumi breathed a sigh of relief, but she didn't dare to go outside yet. They could still be in the park.

But why had Eiji run off? Had he been scared of those kids? Or was it because he thought so little of her? And those kids had been too much, treating Eiji like he was invisible.

And then Fumi realized something she should have noticed much, much earlier.

Why hadn't she thought of it? Those children in the field, they hadn't seen him either, had they? Otherwise they would've asked him to throw the ball, not her. And of course, Eiji had a reason he couldn't go to Yokohama with her, couldn't find a job, never ate, and insisted on hanging around in the house. All the pieces clicked into place.

Closing her eyes, Fumi thought of someone she had tried so hard to forget.

Ruri.

2 2

Images
of
Fans
and
Flowers

Ruri had been in the backyard when Fumio had come to do his usual sweeping duty. The sky was dull, as if it was going to rain soon. It was a cold, gray morning. Yet Ruri was still lightly dressed in a floral one-piece and her usual pair of worn-out shoes.

"Good morning," she greeted him. "You're late."

"I couldn't sleep," he said.

"Something bothering you?"

Fumio shook his head. He couldn't tell Ruri. He didn't want her to know what awaited him once school started. He was afraid her opinion of him would change. "Everything is fine. I'm just nervous about going back to school."

"Ah, that's right, the new semester is starting. Are you going to forget me once you see your school friends?"

"Of course not." It wasn't a lie, since he had none.

She offered her pinky finger. "Promise?"

Fumio nodded and was about to link his pinky with Ruri's when he heard his mother's voice.

"Fumio, where are you?" she called.

"Out back!" Fumio shouted and turned to Ruri. "Wait here."

Putting down the broom, he ran inside. His mother was walking toward him, a gift box in her hands.

"How many times have I told you to walk slowly and quietly in the hallway?" she said, frowning. "This is a shrine. You're disturbing the visitors."

"There are no visitors this early in the morning," he protested.

She glared at him. "As the son of the priest, you need to behave well all the time. One day, you'll inherit this shrine from your father."

Fumio rubbed the nape of his neck.

If his mother noticed his reluctance, she pretended not to. "Come here. Your father bought you some sweets from Fujiwara yesterday."

"Really?" Fumio took a closer look at the gift box. Decorated with Japanese paper, it bore images of fans and flowers. His eyes widened. "This is for me?"

His mother nodded. Fumio took the box from her, but when he opened it, only a quarter of the sweets were left. He sighed in disappointment.

"Don't be greedy," his mother said. "We have to share with everyone else here."

"I know. I'll share it with my friend too."

Her eyebrows rose. "Which friend is this?"

Fumio hadn't told anyone about Ruri, but he was finally ready to tell his mother. "She's a girl who comes to the backyard to play with me every day. She lives nearby."

"How nice! Is she a friend from school?"

The mention of school triggered nausea. "Ruri doesn't go to school."

"How strange," his mother said. "Why don't you introduce her to me?"

Her face beamed as she said it. Fumio's mother was clearly happy her son had made a friend. Although Fumio tried his best to hide the rooftop bullying, his mother probably knew something was wrong. After all, he had asked to skip school several times without explanation.

To be honest, Fumio was relieved too, to have someone to call a friend. He finally felt like he was normal. He could make friends just like everyone else. It took him longer, but that was all.

Fumio led his mother to the backyard and waved to Ruri. "Look, she's over there."

"Where?" Fumio's mother narrowed her eyes. "I don't see her."

"There, near the bushes." Fumio pointed. "Hey, Ruri!" he called. "My mother brought us some sweets."

Ruri turned to them. Her eyes widened and she froze.

"What's wrong, Ruri?"

Fumio walked over to her, but she edged away. He frowned. Why was she avoiding him? Before he could ask, she turned and ran into the bushes.

"Ruri," Fumio shouted. "It's all right. She's my mother!"

He wanted to run after her, but his mother caught his arm. Her face was pale.

"Fumio, we need to talk," she said.

THAT NIGHT, FUMIO YANAGI learned about the curse that ran through his blood. It was probably the hardest moment of his life. It wasn't so much about his unwanted ability as the fact that the only friend he'd ever had wasn't real.

Ruri probably knew what was happening too, because the next day, she was back to standing in the bushes, staring at him without saying anything. Fumio continued to clean the shrine grounds as usual, as his father had advised.

"Nothing should change," he had said. "Do everything like you normally do."

But it was far from normal. The silence was intimidating. Fumio's steps were heavy. He skipped mopping and went inside the shrine, only coming out when it was time for him to do his afternoon sweeping.

Ruri wasn't looking at the sky anymore. Her head hung down. Her lips were shut. The glow Fumio had always seen in her was gone, replaced by a white and ghastly paleness. She had the color of death running in her veins.

A FEW DAYS BEFORE the new semester started, Fumio saw Ruri crying.

"Why are you ignoring me?" she said. "Aren't we friends?"

Fumio's throat went dry. It was hard to breathe. Against his father's advice, he told her, "We can't be friends, because you're not real."

Ruri gritted her teeth and glared at Fumio before running away.

Fumio continued to sweep. When he was done, he returned to his room. He didn't want any dinner, but he couldn't sleep, either.

"Don't worry, they can't hurt you," his father had said. "They can't even touch you."

Fumio had no idea why he was crying. Ruri wasn't a real person, anyway. She was a wandering spirit who had found her way to the shrine. No one was able to see her except Fumio. He'd trusted that she was a friend and gotten hurt.

But now that he knew, he just had to accept that she wasn't part of the living world, and then, the pain would disappear, wouldn't it? For better or worse, Ruri stopped showing up. Fumio's father thought she had probably been reincarnated.

"It happens to everyone eventually, but it's usually faster for children," he explained after one of his meditation trainings. "Most of the time, they have fewer sins to atone for and less to tie them to this world than adults."

Fumio was silent, his eyes fixed on the altar. A pair of huge lanterns gave the tatami room a warm, golden glow. The smell of incense lingered in the air. It was already noon, but in that darkened room, the time wasn't immediately clear.

"A lot of the spirits believe staying in places of worship will help them reincarnate faster," his father continued, "but we can't be sure. Still, it's worth trying if you have nothing to lose."

"Do you think that was the reason Ruri came here?" Fumio asked eventually.

"Possibly," his father said. "I doubt she died in the vicinity of this shrine. Otherwise we would've heard about it."

Fumio's throat felt dry. "How do you think she died?"

"There are a lot of possibilities. You said she was young, so most likely illness. She spoke to you about not needing to go to school, didn't she? There are also other possibilities, like traffic accidents. As a general rule, if they don't tell us on their own, we don't ask. It's best not to know too much or get involved. They live in a different world than we do."

Nodding, Fumio thought of the days he and Ruri would talk in the back courtyard of the shrine. She could have told him the truth on any of those occasions. There were so many opportunities, but she'd chosen to hide it.

"Fumio?"

He raised his head and saw his father's creased brow.

"Are you all right, son?"

Fumio nodded again.

"I need to explain what's been happening."

He kept his head hung low.

"This ability has been passed down through our family for generations to the firstborn men, along with the responsibility of serving in this shrine. It was first bestowed upon our ancestor as a gift for his devotion and self-sacrifice."

Fumio's father proceeded to tell him a tale from centuries ago, when there had been a plague in the region that had wiped out more than half of the residents. Those left alive were wallowing in sorrow and regret, and restless souls roamed the area, plaguing its population with negative energy. The head priest was deeply saddened and sealed himself inside the shrine, praying and fasting for days. On the hundredth night, the gods gave him the ability to communicate with the dead so he could help them cross over to the other side.

"Normally, the ability manifests when we become adults. I didn't know this would happen to you so early." Fumio's father took a deep sigh. "If I had, I would've talked to you about it. I thought I had plenty of time, so I haven't yet taught you the history of this shrine or our family. I'm sorry this has caused you pain."

"I'm fine," Fumio insisted. "Like you said, she's not a real person. How can something that doesn't exist hurt me?"

After that day, they never spoke of Ruri again.

Fumio's parents solidified their preparations to make him successor to the shrine. The early manifestation of his ability only confirmed to them that he was the most suitable candidate.

"You need to learn the proper way to use this gift," his father told him. "In the past, there have been cases in which the selected ones have neglected to follow the rules of the spirit world and been driven to insanity as a result."

"Uh-huh."

"No one can know about your ability. Not even Ryu. This is a secret that we, the priests of this shrine, guard closely and share only with our successors and life partners."

Fumio spent his nights and weekends meditating, saying prayers, and reading scriptures. Even though these things made him feel increasingly empty, he did as he was told. He didn't want to worry his parents.

As for what was happening at school, one day Fumio finally decided he'd had enough. The group of girls called him up to the rooftop yet again. But when they started beating him, he stood tall and grabbed one of their wooden sticks.

Fumi could still remember their frantic shrieks. The girls had dropped their weapons and run, but Fumio came after them, swinging the stick wildly. Their high-pitched screams pierced his ears as they scampered in different directions. He chased the skinny girl who led the pack. She tripped and fell as her friends escaped. He pinned her to the ground with the stick. For the first time, she looked at him with fear in her eyes. The expression of disgust he was so used to seeing was gone.

Standing over her, Fumio swung the stick high, ready to strike. All the anger and rage that had been building within him for the past few months was packed into his swing.

And then he stopped.

Hands over her face, the girl was shaking and in tears.

Fumio threw the stick away and said in a stern voice he'd never known he had, "Don't you *ever* mess with me again."

And with that, he left her alone on the rooftop.

For the first time in weeks, he felt free. The invisible burden that had weighed him down was gone. He raised his head. The sun's rays filtered through the cloud. The sky had never looked so beautiful.

When Fumio entered the classroom the next morning, everyone

averted their eyes. The atmosphere around him had changed. He could feel it as he walked to his seat. His desk wasn't flipped over, nor was his chair. No one had scribbled anything on either, and his books were also untouched. Overnight, he had gone from the bullied to the delinquent.

In the end, Fumio Yanagi still didn't have any friends, but no one ever picked on him again. And to him, that was enough.

23

Isn't It Sad to Force Yourself to Laugh

Fumi found Eiji lying on the sofa. He didn't greet her when she entered the apartment. She took her house slippers off. Both were dirty, and one had a tear now. Pulling up a chair next to Eiji, Fumi sat with her arms crossed and waited for his explanation. She didn't want to be the first to talk.

"I suppose you're angry," Eiji said. "Will it make you feel better if I apologize, or will it just make things worse?"

"What do you think?" she asked rhetorically. "Anyway, what else could you have done? It's not like you could've stepped in and beaten up those boys."

He smirked. "You've got a pretty low opinion of me, Fumi-nee."

"It's not that."

"What is it, then?"

"Are you sure you want me to tell you?"

He nodded. "Come on, entertain me."

Taking a deep breath, she looked into his eyes. "You're dead, Eiji."

His expression shifted just slightly—barely visible enough for her to catch, but it was there.

"You're already dead," Fumi repeated. "That's why you avoid going outside. Because no one can see you but me."

Eiji averted his eyes, then started to laugh. "You really should consider that career as an investigator, Fumi-nee."

She sighed. "Is this really the time to be laughing?"

"What do you want me to do? Should I cry instead?"

Fumi shook her head. "Isn't it sad to force yourself to laugh when you're feeling down?"

He stopped and glared at her. "Don't pretend that you understand."

"I never said I did."

Looking away, Eiji shoved his hands into his pockets. "I also have a theory about you, Fumi-nee."

She pressed her lips together and frowned.

"The reason you haven't gone through with the gender reassignment procedure is because of your brother."

Fumi felt a sting. "Who told you that?"

"No one," he said. "I figured it out myself. You're the first son of a priest, aren't you?"

"How did you know?"

"I saw your family photograph earlier when it slipped out of the album. You know, the one in front of the shrine." He licked his lips. "That boy was you, right?"

Fumi placed her hand on her neck. "I thought you missed it."

"I've figured out a lot more than that," he said. "I think I know why you can see me."

She clicked her tongue. "So now you're the one playing detective."

"I reckoned there was something in your lineage that caused you to see spirits. Or rather, your male lineage. You're worried that the procedure will eliminate that ability, and it will be passed to—"

Fumi stood and raised her voice. "Stop calling the curse an ability."

"I—" Eiji mumbled.

"Just because you've got an explanation for what's happening, doesn't mean you actually understand," she said. "You have no idea what I've been through. I saw spirits appear and disappear, roaming among the living. A few of them don't even know they're dead. Other times, they'll take the form of someone else to trick me. Wandering spirits like you are everywhere, and I'm the only one who sees them." Fumi's vision blurred with tears. "I'm cursed, but I've gotten good at pretending that I'm just a normal person. Even my brother doesn't know."

Eiji stepped forward and tried to hug Fumi, but his arms passed through her body. He stared in shock.

"I'm sorry," he said. "I never meant to hurt you."

Fumi started to sob.

"I'm sorry," Eiji whispered. "I'm so sorry."

His gentleness only broke her. She sank to the floor, weeping, as Eiji sat helplessly next to her.

Fumi lost track of how long she cried, but she remembered crawling into bed. Eiji followed her and sat at the edge, and she fell asleep right away. When she woke up the next day, he was asleep on the floor below her. She stared at the scar on the bridge of his nose until he opened his eyes.

"Good morning, pretty girl," Eiji said. "Have you been watching me sleep for a while?"

"Aren't you full of yourself." She turned away from him, feeling embarrassed about last night's burst of emotions. "Can we forget everything that happened yesterday?"

"Of course, but I have a favor to ask in exchange."

She looked at him. "What do you want now?"

He grinned. "Let me stay here another few months."

"Don't you have some other place to loiter?"

"It's fun being here with you, Fumi-nee. I really like you."

His words moved her, but she reminded herself they lived in two different worlds, which had just happened to collide during this brief period.

"It's up to you, Eiji," Fumi said. "You can't stay here forever, anyway."

He furrowed his brow. "What do you mean?"

She rubbed her neck. "After you've made peace with your past, you'll be reincarnated."

"What?"

"You'll be reborn. You didn't think you'd remain a wandering soul forever, did you? If that were the case, the world would be overcrowded with lost spirits."

He paused. "Makes sense. How much longer do I have?"

"I have no idea. I don't know how you died or why you're still here. Or what might have happened in your previous life."

"I committed suicide," he answered right away. "After I killed someone."

Fumi stared at him. She couldn't tell whether he was making it up, but who joked about such things? Yet coming from Eiji, it was hard to believe. He seemed so easygoing and cheerful. What kind of reasons could he possibly have had for making such choices?

"You can go to places of worship, like shrines and temples, to speed up the cleansing process," she continued. "I've heard it's because of their positive energy. I'm not entirely sure it's true, but it's worth trying."

Eiji didn't respond.

"Why so quiet?" Fumi asked. "Do you have more questions?"

He turned to her with downcast eyes. "Aren't you afraid of me?"

"Why would I be?" she said. "You're dead. You can't physically harm me. And if I decided to stop acknowledging you, unless you found someone else who could see you, you would basically cease to exist." As soon as the words came out, Fumi regretted them, but she couldn't take them back.

Eiji glanced sideways. "You must think I'm a terrible person for killing someone. Have you ever wished for anyone to die, Fumi-nee? Just . . . felt that the world would be better off without that person?"

Fumi recalled the girl who had bullied her in high school. Had she ever hoped the girl would just disappear? Yes, all the time, but actually wiping out her existence had never crossed her mind.

"Why did you kill this person?" Fumi finally asked.

Eiji didn't answer at once. Eventually, he mumbled, "I thought I knew, but recently, I'm not so sure anymore."

"No matter what, everyone has someone who will miss them," she said, "a child or sibling or parent or lover or friend. I'm sure someone misses you right now."

He nodded slowly. "Are you trying to make me feel guilty?"

Fumi forced a smile. "Trust me, it's a good thing to know you still have feelings."

"When you put it that way . . ." Eiji sat at the edge on the bed. "Fumi-nee, why are you so against having your brother inherit your ability? I'm sure he'll manage, just like you and your father."

"I told you, it's a curse," she said. "Not an ability."

"Fine." He shrugged. "Whatever you prefer."

"About my brother." Fumi paused to pick her words carefully. "He seems mature, but I worry about him a lot. He always puts up a strong front. When our parents died and we were sent to the orphanage, he never shed a single tear. He's the type who keeps everything to himself."

Eiji leaned in toward Fumi. "Aren't you the same?"

She ignored him. "Ryu shouldn't inherit this curse, especially after Miwako's death."

"Who's Miwako?"

"The girl my brother loved," she said. "Even now, he's still in love with her. He certainly won't admit it, but everyone we know sees it."

"Do you think a wandering soul might take Miwako's appearance to manipulate him?"

"It may even be simpler than that," she lamented. "I suspect the girl is still roaming somewhere in this world. I haven't seen her, but I doubt she's left yet."

He pressed his lips. "What makes you so sure?"

"Well, like you, Miwako committed suicide. Cutting a life short, even your own, is essentially murder. Coming to terms with whatever led you to it isn't easy."

A silence descended upon them.

Eiji cleared his throat. "How did she die?"

"She hanged herself," Fumi said. "What about you?"

"Motorcycle crash. Just your standard traffic accident."

"It's not an accident if you crashed it on purpose."

"I know that," he said. "Of course I know."

FUMI STARED AT THE calendar on the wall. It had been two months since Ryu had left Tokyo. If he were to turn up right now, would he notice that his sister was harboring a wandering spirit? Fumi sighed. Even though she missed her brother, she was glad he wasn't around for Eiji's visit.

"Are you done vacuuming yet, Fumi-nee?" Eiji asked. "You've been working on the same spot for quite a long time."

Fumi turned off the vacuum cleaner. "Stop complaining. You're distracting me."

"You really love housework, don't you? You would make a great wife."

"You never learn, do you? Empty flattery gets you nowhere."

"Hey, these are sincere compliments." Eiji laughed and curled up on the sofa. "By the way, a girl came by and delivered a bag of mail this morning."

"A girl?"

He nodded. "Short hair with freckles. She came when you were in the studio. She left the bag next to the front door, which I didn't think was very safe. Anyone could just take it. Didn't you see it when you got back?"

Fumi went out to retrieve the bag and brought it to her room.

Even though she and Ryu had left the orphanage years ago, from time to time, mail would arrive for them there. Once in a while, a staff member from the orphanage would drop it off in bulk at their apartment.

Fumi opened the bag and went through the mail. Most were advertisements. A company selling plastic containers, a charity soliciting donations, a religious sect offering a way to find peace and happiness. There were a few letters for Ryu, too, but none seemed urgent.

Among the letters, Fumi recognized a logo. It was from her alma mater. She tore open the envelope. Inside was an invitation to her high school reunion. She gripped the letter tighter.

Could she bear to face those six girls again? What would she say if she saw them?

Fumi put the invitation down. It would probably be wise not to go. No point in reopening old wounds. What was in the past should remain in the past, even if she had never really made peace with it. But all these years, she had never learned the reason she was bullied, and at times, the question continued to nag at her.

She sat at her dressing table and found herself rubbing her neck again. The woman in the mirror stared at Fumi as if challenging her.

You're now a different person. Don't be afraid. Seek the answer you've been looking for.

Fumi stood, still looking right at her reflection. "You're right. I must go to the party."

24

Even
If
I
Wanted
To

The reunion was at a typical three-star business hotel, the kind of establishment with reasonably priced rooms and basic amenities. Classy and adequate, but not fancy enough to impress a date.

Fumi's crystal-studded heels clanked against the glazed tile. The marble was polished to a sparkle, and the air-conditioning was blasting. She adjusted her shimmering silk shawl to cover her bare shoulders.

"Good evening." A hotel employee in a sleek dark suit greeted her. "Are you here for the reunion?"

"Yes." She flashed her invitation.

He stretched out his hand. "Please go straight and take your first left onto the corridor. The party is in the main banquet hall."

Fumi thanked him and followed his directions. It wasn't hard to locate the massive hall. A huge framed poster announcing the reunion was perched on a wooden easel, and a short queue had formed at the reception table. Fumi joined in and waited for her turn.

Because of her heels, she towered above everyone. She had purposefully overdressed for the occasion. Most of the other guests had turned up in officewear, probably coming straight from work since it was a Friday night, while she stood tall in an elegant, stylish pearly white evening dress.

"Excuse me," the girl waiting next to Fumi greeted her. "You look so familiar. Are you an actress?"

Fumi shook her head. "You must be mistaking me for someone else."

The girl turned red. "Oh, I'm sorry."

Then it was Fumi's turn to sign the attendance book. She signed her name next to "Fumio Yanagi," while discreetly glancing at the young man manning the registration counter. He wasn't paying attention, so he didn't notice Fumi was signing in on the men's registry instead of the women's.

Stepping into the hall, Fumi was greeted by large pillars and sparkling crystal chandeliers. Waitresses in black vests and satin bowties made their rounds with fizzing champagne flutes and glasses of wine on trays. Fumi reached for a glass of champagne and strolled around the hall. She tried to spot a familiar face, but she didn't recognize anyone.

Well, twelve years had passed. Everyone had changed. She certainly had.

But those girls, especially the one who had started it all—there was no way Fumi wouldn't recognize her. But what if they hadn't come? It was possible. As much as she didn't want to admit it, Fumi had dressed up for them. If they weren't here, then all her efforts were for naught.

Fumi wondered why she had bothered to doll herself up so much for her adolescent enemies. She smiled wistfully, disappointed in herself. And then she saw her. The person she had been looking for, the one who had made her dread school every day, who tormented her for no apparent reason and made her the school's trash.

Looking at this woman now, no one would suspect she had

once committed such atrocious bullying. She looked harmless, not unlike any other housewife in her neighborhood. On the short side and slightly plump, the woman wore a long, flowy beige dress with gold flower embroidery and a white fur shawl. Judging from her non-businesslike attire, she wasn't a working woman. Fumi remembered rumors that the girl was from a well-to-do family, so she had probably married money. Her soft brown leather handbag—designer, of course—seemed to corroborate that, but the expensive accessory did nothing to change the fact that she was unremarkable looking.

Fumi waited for the crowd around her to disperse before inching closer. Their eyes met, and the woman smiled. Her unguarded expression made Fumi furious. Tightening her grip on the champagne flute, she considered throwing it into the woman's face. She almost wished she'd asked for red wine instead.

Before she could reach the woman, an arm circled her waist.

"Fumio, it's been a while."

She turned around to see a man in a gray suit. His face was angular, and he had prominent dark bags under his eyes. He gave Fumi a grin that made her uncomfortable. It took her a while to recognize him as her high school classmate. He was actually a year older, but he had been held back into her year, and he had also been Fumio's first boyfriend.

He used to take Fumio to his house when his family wasn't around. He'd ask Fumio to put on women's clothes before they had sex. Fumio never asked whose garments they were.

"It's really you, isn't it?" he said, his breath reeking of alcohol. "You're so beautiful, I almost didn't recognize you."

"Quit it." She moved away from him. "Also, my name is Fumi."

"Ah, cute name. It does suit you better. If I'd known you were going to be this gorgeous, I would've held on to you back then."

"You cheated on me, remember?"

He laughed as if what she'd said was funny. "What about now? Shall we give it another try?"

She glared at him, but instead of moving away, he came closer.

Even back then, Fumi had known going out with him was a bad idea. But she was always alone, and she had been so thrilled at the prospect of having someone special to spend time with.

"I heard you're working at a bar now," he said. "Can I come visit?"

Well, news traveled fast. Calming herself, she leaned to him and whispered, "Of course you can. But as a former acquaintance, I have to warn you, it's expensive. Are you sure you're ready to spend that kind of money?"

He snickered, but finally walked away. She sighed in relief. That guy had always been too aggressive, and she'd actually been glad he'd dumped her for a freshman.

Fumi turned to her original target. The woman was now heading toward her.

"By any chance, are you Yanagi?" she asked in a small voice.

Fumi flashed her sweetest smile. "Yes, I am."

The woman's face went pale. "Do you . . . remember me?"

"Of course. Even if I wanted to, I couldn't forget." Fumi hadn't been aiming for sarcasm, but her voice came out sharp and full of hatred.

"I . . ." The woman fumbled and looked down.

Not wanting to back down, Fumi leaned forward. "Yes?"

Before she realized what was happening, the woman lowered her head to Fumi. "I know it's too late, and this probably won't be any consolation to you, but I've always wanted to apologize." Her voice cracked. "I'm so, so sorry for what I did. I deeply regret it."

Fumi was taken aback, but she forced herself to maintain

composure. She rested her hand on her neck. "Stop that," she whispered. "Everyone is staring at us."

The woman continued to bow. "I'm so sorry, Yanagi. I've never forgotten what I did. I was so horrible to you. I know my apologies aren't enough, but I don't know what else to do."

Initially, Fumi had wanted to shame her. But seeing the woman's remorse, she wasn't sure what to say or do. She had only been ready for a fight.

"I'm so sorry. Will you forgive me, Yanagi?"

Crossing her arms, Fumi took a deep breath. "Look up and face me, will you?"

The woman did so.

"I always wondered, why me? You could've chosen anyone. Did I do something to offend you? I tried to recall a single interaction between us before what happened, but I couldn't think of one."

The woman's face turned red. "It had nothing to do with you."

Fumi frowned. "What do you mean?"

"Back then, I liked a boy," she said, slightly stuttering. "He turned me down, calling me skinny and ugly, and saying even a boy like Yanagi was much prettier than me."

She gasped. "What?"

"I know. It was unreasonable of me. I shouldn't have taken it out on you, but I was hurt."

"That was the reason?" Fumi couldn't believe her ears. "What about the other girls?"

The woman shook her head. "They didn't know anything. I only told them you got on my nerves, so they followed my lead."

Fumi clenched her fists.

"I'm so sorry, Yanagi. We were young. We didn't know better. Each of us kept trying to outdo the others, and in the process, we went overboard."

Went overboard? It had been so much more than that. They had made Fumi's life a living hell. They had made her fear school. And above all, they had made her hate herself, all because of a single thoughtless remark from a boy. Fumi shuddered, finding it hard to grasp that months of bullying had stemmed from something so petty.

Fumi ran her manicured fingers through her long, permed hair. "I hope you're not expecting me to say that everything is okay, that we're all friends now."

The woman froze. Her face was pale. Fumi turned and walked away. She didn't want to stay there another second. She felt sick.

Don't you cry, she told herself as she climbed into a taxi in front of the hotel. *Don't cry because of her. She isn't worth your tears.*

EIJI LAY IN HIS usual spot on the sofa. He stood up and greeted Fumi with a warm smile.

"You're home early," he said.

She took her high heels off. The straps had dug into her skin, leaving raw red lines. "I wasn't feeling well, so I left early."

He furrowed his brow. "Are you okay?"

"I'm fine," she said. "I want to be left alone for a while."

Once she was inside her room, Fumi dropped her handbag on the floor and threw herself on the bed. Staring at the ceiling, she replayed what the woman had said. *It had nothing to do with you. A boy turned me down and said I was skinny and ugly, that even a boy like Yanagi looked much prettier than me.*

Had that really been the only reason for her suffering?

Flashes of that day flew into her mind. Fumi could still recall every detail of the first time that girl had come to Fumio's seat during recess, her five friends tailing behind her. She banged on his desk.

"Fumio Yanagi?" she asked, louder than necessary.

"Yes," he answered timidly.

"Follow us."

Fumio was scared, but he tried not to show it. "What did I—"

He felt a hard slap on his left cheek and fell off his chair. There were audible gasps. All of his classmates stared at him lying on the floor.

"Do you have any more questions?" the girl asked.

Still shocked, Fumio didn't react.

Another girl kicked him in the stomach. "Answer when you're asked."

"No." He shook his head. "No, no."

The first girl clicked her tongue and walked out.

"Come with us while we're still being nice," one of the girls said. "Unless you want us to beat you up in front of everyone."

The group walked out and Fumio Yanagi followed, his classmates whispering all the while. Even with his head hung low, he could feel their looks of pity. On the way to the rooftop, Fumio knew the girls were going to beat him up. But he didn't know they were going to do it over and over until he broke.

Clenching her teeth, Fumi struggled to suppress her tears. She still couldn't believe it, that all that suffering had been for one stupid offhand remark. Fumio had probably never even spoken to that boy. But because of those words, she was a different person.

Fumi took a deep breath. She had promised herself never to show weakness.

But it had been Fumio's fault too. If he had stood up to the girls earlier or told his teacher or his parents, the bullying might not have lasted so long.

"Fumi-nee, are you all right?" Eiji asked from the other side of the door.

"I'm fine," she said. "Leave me alone."

There was a brief silence. "How can you say you're fine when you're crying?"

Fumi realized her face was wet. Wiping away her tears, she hoped she had used waterproof mascara. "Go away, Eiji."

"What if I don't?"

She kept quiet, noticing for the first time that the white pendant lampshade on the ceiling had gone yellow.

"Please let me in," Eiji said.

"Why do you need me to open the door?" Fumi asked. "You can just pass through it, can't you?"

There was a pause. "Just because I can, doesn't mean I should."

Standing up, Fumi checked her reflection in the mirror over her dressing table. Her hair was a mess and her eyes were bloodshot, but her makeup was somehow intact. She reached for the doorknob and thought about what Eiji had just said.

Just because I can, doesn't mean I should. Fumi had been the victim back then, and she knew she wasn't supposed to blame herself, but she did. Every single day. She had suffered enough.

"Fumi-nee?"

She opened the door. "I'm fine."

"Is that so?" Eiji looked at her with concern. "You don't look fine."

"That's none of your business."

He gave a chuckle.

"I don't know why you're such a busybody." Fumi crossed her arms. "No matter how nice you are, you still have to leave when my brother returns. You know that, right?"

He gave her a reassuring smile. "Yes, I know."

Fumi raised an eyebrow at Eiji, who had agreed far too readily.

"I don't want to be here when your brother comes back," he continued. "You don't need to worry."

She grew suspicious. "Do you happen to know Ryu?"

"Ah, I wonder if I did." He spaced out for a moment before returning his gaze to her. "Do you want to tell me what happened?"

She shook her head. "Not really."

"Then why did you let me in?"

"You asked me to open the door, didn't you?"

Eiji broke into a smile. "Fumi-nee, you're not the type of woman to do something because someone asks."

She smiled too, and soon she was laughing. It infected them both, even though there was nothing particularly funny about what he'd said. Fumi laughed until her stomach hurt. She laughed and laughed until she got sick of it. Then, sitting down on the bed, she curled up and sobbed.

Eiji waited for her to calm down. When she finally did, he asked, "How do you feel?"

"Much better," she said, wiping her eyes. "Thanks for being here with me."

"This is one of the few things I can do for you before my time runs out."

She nodded and raised her face to look at him. "You know, I've been wondering, why did you choose to stay here? I'm not the most hospitable person in the world."

"At least you're aware of it." Eiji flashed a dimpled smile. "I don't have much of a choice, do I? You're the only person who can see me."

"There should be others. You might find them if you wandered around more, but it's not so simple. It's not like you can tell at a glance whether a person can see spirits. And anyone like me would probably ignore you once they figured it out. It's easier that way. Wandering spirits often attempt to get the living to assist them, but we're not supposed to interact. We belong in different planes of existence."

"Then why are you talking to me?"

Fumi rubbed her neck. "I'm not sure. But I figure there must be a good reason you showed up at the studio. You must have some regret that ties you to this world, and maybe whatever holding you back is related to me or Kenji."

"You're playing detective again, Fumi-nee."

She ignored him and continued. "We can probably rule out Kenji, since you don't even know what he looks like. So the one you're looking for must be me." Fumi paused. "Or my brother."

Eiji averted his eyes.

"It's my brother, isn't it? How do you know Ryu?"

"What is this, an interrogation?"

Fumi closed her eyes, recalling the first time she had met Eiji in the studio. He was alone, armed only with a giant rucksack, crouching down near Tama as the cat circled him. Wait, how could she have missed it? Tama had never been good with strangers. The only people she'd ever gotten along with were Fumi, Ryu, and Miwako. But Miwako was dead.

No, that couldn't be it. There had to be another explanation.

Yet the more Fumi thought about it, the more she understood it was the most likely answer. Clearing her throat, she turned to Eiji.

"So, who are you pretending to be right now, Miwako Sumida?"

Crush . . .
Or
the
Taste
of
It

Eiji smiled, albeit insincerely. "What do you mean, Fumi-nee?"

"Stop it," Fumi said. "You're Miwako, aren't you? I have no idea why you've chosen to take on somebody else's appearance."

"It's over, isn't it?" Eiji looked down. Slowly, his features seemed to melt away, and the contours of his body changed. When he finally lifted his head, it was Miwako who was staring at Fumi. "I should've told you the truth from the beginning."

Fumi sighed. "But really, whose appearance was that?"

"My older brother," she said. "I was thinking about him when I heard you calling for Tama."

"He doesn't look like you."

"We weren't blood-related. My mother remarried when I was in high school. He's my stepbrother."

"I see," Fumi said. "Was Eiji his real name?"

"Yes. Eiji Sumida."

"And he died in a motorcycle accident?"

Miwako's expression darkened. "It's not an accident if it's on purpose."

"Your stepbrother committed suicide?"

"Yes."

"What drove him to do that?" Fumi asked.

Miwako didn't respond.

"What happened, Miwako?"

She remained quiet.

"At least tell me why you're here. Why did you pretend to be someone else to get close to me?"

"I don't know," she whispered. "I was confused."

"Why don't you tell me everything? You know I'd never judge you."

Miwako shook her head. "I know, but . . ."

Fumi sighed and wrapped her arms around Miwako's shoulders, forgetting she couldn't touch her. Her arms simply passed through the girl. Why had she done that? How stupid. Looking at Miwako, Fumi knew something bad had happened to her—enough to drive her to end her life.

She wondered where Ryu was, and what he would tell her to do.

Miwako lowered her head and started shaking. She didn't make a sound, but Fumi could tell she was crying. Those tears were the kind that tore you apart. Fumi took a deep breath. Her chest ached. She could feel sadness bubbling deep inside her, filling her whole body, threatening to spill out. For the first time, she glimpsed what was beneath Miwako's hardened façade. Beyond her stubbornness and seemingly nonchalant attitude, the girl was hiding a terrible secret, not unlike herself. Fumi suffered in silence, and that silence did her no good. It hadn't done Miwako any good either.

"I was bullied in high school," Fumi eventually said.

Miwako raised her face.

"It was a group of girls," she continued. She tried to control her voice, but it still came out like she was choking. "They would drag me to the school roof and beat me up almost every day."

"Didn't anyone help you?"

Fumi shook her head. "I was a shy, quiet kid who didn't fit in. I didn't have any friends. My classmates thought I was strange. When those girls picked on me, no one in my class said a word. They didn't want to get into trouble. They acted as if nothing was happening. And for a while, I pretended those bad things weren't happening too. It's easier to tell yourself that everything is all right." She took a deep breath. "But it hurt. A lot."

Miwako furrowed her brow.

"I never told anyone about it. If I had, perhaps someone could've helped me."

"Did the bullying eventually end?"

"Yes."

Miwako looked up. "What made it stop?"

"I hit back." Fumi forced a smile. "One day, I just snapped. In a rage, I managed to overpower them. It really freaked them out." She chuckled. "You should've seen their faces. It was like they'd seen a ghost. It felt so good."

Miwako laughed, and Fumi found herself laughing too. Fumio Yanagi would never have thought it would be possible to joke about the incident, but Fumi was glad she finally could.

"You saw those girls at the reunion, didn't you?" Miwako asked.

"Smart girl," Fumi said. "Yes, I met their ringleader—the one who started all of it. She apologized to me."

Miwako tilted her head. "Can you forgive her?"

Fumi shrugged. "I had my revenge that afternoon. In a way, I think I've already made peace with them, even though I couldn't bring myself to tell her that."

"That's really generous of you," Miwako mumbled. "But have you forgiven yourself?"

"I'm trying to."

"Do you feel better now?"

"I do, especially after sharing this with you."

Miwako nodded and looked like she was about to cry again.

Fumi turned to her. "I know you're hurting," she said. "You don't need to keep it all inside. I want to share your burden."

She waited for Miwako to speak. The girl was quiet for a long time.

"I fell in love with a man I shouldn't have," Miwako eventually said. "He was my stepfather."

MIWAKO KOJIMA FIRST LEARNED of Mr. Sumida the spring she turned sixteen.

"There's someone I've been seeing at work," her mother said when the two of them were having dinner. "I'd like to introduce him to you."

Miwako's eyes widened.

"He's a divorcee, and he has a son who's in college," her mother continued. "Mr. Sumida is very kind, and I'm sure you would like him. But if you're against this, I'll understand, and I won't pursue it further."

"That's not it," Miwako quickly said. "I'm just surprised." Not once had her mother shown interest in another romantic relationship since her father's death. "Of course I'd like to meet him. If you're happy, I'm happy too."

Her mother broke into a wide smile. Miwako hadn't seen that expression on her since before her father had been diagnosed with cancer. It suddenly occurred to Miwako that her mother had changed recently. She was more cheerful. She carefully chose her clothes and accessories each morning. Even before meeting this man, Miwako had decided to support her mother in whatever decision she made. Even if it turned out that she hated this man, if he could make her mother happy, she would put up with him.

Later that week, the two families met in Ueno for lunch. They went to a traditional Japanese restaurant for kaiseki and were seated in a private room with a view of Ueno Park. At the peak of autumn, the leaves had turned to gorgeous shades of red, yellow, tangerine, and magenta.

True to her mother's words, Mr. Sumida was warm and courteous. An avid runner, he was tan and lean and looked much younger than his age. His son, Eiji, was friendly and chatty. The young man easily engaged Miwako's mother in conversation and made her laugh.

Miwako had thought the meeting would be awkward, but it wasn't. Everyone got along well, and the Sumidas didn't seem to mind Miwako's reserved disposition. After the delicious multi-course lunch, they went for a stroll in Ueno Park before parting ways.

"How do you think it went?" her mother asked Miwako on the way home.

"They're nice," she answered. "Mr. Sumida seems like a good man."

Her mother smiled. "Is that so? You have no idea how glad I am to hear that. But of course, we're still in the early stages of the relationship. We'll see how it goes from here."

Miwako said nothing. It was obvious her mother was already in love with Mr. Sumida, and their marriage was inevitable with time. She was just glad he seemed like the sort of man who could make her mother happy, and hoped her intuition was right.

Three months later, Miwako Kojima moved into a bigger two-story house, and her name changed to Miwako Sumida.

FUMI COVERED HER MOUTH. "Miwako, how did you end up . . ."

"I don't know. Even now, I can't really explain it," she said. "It's not like I was planning for it to happen."

"If you had feelings for him, you shouldn't have agreed to your mother's remarriage."

"It wasn't like that in the beginning. At first, I saw him as a friend. He made such an effort to get to know me, and we became closer. We talked for hours about books, something my mother and Eiji have no interest in. He was knowledgeable, and he had a deep passion for language and contemporary Japanese literature. I learned a lot from him. It was fascinating to hear him talk, even on topics I had no interest in. And then, before I realized it . . ." She looked down and continued in a small voice, "When we were together, my heart jumped."

Fumi's throat went dry. "Did the two of you—"

"Of course not," Miwako interrupted. "He has no clue to this day. Plus, he was completely devoted to my mother." She paused, brushing her hair behind her ear. "He never saw me that way."

"Hmm. So what happened then, if he never found out?"

"Nothing would have happened, if not for that day."

ONE WEEKEND, MIWAKO RETURNED home to find Mr. Sumida asleep on the sofa. The house was quiet. Her mother was working that day, and Eiji usually hung out with his friends on the weekends.

Miwako went over to the sofa and crouched next to her stepfather. Her heart raced. She stared into his peaceful sleeping face. He usually sported a clean-shaven look, but that afternoon, there was a thin layer of stubble on his chin.

She inched closer. Just being next to him was enough to make her flush. She knew she shouldn't linger too long. He could wake up at any moment, and she didn't want him to suspect anything.

Getting up, Miwako saw a half-drunk mug of coffee on the table. She picked it up, caressing it lightly. The coffee had turned cold and left a ring mark on the inside of the cup.

Better wash it now, before it leaves a stain.

She was about to go to the kitchen when her stepfather shifted and mumbled. She froze for a moment, wondering if he'd woken up, but he hadn't. He was fast asleep. And then something inside her stirred.

Bringing the cup to her lips, Miwako took a small sip. *It's so sour,* she thought as she had another sip. And another.

Then she turned to her sleeping stepfather. His breath was even. He was in such a deep sleep. He'd probably pulled another late shift yesterday. It must be so tiring. She inched closer to his face. A warmth spread inside her, and she felt the nape of her neck go hot. Leaning closer, she brushed her lips softly against his.

When Miwako realized what she had just done, a lump formed in her throat. She touched her neck, recognizing it for what it was.

Guilt.

Miwako sat on the floor as she felt her eyes tear up. What was she thinking? That had been so, so stupid, she cursed herself. She would never do anything like that again. She stood, silently wiping her tears with her wrist. She walked to the kitchen with the coffee cup.

But what waited there was her stepbrother, his expression cold.

Her heart skipped a beat. Had he seen? No, he couldn't have from here. Miwako forced a smile. "I didn't know you were home."

Eiji continued to glare at her. She had never seen him look so unfriendly.

"Have you had your lunch?" She went to the sink and put the cup down, eager to leave the room. "Maybe we should—"

Her words were cut short when Eiji forcefully grabbed her wrist and pulled her around, pinning her against the wall. His lips met hers. Miwako shoved him away in surprise.

"What are you doing?" she hissed. "Are you crazy?"

Only inches away, he stared into her eyes and said, "I saw."

No. It couldn't be true. "I don't know what you're—"

"You don't want our parents finding out, do you?"

Miwako clenched her fists.

"Keep your voice down, Miwako. Father is still sleeping." He came closer to her, cornering her between the cabinet and the wall. "Is this the reason you asked for his old watch?"

Eiji grabbed Miwako's wrist. She was wearing her stepfather's black Casio watch.

He sneered. "Of course it is. Everything makes sense now."

Pulling her hand, she said, "You have no proof. Who would believe you?"

"Think wisely. Why would I make that up? And even if it's just a seed of doubt, are you sure you can afford it?"

Miwako went pale.

"Listen to me," he whispered. "If you don't say anything, I won't say anything either. I'll never betray you, as long as you don't betray me."

"HE CAME TO MY room that night," Miwako said without looking at Fumi. "At first, it was just another kiss. I let him do it. That may have been my biggest mistake. Over time, it got worse, until I'd lost sight of myself."

Fumi furrowed her brow. "How long did that go on?"

"Until I went off to college."

She shook her head. "How did you manage to keep quiet about it for so long?"

"I was terrified of the consequences," Miwako said. "I didn't want to destroy my family. Mr. Sumida was such a good man. He treated us well. And my mother . . ." She took a deep breath. "She was so happy in her second marriage. Even though she'd never said a word, I knew she had been lonely after my father's passing. She needed Mr. Sumida. I couldn't afford to break up our new family, all because of my own stupidity."

Fumi looked into Miwako's eyes. "But this isn't about breaking up your family or what started all this. It's about protecting yourself, isn't it?"

"I know, but I realized that too late," Miwako said. "I had already endured so much, and I used that to justify my silence. I would go off to university soon anyway, and I could finally live on my own, so it would be over. But even after I moved out, he visited me from time to time. In the end, I was just manufacturing more excuses."

"Did you eventually tell your parents?"

"I did, though I didn't tell them how it had all started. I only told them that Eiji had been forcing himself on me," she said. "My mother was enraged, but my stepfather couldn't believe his son would do such a thing."

"Your stepbrother must have denied it."

Miwako shook her head. "I was surprised, but he actually admitted it without attempting to defend himself. After that, he walked into the garage and left on his motorcycle. I'd expected him to tell our parents about what I had done on that day, but he didn't."

EIJI DIDN'T RETURN HOME in the next couple of days. Miwako's parents agreed to ask him to turn himself in to the police once he came back, and if he refused or didn't show up after a week, they would file the report themselves. Even though Miwako insisted they should just move on, they felt strongly it was the right thing to do. Her mother and Mr. Sumida also decided to separate amicably.

Instead of relief, Miwako felt an overwhelming sense of guilt. Her parents' separation was the last thing she wanted, but she knew nothing she said could convince them otherwise. Mr. Sumida apologized profusely to Miwako, but all she could do was avoid his gaze. It hurt her to see him like that—he probably thought she hated him.

To keep Miwako safe, her parents changed all the house locks and asked her to temporarily return to the family home. They also instructed her to call them once Eiji turned up. But he never did.

One afternoon, when Miwako was home alone, she received a call from Eiji. On hearing his voice, she immediately slammed the phone down. But he kept on calling and calling, and eventually she answered.

"What do you want?" she asked coldly.

"I need to talk to you," Eiji said. "Just talking, all right?"

"There's nothing for us to talk about."

He sighed. "Please, just this once, Miwako. And then I promise never to bother you again."

Miwako hesitated. She hated her stepbrother, but she knew he was the type who kept his word.

"I know you hate me. I don't expect you to forgive me. What I did was wrong, and I know I shouldn't have done it, but . . ." He paused. "I was so angry and hurt."

"*You* were angry and hurt? I'm the only one with the right to feel that way, Eiji."

"Of course, and that's why I want to apologize. To you, and Father, and Mother, but especially to you. I'm so sorry."

As if apologizing changed anything.

"I know this is the most despicable, unforgivable thing I've ever done. I discovered one of your secrets and used it to completely take advantage of you. You probably see me as a heartless monster. I get that. But at the time, I just felt misguided. I was desperate."

"I don't understand what you're talking about."

"That's the thing, Miwako. You don't understand," he said. "Have you ever thought that I actually cared about you, maybe a little too much? That what I felt for you might be real?"

Miwako put her hand against the wall to steady herself.

"I . . ." He paused and took a deep breath. "I just wanted the girl I liked to look at me. Even for a split second. But no matter what I did for her, her eyes were on someone else. So I started doing things to break her, to get her attention. And I guess in the process, I broke myself too. I turned into a monster who wanted to destroy her."

Miwako was crying, but she was careful not to let it slip into her voice. "I don't want to talk to you anymore, Eiji. You should just come home and speak to our parents."

"Miwako." His voice was soft. "I'm not coming back."

"You can't run away forever."

"Oh, I think I can," he said, chuckling.

Miwako clutched the phone tighter. "Fine. I don't care what happens to you."

"You don't, huh?" He laughed. "All right, then."

"Goodbye," she said. "Please don't call again."

Eiji was quiet for a moment. "I understand. Goodbye, Miwako. I know it's not my place to say this, but please be well."

"THAT WAS THE LAST time I spoke to Eiji," Miwako said. "That night, he was involved in a traffic accident. The police said he was drunk, but Eiji was always a safe rider and not a big drinker. I knew what happened to him had been because of me."

Fumi shook her head. "Miwako, it wasn't because of you. You didn't ask for it, and I'm so glad you told your parents what had happened. You did the right thing."

Miwako looked down. "I'm not so sure about that."

Fumi was about to say that Eiji had gotten what he deserved, but she stopped herself, knowing it wouldn't make Miwako feel any better. "Was that why you left Tokyo?"

"Yes. I felt trapped. I wanted to get away from everything. I thought I could start over, but Eiji's death and my parents' separation stuck with me. I hated myself for what I did and what I didn't do."

Miwako started to sob. Fumi wished she could hug her, but all she could do was stay here, be there for her.

For a moment, everything was still. Fumi felt as if Miwako and she were drifting away from their current dimension. They were far away in a quiet forest where no one could hurt them.

"I shouldn't have lied to myself, or to everyone else." Miwako's voice shattered the silence. "I shouldn't have pretended everything was perfect."

26

Looks
Like
It's
Going
to
Rain

There are two types of farewells: the expected and the unexpected.

Miwako Sumida's death had been unexpected. Her final passing, on the other hand, Fumi had long anticipated.

I'm going to miss her, Fumi thought as she stared at Miwako, who was sitting idly on the couch.

Miwako turned to her. "Fumi-nee, I'm curious. Why did you name the company Studio Salt? Is it because of the sweat and tears going into it?"

"Perhaps," she said, even though that had been precisely the reason. Kenji had been the one who had come up with the initial idea. She'd visited his warehouse to make a commissioned sculpture, dragging Ryusei along. At that time, she told him she planned to open an art studio.

"Sounds great," Kenji said. "What will you call it?"

"I don't know. I've been thinking about that all night, but none of the names stand out. I want something simple and memorable. Do you have any suggestions?"

"What about Studio Salty?" he suggested. "Because it's made from your sweat and tears."

She thought about it. "Not salty. That leaves a weird impression."

"What about salt? Studio Salt," Ryusei said.

"Not bad," Kenji said. "Let's use that. Studio Salt. Nice and catchy."

She laughed. "The two of you decided without me."

And just like that, the name stuck. Some customers asked about it, but Fumi never told them the real story. To her, it was a little secret shared by the three of them. Yet Miwako had figured out the meaning without any hints. The person Ryu had loved was no ordinary girl.

Fumi stared at Miwako, who was laying down on the couch. "Even though you're not in love with my brother, you still really care about him, don't you?"

Miwako continued to stare at the ceiling.

Fumi furrowed her brow. Had she been wrong? Could it be that this entire time, Miwako had been in love with Ryu too? But it was already too late for them. Fumi felt a pressure in her chest.

"Ryu will be fine, if that's what you're worried about," Fumi said. "He's a tough kid. He's been through a lot. If my brother's well-being is what's holding you back, you should know your concerns are unfounded."

Again, Miwako kept quiet.

"Actually, I have a small request," Fumi said. "Can I draw a picture of you?"

Miwako got up and smiled. "Of course."

"All right, keep that expression and try not to move too much."

Fumi reached for her sketchbook and a box of pastels, trying her best to hold back her tears.

THE DAY MIWAKO SUMIDA left began like any other day. They had a casual conversation over breakfast. Nothing important—Fumi couldn't even remember what it was about. Probably the weather, since the temperature had started to drop. Fumi recalled checking the clock, realizing she was about to be late for an appointment.

"You'd better go now," Miwako said, glancing out the window. "Looks like it's going to rain."

Yes, those had been her last words. *Looks like it's going to rain.*

Fumi grabbed a folded translucent umbrella and dropped it into her tote bag. Miwako waved to her as she left the house.

At that moment, Fumi hadn't felt anything was amiss. She went to her meeting at a family restaurant owned by a potential new customer without a single thought of Miwako. She was trying to convince the old man before her to commission a painting. When he sat, the gaps between the buttons on his shirt opened. The gingham pattern was slightly faded—likely a shirt that had lasted a good few years.

After browsing Fumi's portfolio, the restaurant owner praised her landscape paintings, especially the western-style ones.

"I used to live in Prague," he said. "I was there for over a year."

"Was it for business?" she asked, watching his body language closely. Over the years, she had learned that the key to securing a sale was reading the customer's reactions and making tailored recommendations.

"Not really," he said. "I wanted to experience all four seasons in a faraway country. My relative owned a Japanese restaurant there. He let me eat for free and sleep on his couch in exchange for helping out with the kitchen work. In fact, that was how I became interested in this business. You could say my restaurant was born in Prague."

"Shall we do a landscape painting of Prague, then?" Fumi suggested. She didn't know much about the place, but she remembered a picture of Charles Bridge from the gigantic calendar in her studio.

"Sounds like a good idea, but would that suit the décor?"

"Absolutely," Fumi said. "We can choose a scene with warm colors, like during sunset or sunrise. It will pair well with the wooden furnishings."

The restaurant owner's eyes lit up. Fumi knew she was moving in the right direction.

"The churches, the bridges, the rivers, the houses, the trees. Can you picture it? I'm sure it would be stunning," she continued. "Is there a particular view that you love, or perhaps one that holds a special meaning?"

"Yes, I enjoyed the winter in Prague. You know, when the snow covers the city and the rivers are frozen. It's beautiful."

"Let's do that then. A romantic sunset in winter."

"Ah, yes, yes."

Fumi took out her sketchbook and did some rough outlines. The restaurant owner made a few suggestions and the two of them discussed the color palette, and then they made an appointment a week later for Fumi to return with a detailed sketch.

After the meeting, Fumi went straight to the studio. She wanted to look at that calendar. If memory served her right, it should be the reference she needed.

Fumi put her things down in the office upon arriving. She looked around for Tama, but the cat was nowhere to be seen.

"Tama!" Fumi called aloud, wondering where she might be.

The cat didn't appear. Something was wrong. Fumi kept calling Tama, circling the premises, but she wasn't there. Not knowing where else to search, Fumi returned to her apartment. She opened the door to find the place empty.

No Tama. No Miwako. She was all alone.

Fumi grazed her fingers on the couch. Was she really gone?

As Fumi tried to come to terms with what had just happened,

the phone rang, startling her. She ignored it and continued to look around for signs of Miwako. When she found nothing and the phone rang again, Fumi finally went to pick it up.

"Yes?" she answered.

"It's me," a familiar voice greeted her on the line.

"Ryu," she said, relieved. "Where are you?"

EPILOGUE

I had told my sister I would be back before dinner, but I ended up returning later. It was almost ten when I reached the apartment.

The moment I opened the door, she ran to me.

"Ryu." She hugged me. "What took you so long?"

I mustered an awkward smile, still carrying my bags. "An accident disrupted train service. Some of the lines were down, so I had to take a different route."

"I thought something bad had happened to you."

"Nah. Look at me, I'm fine." Behind her, I saw plates of food on the table, neatly shrink-wrapped. "Have you had your dinner yet? Or have you been waiting all this time?"

She rubbed her neck. "I had a late lunch, so I wasn't hungry. Why don't you put down your things first and take a shower? I'll heat up the food."

Her words made me realize how sticky I was and how awful I must have smelled. I rubbed my chin, which was covered in short stubble. "You're right."

"I want to hear all about your trip," she said, "but only if you want to share."

I smiled. "I'll give you the details later, but it's a long story. It might take a while."

"Don't worry. Your sister runs her own company. She can take tomorrow off."

I laughed and went to my bedroom. Setting my bags down, I felt a sense of comfort. After three months, I was finally home.

THAT NIGHT, I TALKED for hours with my sister. It began with the train ride to Kitsuyama and went all the way to the day I had decided to return to Tokyo, but not before making a side trip to Nara.

"I went to Todaiji Temple," I said. "Remember that time we went there together? After I was accepted to Waseda."

My sister listened patiently, not interrupting even once. I noticed she had cooked all my favorite foods—grilled eel, shrimp tempura, fried pork cutlet, simmered vegetables, sliced pickles, and miso soup—so I ate slowly, savoring each bite. I hadn't had a good home-cooked meal in a while.

By the time we were done eating, and even after we had milk pudding for dessert, there was more to tell her. I helped her with the dishes while continuing the story. After that, she made coffee and we sat together on the couch until I was done.

"That's all," I finally said.

"So you traveled to Kitsuyama with Chie, but when she went back, you chose to stay. Until one day, you simply decided it was time to come home?"

"More or less."

"But you stopped to visit Todaiji Temple first."

"Correct."

"Why there?"

I didn't have a concrete answer. "I just felt that I needed to go there to pray."

"That sounds a bit strange," my sister said, narrowing her eyes and smiling. "You had quite the journey, didn't you?"

"Yes, it was exactly what I needed."

"The most important thing is that you're back safely."

I nodded. "What about you? How is everything?"

"I'm good." My sister rubbed her neck. "But Tama is missing again."

"Don't worry about that."

"What do you mean?"

I cleared my throat. "Tama is fine. She'll be back next week."

"Hang on." Her eyes widened. "How do you know that?"

A silence followed.

"Ryu?"

"I can't really explain," I finally said. "Intuition?"

She chuckled. "Don't be ridiculous."

I laughed and reached for my coffee, but the cup was already empty. Setting it back down, I glanced at the clock. Three in the morning. "We should sleep now, or you'll wake up with dark circles under your eyes."

My sister turned to look at the time. "I didn't realize it was so late." She got up and collected the cups. "Go to sleep, Ryu. I'll clean up."

"I'm not tired yet," I said, and it was the truth. Despite the long journey and the late hours, I was surprisingly alert and energetic. "Let me do the dishes. You should rest."

"You're all grown up, aren't you? Not listening to your older sister anymore."

I laughed, but then I recalled a question that had weighed on my mind for years. I had never been ready to ask it, or rather, I had been afraid to hear her answer, but somehow, at that moment, I felt it was time.

"Fumi-nee, can I ask you something?" I asked.

She turned to me. "What is it?"

"Back when we had just moved out of the orphanage, you used to cry in the middle of the night."

My sister froze for a moment. "So you knew."

"What were you thinking about?" I asked.

She paused for a while, seemingly thinking it through. "Our misfortune. I used to wonder what we had done to deserve such tragedy. Why was it us who'd lost our parents? It could have been anyone, so why us?"

I was at a loss for words. The same question had replayed itself in my mind for years. Why had it been our parents' car that had skidded in the mountains? Why on that one stretch of road bordering a deadly cliff? Why hadn't they taken us along that night, so we could have died together as a family? Then no one would have been left behind.

"But," my sister said as she put her arm around my shoulders, "I've come to terms with it since then, and it was you who gave me the strength to carry on. So thank you, and don't you ever forget how important you are to me."

I felt myself flush. I knew my sister was the reason I was still here too. The reason I had been able to make friends, to go off to college, to meet and fall in love with Miwako Sumida, and finally, to let her go.

Fumi-nee had supported me all my life and asked for nothing in return. I should have been the one thanking her. I loved her, but those words were so heavy to say aloud. Yet the warmth of her arm around me made me feel that she knew.

My sister put her head on my shoulder. "Was there something else you wanted to ask?"

I paused, remembering the dream I'd had the night before. In my dream, I'd been with Miwako and Tama in the studio.

"Ryu?" She moved away and looked at me. "Why are you so quiet all of a sudden?"

I tilted my head. "Actually, I was wondering if Tama could stay with you for good in the studio."

My sister thought for a moment, probably caught off guard by the sudden change of topic. "Sure. I wouldn't mind that," she eventually said. "Tama and I, we get along fine."

"That settles it, then."

She nodded. "But are you sure Miwako would be happy with that?"

"Of course. I think it's what she wanted. It just took me a while to figure that out."

MIWAKO LOOKED RADIANT AS she smiled and laughed, watching Tama rolling around on the floor. She wore a loose beige sweater and pastel-colored chiffon skirt, the same one she'd worn the day she first met my sister. Her long hair was tied up with a plain black hairband, but the wind had made it messy. Some of the stray hairs stuck to her face, but she didn't seem to mind.

I came over and sat next to her.

She turned to me. "Ah, Ryusei, you're here."

Coming from her, my name sounded so tender, even if laced with pain.

"Thank you for taking care of Tama," she said.

"You don't need to thank me," I said. "Fumi-nee does most of the work."

"Is that so?" she said, seemingly surprised. "If that's the case, do you think we could ask Fumi-nee if Tama could live with her?"

My sister and Tama? I wondered why I hadn't thought of it. They were perfect together. "Of course," I said. "I'll ask her."

Miwako gave a slight smile. "Thank you. I know I can always count on you."

I looked at her. "What are you going to do now?"

"That's a good question." She picked Tama up. "If it's all right, I want to spend a week with this young lady first, and after that . . ." Her words trailed off.

"After that?"

"I have to leave," she said. "I'm not sure what's waiting for me, but I'm looking forward to it."

"I'm glad," I said.

We fell into a long silence before she asked, "Do you hate me for what I did?"

"Of course not," I said, "but I am angry sometimes." She had killed the most important person in the world to me.

She tilted her head. "Can you forgive me?"

"I don't know," I said. "I'll try, if it makes you feel better. Is that enough?"

Miwako nodded. "It's enough."

Stillness descended upon us again until I called, "Hey, Miwako."

She raised her head. "Yes?"

As I looked into her eyes, the words disappeared. "Nothing," I said. "It's nothing."

For a split second, I wanted to tell Miwako Sumida that I still loved her. But I couldn't. I didn't want to burden her with my feelings.

Instead, I decided to remember her every detail. Her bright eyes behind black-rimmed glasses, her silky straight jet-black hair, her long neck, her collarbone, her slim fingers, her unpainted nails, and her smile, which never failed to convince me that the world was a perfect place.